HELL AND HIGH WATER

—.—

Fae Fatales: 1

Charlotte E. English

This one is for you, Dad
Because if I grew up to be a tough, go-getting kind of dame,
I couldn't have done it without you.
Rest in peace.

FAE
FATALES
FIONN
STILL WATERS RUN DEEP

1

FIONN

'FIONN!'

Jane's voice, rising above the hubbub around me; I paused in pinning a rippling azure skirt to the model before me, and looked up.

There she was, shoving her way past the model wearing my summer lake-water ensemble, clutching her phone like a lifeline. She'd probably been calling me, and I hadn't noticed.

'*Fi*. Girl number eight's put her arm through the morning mist shirt, and no one's seen girl twelve in half an hour. Previously spotted heading for the ladies at an unseemly pace. What do you want to do?'

'Right.' I took a second to breathe. The show began in twenty minutes, if not less. Now wasn't a great time for complications, but these were fixable problems. 'Gina can do nothing with the shirt?'

Jane shook her head, emphatic. She has the kind of hair, buoyant and exuberantly curly, that has a life of its own; it adds emphasis to gestures like this one. 'It's a wreck. Only you can sort it, if anyone. And before you ask, I've sent runners to the bathroom. Can't locate the girl.'

"The girl" had a name, but I swallowed my objections to the moniker; Jane had too much on her plate to remember everybody. 'We'll slot me in for twelve,' I decided. Not a problem. The outfit the missing model was wearing would be a loss – sea-green tulle and frothing sea-foam, that kind of thing – but this wasn't the first time something like this had happened. I'd got into the habit of making up a secret, additional ensemble with every collection, just for me. I took a great deal of pleasure in doing so, and usually I didn't need to employ it for the show.

Times like this, I was glad of the custom.

'As for the shirt.' I handed over the model I'd been working on – Melly, a fellow selkie, though her colouring was markedly different to mine – to one of my sewers, and turned back to Jane. 'Let me at it.'

We'd booked a stunning, urban garden space for the show, right at the top of the skyscraper they call the Walkie Talkie. Striding through the venue in search of the beleaguered shirt and its no doubt mortified model, I received a heart-lifting glimpse of stunning, gold-drenched London through the mile-high glass walls. The sun was on its way down; I'd timed the opening of the show deliberately to coincide with it. Golden hour, followed by twilight, and the rippling waters of the Thames only a short walk away; it did things to the soul. Mostly good things, though there were times...

Number eight was Jessamy, a dryad, and a regular at my shows. I'd used her several times before; she was reliable, so the wreck of the shirt could only be a mistake. I found her close to tears.

'So damned *clumsy* of me,' she said, looking at me like I might be expected to swing an axe at her face.

Not sure why. I'm not exactly known for flashes of temper.

'It will be all right,' I told her, though from the look of the thing I wasn't as sure of that as I sounded. She placed the flimsy garment into my hands and stood by my elbow, gnawing a lower lip and looking hangdog.

I focused, filtering out the ruckus made by the swarm of people around me. It was a big show; we had thirty-two models set to walk, and a small horde of sewers, dressers, assistants, and set designers to make it all work. The milling about, chattering, panicking and last-minute organising of it all might get under my skin, were I to let it, but the hubbub rolled off me like water.

Pity that it had to be the eighth in the line-up to throw out complications, though; were it the twenty-eighth, I'd have had more time.

'Might have to cheat a bit,' I murmured, for half the sleeve hung free of its armhole, and there's no darning fabric that fine in a hurry. 'Can you get me Sunny?'

Jessamy nodded and dashed off, her mass of sage-and-grass hair flying. Ordinary humans thought it was dyed. It really wasn't.

Sunny came sprinting up a few minutes later, Jessamy trailing after, and I stuffed the mess into her hands. 'I know I said we wouldn't do this,' I told her with a rueful smile. 'But needs must.'

'You want me to witch it?' She didn't wait for an answer, but nodded and set to work. A subtle ripple of magic teased at the edges of my senses, and as I watched, the wispy fabric wove itself back together and neatly realigned with the armhole.

I wasn't usually in favour of "witching" up the ensembles, as Sunny put it. It was risky; not everyone involved with the show, or the venue, was fae. And it didn't seem right, somehow. A fashion show was a display of skill and artistry, not magic.

But the shirt was back on Jessamy in a trice, perfect again, and the smile was restored to her face. I ran a quick eye over her and nodded, satisfied. The shirt was ideal on her, wreathing her slight frame in puffs of gossamer like dawn mist. She wore a trailing skirt with it, all twinkling green velvet, and just the right skyscraper heels to elevate her diminutive frame. Make-up had done a fabulous job on her eyes, too.

'Right, I must go, if I am to be walking twelfth,' I said.

'What?' said Jessamy. 'Where's Narasel?'

'Last seen heading for the bathroom,' I said, already walking away. 'Nowhere to be found.'

In truth, I was a little worried. Narasel, another of my selkie girls, was a regular. I had never known her to bail on a show before. But she couldn't help it if she was ill, of course. I would send somebody to her house shortly, and make sure she was okay.

I missed the opening of the show, to my regret; I was still getting changed. I can't switch outfits as fast as some of my models do. Out of the habit, perhaps. All that pale gold charmeuse proved a challenge to don quickly; I hadn't exactly designed it with a quick-change in mind, and I had Jessamy's mishap with the sleeve fresh in my mind's eye. But in due time I was dressed in my rippling, back-bearing gown, all the sea-green tulle properly afloat around me, and my pearls a comforting weight at my neck and my left wrist.

I did something glamorous and gold with my eyes, left my mass of black hair hanging loose to my waist, and swept out to the show-room.

The next twenty minutes or so passed in the usual chaotic haze: lights, music and shimmering fabrics, applause, a rotating blur of faces, the satisfying *swish-swish* of the cool charmeuse around my legs as I took my turn around the catwalk. It's always over too quickly, even when I am not in the thick of it myself.

After the show, when the noise fades, the bustle is over, and peace returns, there is always a mix of feelings to process. Relief, if the show went well; regret and frustration if it didn't. In the aftermath, my mind is already racing ahead to the next collection, the next show. Perhaps it helps to mask the odd sense of loss I always feel. A species of anti-climax, perhaps. A show like tonight's is always months in the making, and it's over in the blink of an eye.

It's the sort of thing that sends me to the bar.

Sunny found me later, lingering over a prismatic gin in a quiet corner. I was still wearing my gold charmeuse, hadn't bothered to change. It made sense for a while, as there were always people to be met with post-show: reporters looking for comments from the designer; boutique owners expressing interest in displaying or selling some part of the collection; fellow designers coming to congratulate, or possibly to pick my brains. I tended to let them. It's tough out here.

'Good night for Serenity,' said Sunny, and nodded at my glass. 'Gin?'

'Among other things.' The bartender at the garden knows my tastes, and since he's a clurichaun, he's not bound by the usual rules of mixology. My glittering drink had the salt-tang scent of the sea about it, and refreshed me almost as much as a dip in the ocean.

'I'm getting one,' said Sunny, and vanished in the direction of the bar.

I sank back in my seat, and let my head rest against the plush upholstery. Weariness was setting in. I don't sleep much in the week before a show, as a rule; there's too much to do. I take a great deal of pride in bringing off a show without a hitch, and that takes work.

I'd spend another hour or two at the bar, then I'd slip back to my flat, and spend the next week or two catching up on my rest. Everybody knows not to disturb me too much in that time.

By the time Sunny returned, clutching a tall glass filled with a glittering, bright-blue drink, Jane had tracked me down and taken a chair. Melly wasn't long in following, and soon I had a chattering crowd around me, all excitedly talking about the show. They had reason to be elated: it *had* been a good night for my label, Serenity. I knew tonight's collection to be one of my best yet, and the press had been great.

I had little to add to the conversation, but it was pleasant to sit, blissfully immobile, and listen to the others. We've been doing shows together for years, and have developed a passable closeness over that time. These women know me better than anybody else these days, and I am fond of them.

I tried not to keep looking past them, scanning the glittering crowd for someone else.

Every damned show, I thought, disgusted with myself. Every single show, year after year; always there was the hope, faint but inextinguishable.

Always I was disappointed.

Today was no different. I caught a glimpse, occasionally, of a tall, dark-haired woman with more or less the right carriage, nearly the right skin-tone; a wicked smile, a glimmer of something dark. Always a stranger. And while the short, slight woman coming in the door might have a recognisable air of restless energy, and a suitably riotous style, I didn't know her either.

Absent friends, I thought in a silent toast, and drained the dregs of my drink.

I'd had enough gin. 'Time I left,' I announced, and rose to my feet, teetering just a bit in my exaggerated heels. *Those* I should certainly have changed out of, if nothing else.

'Mind out,' said Sunny mildly, and caught my elbow.

'Thanks,' I muttered, and mustered a smile. 'Ladies. You were, as always, fantastic. Thank you for tonight.' I toasted them, too, albeit with an empty glass, and received a chorus of praise in return.

I achieved a reasonably dignified exit, my silks trailing around me. I briefly considered a trip to the ladies' and a quick change into something more reasonable for a walk home, but abandoned the idea. Midnight had not yet struck, and there was no law against wearing an haute couture outfit all the way from the bar to the bed.

The chill, fresh nightly breeze cleared my head, and went some way towards sweeping away the weight of regret I'd begun to wallow in. Good. A few drops of rain sailed down, cold on my skin, and the charmeuse flowed around me as I walked, rippling and fluid, almost like water; perfect. The streets were far from quiet on a fine April night: too many carousers for that. But the tumult in my mind lessened, quieted, and by the time I arrived at my flat, I felt restored to the more-or-less characteristic serenity for which I named my brand.

I took the lift up to the penthouse floor, and let myself in. Without pausing to notice the emptiness of the place — if I don't dwell on it, it's almost like it isn't even there — I went straight through to my bedroom, slipped out of my catwalk ensemble, and fell into bed.

I didn't stir for many hours.

FAE
FATALES
TAI
NO ROSE WITHOUT THORNS

2

— . —

TAI

Fionn didn't see me.

She never does.

I slipped out of the garden a few minutes before the end of the show, and headed for the river. The cool air hit me pretty hard after the warmth within; I never will get used to the prevailing chill they seem to think necessary in England. I think the good British people believe that April is one of the warmer months. Tell that to my toes.

It's not really fair of me to blame Fi for missing me in the crowd: I go to some trouble to hide myself. A little gramarye. Maybe a hood. I was wearing the latter today, and grateful for it; it was some proof against the night's winds.

Why do I hide myself from Fi? I don't know. I do so out of habit — hoping, the while, that she'll see through the illusions and recognise me. Fearing the same. What I think is likely to happen if she does, I have no idea.

Could be great. Could be disaster.

Hell. If she wanted to see me, she could. It isn't as though I'm hard to find.

I crossed over London Bridge, lingering a while to admire the glitter of moonlight on the dark water. *Cold* waters, never very inviting, although Fionn's never seemed to mind. There is solace in watching the currents, even if I feel no inclination whatsoever to dive in.

I went on after a time, descending into the Tube via London Bridge station. It's quieter late in the evening; I received an unimpeded view of my own face and figure, blazoned across one of the many posters lining the tiled walls. *Farewell Fatales* screamed the headline — my band. We were coming to the end of a run of gigs; we'd be playing the O2 Arena in a week, and then... peace. Sleep. Restlessness, probably, until it was time to work on the next album.

Fionn must have seen the posters. Daix, too. I'd chosen the band's name deliberately, though whether I hoped to impress them or to rile them I couldn't tell you. Maybe just to get their attention.

It hadn't worked.

I've been to most of Fi's shows since she took to the catwalk. I wonder sometimes whether she's ever been to any of mine.

Arriving home half an hour later, I walked up the three brick steps to our back door, and let myself in. My roommate was away in Athens, a development arousing my deepest envy. If I could've joined her, I would. I was left to silence instead, a thing I have never loved, so I didn't stay long.

There's a bar on the corner where they play live music all night long. They let me sing more than is seemly, but we never play the new stuff. Mostly oldies, from better days: Sinatra, Vera Lynn...

I disappeared gratefully into the music, letting the strains of guitar and clarinet carry me far away. Twenty-first century London disappeared; in my mind, I was miles back in the past.

...until I became aware of an insistent buzzing sound, discordant with the melody. Disharmony just slices right through me, so whoever the hell thought 4am was a great time to call my phone was rapidly earning a place on my shitlist.

I ignored the phone.

Half a minute later it rang again.

And again.

Somebody really wanted to get hold of me.

'Hey,' said Ted, looking up from his guitar. 'You going to get that?'

'I could,' I allowed. 'Or I could introduce it to the nearest heavy object, the interesting way.'

'Might be important.'

'Fine. Save me a drink.' I turned from the mic. The bothersome device lay where I'd dumped it on a nearby table, merrily buzzing away. The things are convenient, I grant you, but I sometimes miss the days without high technology. Being constantly on call is exhausting.

I snatched it up and slammed it to my ear as I shoved my way outside. '*Yes?*'

'Tai?'

The voice belonged to Coronis, a nymph of my fairly close acquaintance. She's been in a steady relationship with Mearil, my roommate, for a while.

'Something wrong?' I said, sharply. Coronis sounded upset, and that wasn't like her. Besides, she and Mea should be sunning themselves in Athens by now. What was she doing calling me at four in the morning?

'I was hoping you could tell me,' said Coronis. She was breathing too fast, almost sobbing.

'Not making *any* sense,' I said. 'Take a breath. Talk to me.'

'It's Mea. Tell me she's with you.'

'What? She was meant to be with you.'

'*I know that.*'

'Right.' My turn to take a breath. 'I dropped her at the airport, what, eighteen hours ago.'

'She wasn't on the plane. I haven't heard from her, and I can't reach her.'

'Hold on a sec.' I scrolled through the messages on my phone, none of which I'd answered, but it didn't matter. None were from Mea, and she wasn't online anywhere that I could see.

'I've got nothing,' I said, returning the phone to my ear.

'Shit.'

I dismissed most of the questions I wanted to ask. If there was likely to be a reasonable explanation for Mearil's disappearance, Coronis would not be this upset.

This is... not the kind of thing that's supposed to happen nowadays.

'Called the police?' I said.

'The police.' Coronis took the shaky kind of breath that suggested she was about to yell at me. '*Tai.* I can't do that.'

'You... could, I mean, her cover is pretty good, and so's yours. Right?'

'Not that good. The police will turn our lives upside down. You really think they aren't going to find anything weird?'

Mearil is a selkie. Coronis is a nymph. I'm a siren. Camouflaging ourselves from prying — and mortal — eyes is a necessity we all become adept at, but Coronis had a point. Could their joint cover withstand an intensive missing person investigation?

Could mine?

'Shit,' I said. 'Coronis, I don't know what you want me to do.'

'Find Mea. What else could I possibly want?'

'Just... find her? Me? I'm a singer, Cor. They don't issue those with special detecting powers.'

'A singer. Yes. But you weren't always, were you?'

'You've no idea what you're talking about.'

'Maybe I do.'

A rush of … anger rose, and I had to fight to push it down. I've worked hard to build this life, and I've worked just as hard to bury the old one.

'Farewell Fatales, Tai,' said Coronis softly. 'Something like that name's been heard before, and if you thought I didn't know then you're an idiot.'

'Should've picked a better band name,' I said bitterly.

'Look, I'm in fucking Athens and you aren't. Could you at least go to the airport? If something prevented her from getting on the plane, maybe someone saw something.'

'On it,' I said, curtly. 'Don't call me unless you hear from Mea. I'll let you know if I turn anything up.' I hung up without waiting for a reply.

I stood for a couple of minutes in front of the brightly-lit window of the bar, seeing nothing of the darkened street around me. Really, we were both right. The person I am today has no power to track a missing person. But the person I'd once been… *that* Thetai's still in here somewhere. I just have to be willing to dig deep enough to find her.

There are few things I want less.

'Shit,' I sighed again, and stuffed the phone into my pocket. I left without returning to the bar; I could still hear the faint strains of the music, going merrily on without me. It would keep until I got back.

If something prevented Mea from getting on the plane — something *ordinary* — there are lots of things she could have done. Got on the next plane instead, for one, in which case she would certainly have let Coronis know that she'd be delayed — and she would still have made it to Athens by now. If she'd changed her mind for some reason, or some emergency had come up and called her away, well, ditto. No way would she have gone eighteen hours without talking to either of us. Even if some mishap had occurred to take her phone out of use, she'd have found a way to communicate by now. Mea wasn't flaky. She was sweet, she was thoughtful, and she'd never leave anyone to worry about her.

Coronis wasn't at all prone to fits of panic. Something was wrong. She knew it, and so did I.

I stopped abruptly as a thought occurred to me. Mea's luggage. What might have happened to it? Had she proceeded so far as to check it in — and if she had, had it been offloaded again, when she didn't show up for the plane?

I snatched up my phone and called Coronis back.

'Yes?' she said, breathless with hope.

'Don't get excited. I just have a question. What does Mea do with her sealskin when she's travelling?'

'Wears it. She'd never let it out of her sight.'

'That's what I thought.' I hung up again.

A great deal of a selkie's powers are centred in their skins. They're seals in the water and women (or men) on land, and to lose that skin would be... well, let's take Fi as an example. She'd sooner lose her head than lose her skin again. At least that way she'd merely be dead.

I wished, with a stab of acute regret, that I could just call Fi. She knows what it's like to lose her skin. She could tell me what it means. Maybe she could tell me what to *do*.

Tough luck. I retrieved my backbone from wherever it was I'd left it, and went in search of a taxi. Mea had already been gone for most of a day. I couldn't let another one pass without finding some trace of her.

3

— · —

FIONN

I COULD HAVE SLEPT for another day at least, and gladly. There is little time to rest in the weeks leading up to a major show, and I am disinclined to waste the time on it; there's always an opportunity to make up for a touch of sleep deprivation. Later.

But somebody had other ideas. I understood this from the relentless pounding upon my door, the muffled sounds of which drifted through to my bedroom, and roused me from the depths of my slumber.

Eventually. That there had been some delay seemed indubitable, for as I rose and donned a silk dressing gown and padded to the door, someone began to shout through it.

'Hag's bones, Fionn, wake *up*!'

A terrific *crack* sounded, and the door shuddered. Was someone *kicking* it?

I fumbled with the lock, still sleep-clouded, and yanked the door open. 'Stop, please,' I said mildly. 'I'm awake.'

The person assaulting my front door proved to be Jessamy. I wasted no time questioning her presence, however unusual; her appearance told me clearly enough that something was badly wrong. The hour was still early, not even nine in the morning, and she ought still to be with her bond-tree, a splendid silver maple in Green Park. Yet here she was, dishevelled, distraught, and tear-stained, not to mention committing unusual violence against my property.

'Come in,' I said quickly, and drew her inside. Once I had secured the door behind her — and the protective charms I keep around the flat along with it — I began. 'Tell me what's happened.'

'It's Nara.'

'Narasel?'

'*Yes*. She's...'

'Ill?' I supplied, when the words dried up. A tendril of unease unfurled somewhere within. No ordinary illness would put Jessamy in such a state.

But Jessamy just shook her head, standing there with her small fists clenched and tears pouring down her cheeks.

'Worse,' I said softly. 'Jess. Where is she?'

Poor Jessamy took a choked breath. 'The police found her three hours ago.'

'What?'

'She was... they'd left her in — in the water.' She stopped, wrapped her arms around herself and stood there, shaking.

'She's dead?' I said, gently.

Jessamy nodded, her mouth forming a soundless howl.

I paused a moment, uncertain how to react. The news came as a profound and unsettling shock; Narasel's absence from my show might have been uncharacteristic, but nothing could have prepared me for this. For a long, slow moment my mind and body froze; when thought and feeling returned, I hardly knew what to focus on first.

Jessamy. The poor girl was swaying on her feet, and looked ready to collapse. I towed her further into my living room, and pushed her down onto my blue velvet sofa. I sat beside her, gripping her hand, unsure what to say. I hadn't known that she and Narasel were so close.

She cried hard for some time, great, choking, agonised sobs. With every passing minute, my unease deepened. This wasn't the result of an accident.

They'd left her in the water.

'Jess,' I said, when she had calmed a little. 'Who are "they"?'

Jessamy took a shaky breath, and sat up. 'That isn't known,' she said tightly. 'Whoever it was... they left her body in the *river*, Fionn. A selkie. You *know* what that means.'

A selkie, dead in the water. Dumped there? That would be an irony — or a deliberate cruelty. But Jessamy's words suggested something else.

Was Narasel dead *because* of the water? That should not be possible. In water, selkies take the form of seals; we swim, and breathe, with ease, whether freshwater or salt (though salt is by far preferable). Even in my woman-shape, water cannot kill me — or, it shouldn't.

'Where is her skin?' I said, though I hardly needed to ask. I knew what she would say.

'Gone,' said Jessamy, and went on, as though that one word had not been enough to freeze me where I sat. 'I— I went straight to her house. It isn't there. She didn't have it. Someone took it from her, and — and—'

'Killed her,' I said. 'Jess, I know this is hard, but it is important. Did she drown?'

'If she did, she had — help. She's — she's in bad shape.'

Selkies are fae, but some consider us a... handicapped species. Too much of our magic depends on our sealskin; without it, we are virtually defenceless. We might as well be human.

Worse, if it falls into someone else's hands? Someone who knows what it is, how to use it? We can be... manipulated.

Narasel's had been taken, stripping her of her transformative magic, and trapping her in human form. She was a slim, slight woman, like most models, and to the best of my knowledge, she was — had been — peaceful. Nothing could have prepared her to fend off such an attack.

My stomach twisted. The murder of a selkie is already sickening beyond words, but there is an extra level of cruelty involved in drowning us.

'When I spoke, my voice emerged cold as ice-water. 'Tell me what's known.'

Jessamy mopped tears from her face with the back of one hand. 'Like I said,' she began, sounding weary now. 'Someone found her body a few hours ago. I don't know who, but they called the police. I got there as they were taking her — away — and she —' Jessamy stopped.

'How did you hear about it?' I said, still glacially calm.

'Faerd sent word.'

I nodded. I know Faerd, a little. He is an asrai, a race of fae commonly called water-ghosts. Pale and ethereal, and profoundly nocturnal, they are notoriously elusive; there is no catching up with Faerd unless he wants to talk to you. He's part of a small colony who've been living up and down the Thames for centuries.

I wondered, passingly, why he had sent word to Jessamy, and not to me. He ought to know this would be... my area.

Perhaps that was it. It was *too much* my area.

I forced down a surge of sickness, and focused on Jessamy. 'What else?'

She shook her head, a helpless gesture. 'I don't know anything else. I was getting really worried about her, and she wasn't answering her phone. I went to her house, but she didn't answer the door and I thought she must be really sick.'

'You didn't go in?'

'I don't have a key.'

'Then how—'

'I broke in through a window,' she interrupted, answering my question before I had chance to express it. 'Not something I would do if I thought she was sick in her bed, but now...'

'Has anyone seen or heard from her since the show?'

Jessamy gave me a sick look. 'Fionn, she was still wearing her ensemble.'

'Hag's bones,' I whispered. She had been pulled out of the river wearing *my* designs.

When Narasel had been spotted running out of my show, that was the last time any of us would ever see her.

And I had just *slept* through all the long hours since.

'Where in the nine Hells *was* she?' I said.

'I have no idea.' Jessamy was shaking her head again; she looked drained and sick. 'She wasn't at home. She could have been anywhere.'

'Were there any signs that anyone else had been there?' I said quickly. 'At her house?'

'I didn't — I don't know. I barely beat the police there. I had time only to confirm her skin was gone, and I had to get out.'

'You knew where she kept it?'

Jessamy nodded. 'She used a glamour. It's hidden in a pile of shawls she keeps on the second shelf of her wardrobe, looks like one of them. Cheap cotton things, nothing anyone would think to steal.'

'Were any more of them missing?'

'No. Just that one.'

Either someone had known, somehow, exactly how Narasel hid her sealskin — or Narasel had removed it herself, though how she had been divested of it later remained under question.

A moment's fierce, intense regret hit me like a punch to the stomach. I had been concerned for my model's well-being when she ran out on the show. If I had gone after Narasel last night...

Useless, useless.

I stood up. 'It would be of no use to go to her house again at present,' I said. 'The police will have cordoned it off, and I cannot think of a way to persuade them to let us look at it. But if they've removed her body from the water, then perhaps it will be possible to get a look at the site.'

Jessamy looked up at me. 'Why? What are you going to do?'

'You came to me for help, didn't you?'

'I — don't know what I was thinking. I just... I knew you would understand.'

If she meant I would understand what all this *meant*, she was more right about that than she probably had any idea of. 'I do,' I said. 'The police will never find her killer. They will see her as an unfortunate human woman, nothing more; they'll never know to look for her sealskin.'

Jessamy stood up, but she looked uncertain. 'Are *you* going to find who did it?'

The words stung, but only a little. She saw me as her employer, and perhaps a friend; an artist, talented with a bolt of silk, passingly comforting to run to in times of crisis, and that was all. She could not be expected to know the first thing about my history.

I wished again for Tai, and for Daix, far more fiercely than I had under the influence of too much gin. I'd never had to do anything like this *alone*.

Still, it did not take too much effort to cast my mind back eighty years or so, to another time, and remember another Fionn. Once, the three of us had been equal to anything. Tracking a lone killer across London would have been a piece of cake.

It might be more difficult to pull it off without my partners, but what choice did I have but to try? No one else was going to do it at all.

'I'll dress,' I said to Jessamy. 'And then we're going to the river.'

I DONNED SLIM BLUE jeans, a loose shirt and a light, pearl-grey jumper. Nothing to attract attention, nothing to restrict movement. Easy enough to discard if — or more likely, when — I needed to investigate the river-water more directly.

By the time I was dressed, Jessamy had got herself under better control. I'd turned her loose on my kitchen, and she had downed half of a large mug of tea by the time I reappeared. She swallowed the rest in three gulps, set down her mug, and headed straight for the door.

I paused only to pick up my keys — and phone, Fionn, don't forget the phone — and we were gone.

Jessamy took us down into the Underground. We picked it up at Sloane Square, emerged into the air again at Canning

Town, and headed south. We walked in near silence, grim and quiet, Jessamy with her gentle face set into a mask of mingled heartbreak and rage. The morning was clear, bright and fresh, the more so the nearer we drew to the silver expanse of the river. It began to call to me from the moment we exited the Tube: that cool, familiar scent, the way the river-breeze ruffles my hair.

Jessamy led us into Silvertown, and, finally, the Thames Barrier Park. I did not need her to tell me when we neared the scene: a quantity of uniformed police, crime-scene tape, and gawking bystanders informed me of that. They made a cruel contrast against the rich green verdure of the park, its ornamental hedges and brilliant green-grass splendour far too pretty a backdrop for the harsh scene.

Narasel's body was gone, but a section of a low railing at the water's edge was cordoned off. One or two officers were still at work there, questing for... something. Information. I paused to watch them for a few moments, intrigued. It's so long since I have conducted anything like investigative work, I am out of touch with the ways things are done in the twenty-first century. Forensics. It would fascinate Daix to no end, but I have been devoting my time to more aesthetic pursuits.

Still, nothing they were doing could help me, at this moment; I turned my attention away. Leaning nearer to Jessamy, I murmured, 'Where?'

She gestured towards the far end of the cordoned-off space. We pushed our way past several men and women with strange, avid expressions — what *is* it with mortals and their fascination for the macabre? — and stopped right at the shore. The water gleamed in the thin, morning sun, burnished silver, and I felt the familiar need to submerge myself in it.

Soon.

There was, of course, nothing much to see. I could picture poor Narasel's lifeless, drifting figure; that meant, of course, that she could have gone into the water somewhere else entirely. She might have been adrift in the river for most of the night, as far as anybody could tell.

Well, perhaps that *could* be judged, to a point. I would have to try to discover what conclusions were made once her remains had been suitably investigated. How long she had been dead before her body was discovered, for example, could be a crucial piece of information. If several hours had passed, she could have travelled a long way by water. If not...

Somebody hailed me. 'Ma'am?'

I looked up. One of the police officers stood at my elbow, wearing an expression of firm, but polite, disapproval. Perhaps I had been too obviously scrutinising the scene.

I adopted a wide-eyed expression layered with horror. 'What's happened here? It looks like something *bad*, and I only live around the corner—'

'Nothing to worry about, ma'am,' said the policeman, with a slight softening of his grim demeanour. Good. Even if he was lying. 'Just a bit of an incident in the night, but it's being dealt with now. If I could ask you to step back? This area is off-limits.'

'Nothing to worry about?' I said, permitting my voice to rise a touch. 'It looks like somebody *died* here or something. This is a family park. If I'd known this kind of thing was going to happen I'd *never* have moved here.' I permitted myself to be towed a ways back from the railing, still grumbling. No sense in pushing the police any further at present. There was nothing to see.

The policeman made no further remarks of any pertinence — 'Nothing to worry about at all — keep a clear distance — thank you' — and then abandoned me, safely stowed a clear six or eight feet away from the cordoned off space.

Jessamy was looking at me like I had metamorphosed into an entirely new person. Which, in a way, I had.

'Yes?' I murmured.

Her brows rose.

'I told you,' I said, turning away from the scene. 'I wasn't always a designer.'

'I see that.'

She left an empty conversational space for me to fill with an account of my history.

I passed.

'Well,' she said at last, breaking the silence. 'What did we learn?'

'That there is nothing to be learned here.'

'Great.'

I shrugged. 'It narrows things down, a little.'

'But we got nowhere.'

'Not yet, but we will. I need to find out where Narasel's body was taken.'

Jessamy winced, and I mentally berated myself. I forget that not everybody can be as cold. She took a breath. 'There'll be an autopsy, but I don't see how you can get the findings.'

Autopsy. Right. 'I'll find a way. Meanwhile, I want to talk to Faerd.' All Jessamy had said was that the asrai had got word to her about Narasel's passing; lots lay behind that sliver of information. How had Faerd found out about it? Had he discovered the selkie's body himself? What had he seen?

Still, wanting to talk to Faerd and actually finding Faerd were worlds apart. No easy task.

I was going to have to get into the water after all — but not here.

'You don't need to come with me for this part,' I said. 'I'll be under for a while.'

Jessamy nodded. 'Call me when you know something.'

'If I can manage to go a whole day without mislaying or breaking my phone, certainly.'

Jessamy rolled her eyes, but she said nothing else, and walked away.

Left alone, I wandered on for a space, searching for a quieter spot. It wouldn't do to let anybody see me disappear under the water, and while my glamours are more than strong enough to deal with one or two inconvenient pedestrians, I didn't want to have to blind a whole crowd of them to my doings. That quickly gets exhausting.

But it was still early, and only a few minutes passed before I was stripping out of my clothes. I left them tucked under a hedge, together with my phone, the lot glamoured to resemble an uninteresting pile of desiccated leaves.

Then I dived over the railing in one smooth motion. The blissful, cold waters closed over my head; light faded.

I sank, the glimmer of sun-on-the-water rapidly receding above me. By the time I hit the dark riverbed, I was changed: limbs and hair gone, replaced by the sleek-furred, powerful bulk of a seal. Senses sharpened; the shadowed waters cleared, and I could see again. A medley of scents assaulted my more sensitive nostrils, fresh and clean, shot through with the stench of pollution. I'd have to award myself a long swim in the sea sometime soon, somewhere distant. Somewhere perfect.

But for now... Faerd. I flexed my fins and my tail and shot away through the waters, chasing every hint of asrai I could find.

4

— · —

TAI

THEY *REALLY* DON'T LIKE people asking questions at airports.

Mearil had flown out from Gatwick. I knew this because I'd accompanied her more or less as far as the terminal. She and Coronis had been planning to stay out in Athens for a while, and I wasn't sure when I'd be seeing Mea again.

I hadn't gone inside with her. I'd watched her disappear through the doors, a slight, thin figure determinedly dragging a suitcase far too large. She'd grinned at me over her shoulder just before she'd vanished from sight, given me one last, half-abstracted wave, and then she was gone.

Now I had her suitcase, but no trace of Mea. It hadn't been easy to get hold of the thing, either. An hour's investigating went more or less like this: I collared official-looking people; they responded to my questions with suspicious looks and requests for identification; I privately wished them a bad case of pox, smiled my shiniest smile, and moved on to the next one.

After a while I gave up. Mea was missing. If there was ever a good time to break my no-more-magic rule, this qualified. Right?

So the next time I approached an information desk, I was humming an idle tune. The harassed-looking soul behind the desk would see nothing of my brown skin and cocoa-coloured hair; instead he'd see a fair-skinned façade with Mea's flyaway locks, blue eyes and freckles, her height and her rail-thin build. A cursory glance at my passport would support my imposture.

'Hi,' I said, smiling brightly. I leaned an arm on the counter. 'It *really* isn't my day,' I said. 'I checked in, but I got held up at security, and then I got talking — don't you love it when relatives call you with *serious problems* when you're trying to catch a plane? — and anyway, the long and short of it is I missed my flight. Any chance I can get my suitcase back?'

'Baggage claim ticket?' came the reply, in monotone.

'I seem to have mislaid it,' I said smoothly. 'I'm a scatter brain, sorry. Can you still find my case? I was heading for Athens—'

'Boarding pass.'

Hm. I waited in silence until he glanced up at me, frowning. Then I looked deep into his faded blue eyes, adjusted my smile, and handed him my passport. 'Of course,' I murmured. 'Here it is.'

He took the document with a nod, and turned his attention to his screen. I waited while he tapped and typed.

'Your baggage was offloaded,' he informed me, without looking up. 'It is available for you to collect.' He proceeded to issue directions as to *how* and *where*, through all of which I nodded and smiled, and held my tongue. I didn't even snatch up something weighty and attempt to brain him with it. Really, Fi would be proud of me.

Twenty minutes later (or so...) I had Mea's big, blue suitcase in my keeping, and I dropped the glamour. The case and I went on a quick trip to the ladies, where I contrived — not without difficulty, considering its size — to conduct a hasty but thorough search of the thing. No sealskin. Nothing that felt glamoured, either, and nothing that looked out of place. I zipped everything back in, reasonably satisfied that the sealskin wasn't in there. I hadn't really expected to find it; Coronis knew what she was talking about, and no selkie in her right mind would trust her skin to check-in baggage. But, drifting up from the long-buried memories of my past life came a rule or two for investigating, one of which is: assume nothing. Meticulous, detailed work tends to pay off, even if it is dull as fuck.

I wandered back out into the bustle of the terminal building, and parked myself against a wall. I stood there a while, thinking things over.

Good as it was to get a chance to check Mea's baggage, my heart had sunk a long way the moment it was put into my hands. It... confirmed things, in ways I didn't like. Part of me was hoping Mea had checked herself out of the airport, taking her luggage with her, and there'd prove to be some other explanation for her silence.

But no. The case was here, and Mea wasn't. Any hopes I had of a happy resolution to the mystery disappeared.

So. Think.

Mea had checked herself and her baggage in — and then what? Reason suggested she hadn't made it onto the plane, and this was a thing I *would* cautiously take for granted. They'd offloaded her baggage because she hadn't boarded.

And you know, I *just* don't see how it could be possible to disappear a person from a plane somewhere over the Adriatic. It's also impossible to do it quietly, and I'd been monitoring the news. The flight Mea was supposed to be on made it to its destination on schedule, no disturbances reported.

So, whatever had become of her had taken place somewhere within Gatwick itself. But where? Airport security has really tightened up over the years. Nobody would be dumb enough to try anything while she was getting her carry-on checked through; too many people about, several of whose literal job it is to stand there and watch for suspicious characters (like, for example, me). Ditto the departure lounge. Somewhere between baggage check and security might be a possibly. Or, after security but before she reached the gate. Either way, she'd have been wandering along, just one, unremarkable face among many, her mind happily fixed upon Coronis waiting for her in Athens. Not expecting trouble.

It wouldn't take much.

I watched hundreds of passengers scurry by as I stood there against the wall. Busy, harried people, paying little or no attention to those around them. If I wanted to intercept one of them, what would I need to do? Simple. *Excuse me, ma'am, I think you dropped something. Oh look, yes, your purse is missing, but here, is this it? Saw it fall out of your bag just now. You're welcome, no trouble at all. So where are you headed?* A smile or two, a congenial manner, and now you're walking along right by their side without exciting any suspicion at all. Keep them talking. Gently herd them in whatever direction you want — touch of compulsion if they start to notice — and then, when opportunity presents itself... you're gone, and so are they.

It would be appallingly easy.

It's absolutely the kind of thing I would have done, once upon a time.

Mea's nice. Friendly, trusting — exactly the type to fall easily into conversation with a total stranger, and think nothing of it. The perfect mark.

I spun through several questions in my head, without coming up with any answers. Had anyone seen it happen? Almost certainly not, but if they had... I'd need police clout to find out. What was I going to do, identify everyone who passed through

Gatwick at about the right time yesterday and ask them all? Security footage might help, but getting access to it wouldn't be easy.

If necessary, I could bewitch my way through whatever obstacles lay between me and the digital records of Mea's passage. Maybe. But I doubted it'd help me. Had whoever intercepted Mea known she was fae? Perhaps not, but I had a strong suspicion they did. I had a still stronger suspicion we were dealing with fae abductors. You *could* snatch a woman out of a busy airport without using faerie wiles, but it would be much, much harder. Whoever had done it probably had several ways to bypass, or confuse, mere human security cameras.

Another question. Why Mearil? Was she a specific, individual target? Had somebody known she'd be at Gatwick Airport yesterday, and set out to intercept her? The thought puzzled me. As I've said, Mea's the closest you can get to a bunny rabbit without growing a tail. She's not wealthy. She has no connections, and she works as a sound technician. What possible reason could anyone have for targeting her?

My mind kept coming back to that sealskin. That, and that alone, made sense. If you're shopping for a selkie house slave, Mea would be the *perfect* target. And she'd had her skin with her.

Two options there. Either somebody was out fishing for selkie — someone with eyes to see past the glamours that hide us all — and Mea was unlucky enough to pass by at the wrong time. Or, somebody laid a trap for Mea on purpose.

And if the former was true... maybe Mea wasn't the first. Maybe there were others like her.

That thought went through me like a cold wind.

I was probably overreacting. Just because Mea's present whereabouts was under question, I didn't need to extrapolate that into a much wider problem. They call that catastrophising in the field, and they're not wrong.

But once the idea entered my head, I couldn't dismiss it again. It might, after all, be true.

I retrieved my phone, and stood holding it for a second, thinking. I needed answers, but how to get them? Faerie doesn't have an organised police force, nor a central news agency. Nobody reports on faerie crimes, probably because there's little real structure of law. I couldn't just check the news for similar stories, and while I could consult the mortal police, there's no real way to sort ordinary missing-persons reports from those relating to the fae. We are, after all, incredibly good at camou-flaging ourselves.

That left me with few actual choices, but even so. Did it *have* to be Phélan?

Yes. Yes, it did.

'Well, fuck,' I sighed, and dialled.

The phone rang precisely seven times, then cut off. I tucked it away again, enjoying a moment's brief regret of my choices.

Phélan. I hadn't had occasion to contact him in... a long time. So long. The impulse to do so had faded eventually — some — and... I hadn't had a reason to call on him. Or an excuse, either.

I shivered, momentarily chilled.

Too late for second thoughts; it was done. I grabbed Mea's case and walked away with it, finished with Gatwick for now. If it held any more answers for me, I was out of ways to get at them. It was time to go home. I hadn't gone into Mea's room since her departure the day before, but now I had a really good reason to invade her privacy.

If one of my ideas was correct, Mea had been targeted on purpose, before she got anywhere near the airport — and she'd been intercepted by somebody she knew. If that was the case, maybe I'd find a clue somewhere in the paraphernalia she'd left at home.

Besides that, I needed to talk to Coronis again. She, more than anybody, would have an idea as to who had been lurking around in Mea's life lately.

MEA AND I LIVE in a quietish neighbourhood in south London. Our house is small, but it's enough for the two of us — or the three, I should say. Coronis is often away somewhere about the world; Mea gives her the space. But when Coronis is in England, she lives with us.

Mea's room is at the back, overlooking what passes for a garden with us. Neither one of us being a keen gardener, it's little more than a ragged patch of grass with a few hardy shrubs determinedly clinging on around the edges. Coronis does a better job, when she's around, but she hasn't been for a while. Viewed from the window of Mea's empty room, my thoughts darker than they've been in many a year, our scrubby yard seemed more forlorn than ever.

I shut the blind, and turned my attention to the room. Mea has neat habits, and I found everything as pristinely organised as ever. Her bed's too big for the room, leaving little space to navigate around it. She's also fond of soft things and feels the cold, so I had to step past an excess of white-silk duvet and extra blankets in order to reach the tiny desk set into the curve of the wall.

I went rapidly through the drawers, finding pens and notepaper, but no actual notes. Hair clips, a stray battery or two, a shopping list... below all that, a small stack of papers. Bank statements. A quick perusal revealed nothing that stood out as unusual.

No address book. I laughed at myself for the thought. People don't keep address books anymore; all her contacts would be on her phone, along with everything else pertaining to her personal life and habits. Which would be a useful circumstance if it were not for the fact that Mea's phone was not here.

I sat on the bed, and dialled Coronis's number.

She answered it after three seconds. 'Yes?'

'I have questions.'

'Ask.'

'Did Mea make any new friends recently, that you know of? Any new names dropped in conversation?'

'No. I thought of that.'

'Right.'

'I take it she never mentioned anything like that to you, either.'

'Nope.' That said, I hadn't been around as much as I might have liked. Tours, band business, press — all of that keeps me too occupied to play homebody very much. Mea could have got up to all kinds of crazy new shit and I wouldn't know.

The thought stabbed me, sharp as nails, and I sighed. Quickly, I relayed what I'd done so far to Coronis, leaving out my more disturbing theory. She didn't need to hear about my forebodings; not until I had sound reason to think they might be right, and that would have to wait until Phélan showed up.

If he showed up.

'So that's it, then,' said Coronis, when I'd finished telling her about Mea's suitcase. 'She's really missing.'

'Yep.'

Silence. I waited, while Coronis went through much the same thought process I had at Gatwick.

'I'll be home tomorrow,' she said. 'I can help.'

Perhaps. Where I was likely to end up going, I didn't think Coronis could follow. But she needed to be doing something, and what did I know? I was used to having help. Maybe Coronis could be enough. 'Great,' I said.

I stood up again, stashing the phone. Early morning, still; no chance of seeing Phélan until nightfall. The delay chafed. What was I to do in the meantime? How to proceed?

I was out of practice, out of touch... the whole world had changed, and I'd spent the past few decades drowning myself in music. I used to have a network of connections all across London, and beyond. *We* used to have that. Me and Fionn and Daix. And... and Silise.

Nothing went down in fae London without our knowing about it.

Now, I felt blindfolded, deaf and dumb. I had no one left to call on, no source of information. Only Phélan, *if* he answered my call.

Well. Not only Phélan, perhaps. Who else in London might know, if something was going on with the selkies?

Fionn. Of course. I could... ask her.

Just... ask Fionn.

That thought, curiously, bothered me more than calling Phélan. I was paralysed by it; something like terror held me motionless.

I didn't have Fi's number, but I could visit her. I knew where to find her studio. I could ask her if she'd heard anything, if she had any insight that might help. That would be all right, wouldn't it?

She wouldn't be pleased to see me, but... she didn't need to see me for very long.

And this was for Mea.

I sat down again, perched on the end of Mea's bed. Stood up again. Paced out into the living room. *Think,* Tai. Surely I could come up with some other avenue for investigation. *Some* other way of tracing what had become of Mea.

I had nothing. No witness, no suspect. No leads. Just a woman, vanished without trace, and a head full of fears.

'Shit,' I sighed, and grabbed my coat. No time for dithering and doubting. If I could toughen up enough to summon Phélan, I could face Fionn, too.

I'd just better be ready for a barrage of recrimination when I did it.

5

— · —

Fionn

Selkies are sea creatures. River water isn't the same; I cannot live in it, and it cannot nurture me. Still, it's infinitely preferable to no waters at all, and a long, luxurious swim up the Thames has often refreshed my spirits at need.

So much so that, despite the urgency of my errand, the flow of the currents began to lull my senses. I was in asrai territory before I was aware, gliding along half in a dream, shaded waters slipping smoothly by. No one to witness my passage, at so bright an hour: the asrai are deeply nocturnal. Avoidance of the sun is paramount with them; they would all be sheltered away from the light. If I wanted to speak with Faerd — if I wanted to find him at all — I'd need to pay close attention.

The asrai are not social creatures, and Faerd is less so than most. How to find him was a problem I had yet to solve. Some manner of inspiration would strike once I was in the water, I'd reasoned, as often happens.

Not today. I met with eerie stillness in the asrai grounds, the profound silence of deep slumber; scarcely a flicker of life anywhere. I swam to the far borders of Faerd's domain, swift and silent, and turned—

'Fionn of Cuath-Tor,' came an ashen voice, speaking out of the shadowed depths of the riverbed.

The words shattered the almost oppressive calm of the waters; I started, arrested mid-curve.

Faerd would not emerge from his hiding place, not until the sun sank into darkness. I saw nothing of him, could not even sense from where the voice came.

'It is,' I growled, the words coming with difficulty from lips and teeth not made for the purpose of human speech. 'Am I still welcome in your waters?'

'Fortunately for you, that has not changed.'

Indeed. Faerd would tear me apart otherwise; I knew that.

'I came seeking you,' I said.

No answer yet, but a shift in the quality of the silence; I felt his interest.

'You sent word to Jessamy of the Green Park Maples,' I continued. 'Regarding a—'

'Selkie,' he interrupted. 'Slain.'

The words sliced through the water like bullets. 'Yes.'

Something stirred in the shadows, and settled. 'Your coming surprises me.'

'That such a matter piques *my* interest ought not to surprise anybody.'

'No?' Faerd let the word echo for a long moment. 'There are shadows in your past, Fionn of Cuath-Tor. I had not thought you inclined to disturb them.'

'Not by preference,' I admitted. 'But at need, I will.'

'And this is need.'

'A selkie,' I said. 'Slain. Would you have me sit idly by?'

'I would *have* nothing of you,' he said, and the words might have stung, were they not uttered in a tone of cool indifference. 'Consider me mistaken, and set the matter aside. What would you have of *me*?'

'Information. What brought the incident to your attention? She was not found in your waters.'

'No. But I am known to travel out of them, on occasion.'

'Did you discover her?'

'An hour before dawn. The currents had hold of her. They may have carried her some distance.'

Some distance. Narasel may have been clear on the west side of London, then, when she hit the water — or outside of the city altogether.

But Faerd was not certain. *May. Maybe.*

'What was notable about the scene?' I asked.

'A selkie lay in the river, drowned. Is that not notable enough?'

'She was drowned?' My tone sharpened. 'You are sure of it?'

'She was claimed by waters, and not willingly released.'

I did not know quite what that meant. Asrai can be odd; I have often heard them speak of water as though it were a living thing in its own right, with a character, and whims. Perhaps it is, but so profound a link with the waves lies beyond the selkie's arts.

His words disturbed me anyway, for all their opacity. Narasel was drowned, which meant she was alive when she went into the water. Stripped of her skin, then, and more; of that there could be no doubt. But who could have been cruel enough to force such a fate upon her? She would not — *could* not — have drowned without assistance, even without her skin. A selkie is a strong swimmer even in human form, and the waters of the Thames are not that dangerous.

My silence proclaimed the depths of my disturbance, even without words.

'I have never heard of such a thing,' said Faerd.

'You do not know who is responsible?'

'Who gave her to the water? I do not. I can ask among my people, if it pleases you.'

'Something must be done,' I said, by way of answer.

'Yes.'

He was gone, the moment the word left his lips; I felt his absence. The unnatural murk, barely touched by the sunlight, felt emptied again, and hollow.

I swam slowly downriver, sorely troubled. My mind offered me vivid images of Narasel's fate: the appalling agony of her sealskin's severance, the almost unbearable pain of its absence. I had not forgotten what that was *like*, and never would, no matter how many years slipped away. In such a state — weakened, agonised, afraid — Narasel had been seized, thrown into the waters that *ought* to be a home to her, and... smothered in them.

I shivered, heartsick.

Faerd had said nothing about Narasel's skin. *That* had not returned to the water, then, leaving me with still another burning question in my mind: what *had* become of it?

I RETURNED TO THE Thames Barrier Park, and slipped out of the water. My clothes, and phone, were where I had left them, undisturbed. I contrived to don them without attracting undue notice, employing a little glamour to assist me. Then, my garments clinging to my wringing-wet skin, I left the park behind. I was dry again before I'd taken more than half a dozen steps.

If any of the river's denizens had seen what happened to Narasel, Faerd would learn of it, and inform me. That left me free to pursue alternative avenues of investigation. One thought rising in my mind pertained to what had last been seen of her: the girl distracted, fleeing the sky-high garden shortly before my show. It had been said — Jane had said it — that she had been on her way to the ladies', but was that a fact or speculation? I needed to ask where that information had come from.

The sun was climbing high, heralding the rapid onset of afternoon. Jane would be at the studio, overseeing the myriad of business following a collection-closing show. I had a task for her, besides; I wanted to know if any of the other models at my show had spoken to Narasel that night. If anybody had an inkling as to what was amiss, Jane would discover it for me.

I went straight there, entering the spacious building with a feeling of home-coming. I spend more time in the studio than I ought, perhaps; sometimes I don't go back to my flat for two or three days together. All of my work, my art, is done at the studio, and I am at my best when I am absorbed in it.

The top floor is mine. I took the lift, waiting with mild impatience as the contraption soared smoothly up and up. Glass walls drenched in mild sunshine met me as the doors opened, and a smile lit my heart: here was happiness.

The smile vanished a second later, for the ocean-carpeted vestibule was not empty. Someone stood there, her back to the doors; she had the air of having just stepped out of my studio, with no immediate idea of what to do next.

She was facing the lift, and therefore me, affording us an immediate view of one another.

Thetai Sarra Antha.

Tai.

I'd known it, somehow, almost before I focused on her face. Her height, her figure — the very way she occupied *space*. All so painfully familiar. I couldn't forget.

She looked... changed, yet not. The messy sweep of her deep-brown hair, I knew very well. She had not used to wear it thus, long and loose; she'd favoured shorter hair, last time I had seen her, with the sleek, romantic waves considered glamorous at the time. Now she need no longer care for fashion; or perhaps she had simply lost interest. She wore dark jeans, boots, a black jacket: plain, well cut, unostentatious.

Her eyes were different. Dark as her hair they'd always been, but there were new shadows there now.

'Fionn,' said Tai, and the syllable went straight to my cold-water heart, for I'd never forgotten her voice, either.

'Tai.' I had to pause before I could speak, and breathe, or I could never have uttered her name with such calm.

I stepped out of the lift, and let the doors close behind me. There I stood, uncertain how I felt.

Well, I felt: everything.

We stared at each other for a few seconds only, but it felt an eternity. Finally, Tai produced the faintest of smiles.

'Seems I can put my armour away,' she said.

'Armour?' I repeated, stupidly.

She looked down at herself, and waved a hand. 'I'm not eviscerated! Not even a little bit.'

I blinked. 'I can't even remember the last time I eviscerated anyone.'

'Nineteen forty-five,' said Tai promptly. 'Ravensbrück.'

That silenced me.

'Unless you've made a habit of it since, which is *possible*, of course. Only you do seem more interested in fabrics than sharp objects, nowadays.'

'Yes,' I said faintly.

'I... shouldn't have said most of that,' said Tai after a moment.

My smile was smaller even than Tai's; perhaps it wasn't noticeable. 'Don't mention the war?'

'*Never* mention the war, so of course I go there in about thirty-eight seconds.'

I had a strange, surreal feeling of unreality, and I could barely think through it. Tai couldn't be here, just standing *here*, in my studio. Not after eight decades. I had taken in too much river-water, perhaps. Pollution had got to my brain.

I thought I saw a trace of uncertainty in her face. 'Struck dumb?' she said. 'I'm more used to having that effect on men, but I'll take it.' She spoke lightly, but I know her. Knew her. The more Tai jokes, the more she's trying to hide.

But whatever might lie hidden under this particular bout of entertaining discomfort, I'd resigned all right to enquire into.

'Um,' I said, and passed a hand over my eyes, blinking them hard. Not an apparition. The tai, Tai, once the best friend I'd ever had, was still there. 'Apologies,' I said, pulling myself together with an effort. 'It's been... ah, I have one or two things on my mind today.'

'Funnily enough, so do I,' said Tai. 'I was hoping to talk to you about one of them.'

'Ah.' Not just a social visit. That made sense. Whatever prompted her to show up after nearly a century of silence, it wasn't just a sudden whim to enjoy my company again.

Still, my heart sank a little.

'By all means,' I said, and stepped past her. 'We can go into my office.'

Jane saw me the moment I stepped through the doors, and came bustling over. She stopped when she noticed Tai. 'Fionn, excellent, I — oh, I see you've company.'

Nosy as Jane is, she paused there, giving me an opportunity to explain who Tai was and what she was doing at the studio.

I didn't.

'There are some things requiring your attention—' she said, abandoning the subject of Tai.

'Twenty minutes,' I said. 'And then I'll be at your disposal. I have one or two things I want to consult you about, too.'

Interest deepened; she looked avidly curious, but thankfully she left again. I ushered Tai through the work-space, still littered with the paraphernalia of garment construction and design, and into the small but brilliantly-lit office I keep at the back. The door clicked shut behind the both of us.

I gestured to the seat on the supplicant's side of the desk, but it felt too much to assume my customary position on the power side. I settled for perching on the edge of the desk instead, close enough to Tai for companionableness but not so close as to loom over her.

Tai registered all of this with a glance, and — if I am still any judge — a trace of amusement. But she took the seat, flipped back her hair, and sat with one leg crossed casually over the other. Very much at home, at least by appearance.

'So,' I said. 'I hope nothing is amiss?'

'Very much so,' said Tai. 'It's—' She stopped, and thought, eyeing me with an expression I found unreadable. Wariness? Doubts? 'Perhaps I shouldn't have come to you,' she began again. 'I wouldn't have if it weren't an emergency.'

'You begin to worry me,' I said.

She nodded, and went on. 'I— don't know any other selkies besides you, except just the one, and that's the problem.'

I straightened, suddenly alert. 'What?'

My reaction took Tai aback; she blinked. The wariness deepened. 'If this is going to be a problem, I can just go—'

'No,' I interrupted. 'It isn't that.'

'I know it's a sore subject for you, and I don't want to—'

'*Tai*.' The word emerged more harshly than I'd intended, and I regretted it at once when I saw her eyes widen. 'Please,' I said, more gently. 'Just tell me.'

She nodded once. 'My roommate, Mearil,' she said. 'She went missing yesterday.'

'She's the other selkie you know?'

'Yes.'

I closed my eyes briefly. 'I see.'

Tai nodded again. 'I know. Familiar ground, and I'm sorry for that, but you're the only person I know who might have some insight.'

Tai was being extremely careful of my supposed feelings, and that was odd. Not that it was strange for Tai to care, but considering all the things we'd said to each other last time we talked, it stuck out.

Was she afraid of me?

The thought lodged in my mind, tangled there with the thousand new alarms her revelations brought me. Unhelpful distraction. I thrust it away. 'It's — I said I had things on my mind today. Might be related.'

'What?' It was Tai's turn for alarm; her relaxed posture vanished. She sat forward. 'What is it?'

'One of my models was murdered last night.'

Tai looked sick. 'Let me guess. Selkie.'

I nodded.

'Shit.'

'I've just come from the place where they found her. Her sealskin is gone. She'd been — drowned.'

Tai's sick look deepened. 'Hag's blood and bones,' she said. '*That* possibility hadn't entered my head.'

She did not look pleased that it had done so now. I felt a moment's compunction, but thrust that away too. 'Tell me what happened to your roommate,' I said. 'She's been gone only one day?'

'She was on her way to Athens. I went with her to Gatwick, and... she hasn't been seen since. Never made it to the plane.'

'Snatched from the airport?'

'I think so.' Tai went through a story about offloaded baggage, someone called Coronis and a disturbing lack of communication from Mearil. The picture she drew was a bleak one.

'What worried me *before*,' Tai finished, 'was the possibility she was — slave-taken. She certainly had her skin with her, and it hasn't turned up. But now I'm worried that it's worse.'

With good reason. 'All right,' I said. 'What were you hoping I could do?'

She ran a hand through her hair, her eyes going distant as she thought. An old habit. It fractured my heart just a little bit to see her do it now. Some things don't change.

'I worry that she's slave-taken because I know such things *can* happen,' she said. 'I don't know *how*. Or who... might do something like that.'

I smiled briefly at the latter thought, but it was a mirthless expression. Who indeed. 'The... transferral of a selkie-skin,' I answered. 'Is that what you're asking about?'

She nodded.

'It isn't as simple as picking it up,' I said. 'There's an intent behind it, or there needs to be. It's—' I paused, groping for words. 'It's the difference between closing a door behind somebody, and locking them in. Not something that can happen by accident, if that was your question.'

She sighed, frowning. 'Not... really. I knew it was unlikely. But rule things out, right?'

'Right. So. It's possible her disappearance has nothing to do with her skin. There are, after all, other ways to vanish a person.' I didn't add how unlikely it was, but Tai's face told me she knew.

She'd come in hope that I might be able to reassure her, perhaps. Instead I had all but confirmed that Mearil's disappearance was at least as bad as she'd feared, and possibly worse. There *might* be two totally unrelated selkie disappearances going on in the same city at the same time, but the chances of its being a coincidence were vanishingly small. It's not the sort of thing that *happens.*

Until, that is, it does.

'As for the question of who,' I said into the silence. 'A fair question indeed.' I drew a breath. I had been slave-taken once, as Tai put it, but I didn't think that experience could inform us as to Narasel's or Mearil's fate. My fate had been... personal. 'If we are to be brutally honest, a surprisingly large number of people might be at least passingly interested in a docile selkie about the place. Especially if it's someone they — know, and would like to keep around.' The words thickened in my throat; I paused until I'd calmed. I'd been going to say, *someone they care for.* No. That is not how it ever, ever works, and I was chilled that any part of my mind was still capable of framing it that way.

'The fact, though,' I continued, 'that there are *two* such vanishments casts a different light on the matter. Most of the people I was thinking of just now would have neither need for, nor interest in, multiple such... slaves. It is the difference between a personal crime and a — wider one.'

Tai nodded. 'Some level of organisation.'

'I would say, undoubtedly.' Which raised some unpleasant possibilities.

'Is there some way we can warn people?'

I'd been asking myself the same question. There were more selkies in London, no doubt, but I had no convenient way of getting in touch with them. Whoever, or wherever, they were. It's possible there are not many; I rarely encounter others in the water. But how far did this scheme go, if it was a scheme at all? Were those living outside of London safe? What could I, Fionn of Cuath-Tor, do about it if they weren't?

Tai's face changed. Concern disappeared; her expression hardened, and that dangerous glint blossomed in her eyes. I remembered that look. 'We need to find Mea,' she said. 'Immediately. If we do that, we'll discover who took her, and Narasel too.'

'Probably,' I cautioned. 'Assume nothing.'

For some reason, that caused a smile to pass behind her eyes, if fleetingly. 'We'll discover who *probably* killed Narasel, too,' she corrected herself. 'And we can stop them from hurting anyone else.'

We. She had said it a few times over.

Hags curse me, I'd grown so used to my splendid isolation my immediate impulse was to shove the idea away. I don't do *we* anymore. It isn't worth what it costs.

But another part of me absorbed the idea the way a parched plant takes in water, and relaxed. *We* had made a great team, once. We had made great friends.

I cleared my throat. 'Ah... are you sure we're up to it?'

I didn't need to explain why I'd ask such a question. Tai looked at me, and the memory of Ravensbrück lay heavy between us.

'We are,' she said. 'Of course we are. You think because we screwed up once, we're toast? Fuck that.'

I laughed. It wasn't much of a laugh; a damp, half-choked thing, more surprised than amused. 'You're right,' I said. 'What was I thinking.'

'We're up to it because Mea needs us to be,' she said, more seriously. 'We aren't going to fuck up this time, Fi.'

'I hope not.'

'Right.' She unfolded herself from my chair, and stood up. 'Order of business.' She retrieved a phone from a pocket in her jacket, and brandished it at me. 'Exchange of contact details. Can't work together if we can't talk together.'

A couple of minutes took care of that. 'Great,' she said, pocketing the phone again. 'I've got irons in the fire, namely Phélan—'

'*Phélan*?' I interrupted. 'Tai, you didn't.'

She shrugged. 'I didn't have a better idea.'

'*I* was a better idea.'

That earned me a measuring look. Internally, I winced. She had come to me — but she'd gone to Phélan first. What *that* meant, I didn't want to think too closely about.

'And what,' said I, resigned, 'did Phélan say?'

'Hasn't said anything yet. I expect him somewhere around 3am, because he wouldn't be Phélan if he didn't pick the most deliberately awkward time to appear.'

I smirked. Not quite a smile, but vaguely close. 'I'm awaiting word from Faerd,' I said. 'He's one of the Thames asrai. He'll bring news if anybody saw Narasel go into the water, or who it was that pushed her.' I slipped off the desk, and straightened. 'I was also about to question Jane. I don't know who was the last person to see Narasel, before she left the show.'

Tai nodded. 'So she was last seen at the Walkie Talkie?'

'As far as I know at the moment. I—' I paused, frowning. 'Wait. How did you know where my show was?'

Tai looked vaguely shifty, and said nothing.

'Were you *there*?'

'Er. Yes, yes I was.'

I raised my brows.

'Fi. I've been to every damned show you've ever done,' she said with a sigh.

'What?'

'Okay, no, not quite all. Once in a while I'm on tour and I can't make it. But most of them.'

My mouth opened, but my brain spun and spun. No appropriate response occurred to me.

Tai's eyes danced. 'This is the perfect moment to tell me you've secretly attended a bunch of *my* shows. You see that, right?'

'I...'

'It's okay. Don't hurt yourself trying.'

'*Tai.*'

'Yes.'

'Can we do this later?'

'Do what? Go over the last seventy-five years of *apparently total* estrangement, discover we've been BFFs the whole time, and cry each other into a stupor?'

'What—'

'There can be alcohol. It's a crutch, but that's okay.'

'Tai. Stop.'

She stopped, and waited. I could read her well enough to detect a note of hope behind her words, but ... now wasn't the time. It really wasn't. We had a more urgent problem on hand than the long-ago ruin of our friendship.

'Later,' I said, firmly.

'Right.'

'Do you have any leads on Mearil?'

'Not a fucking thing. If anyone saw her taken, I've no idea who, and I found no trace of her at Gatwick. By all appearances, she went up like a puff of smoke.'

'Unfortunate.'

'Yes, but that's why I want to talk to Phélan. Fi, if somebody's *organising* this kind of shit then you know he will have heard something.'

I grimaced. 'Probable. But can you be careful, please? For all we know, Phélan could be behind the whole thing, and in that case he won't like you asking questions about it.'

Tai waved the idea away. 'Phélan's bad, but he's not *bad*-bad.'

'He was a Nazi spy, how much more *bad*-bad does it get?'

'He was not! Or, no more so than he was an Allied spy, anyway, and I'm pretty sure he was selling *mis*information in the first instance—'

'So he spent the war playing both sides for enigmatic reasons and you're seeing this as a *defence* of his character?'

Tai grinned, the first time she'd done so since I'd walked in to find her waiting for me. I realised this because I caught a glimpse of something out of place: a dark tooth that sparkled slightly in the light. 'I've missed you,' said Tai simply.

I had no time to respond to *that* leveller, because Tai lunged. I found myself swept up into a hug, the kind that makes your bones creak. This surprised me into silence, at least for a moment, and by the time I'd recovered my words — and my motor functions — she'd released me.

It was too late to hug her back. 'Nice tooth,' I said.

One of her brows went up at that. 'Thanks,' she said, and smiled again, affording me a clearer view of it.

Awkward silence returned. I remember when she lost that tooth.

'It's not... diamond, is it?' I said, at last.

Her grin widened. She nodded. 'And,' she said, whipping off one of the thin fingerless gloves she was wearing. She displayed her balled fist for my inspection. Every one of her knuckles bore another such jewel embedded into the skin. Knowing Tai, they were embedded into the damned *bone*.

'Nice,' I said faintly.

'Aren't they?' She flexed her fingers, admiring the jewels with patent satisfaction.

'Must have hurt.'

'Me, yes. Other people on occasion, definitely.'

I winced in sympathy at that. Tai had always had a solid right hook. I didn't want to imagine the effect those bejewelled knuckle dusters would have upon anyone who pissed her off.

'Real diamonds?' I enquired, and that might be said to be my professional interest taking over.

She rolled her eyes. 'Of course not. That would be ridiculous.'

'*That* would be ridiculous. Right.'

She restored the glove to her hand, hiding the jewels. If they were synthetic, they were convincing. 'I'll leave you to interrogate the hapless Jane,' said she. 'I've got another errand.'

'Oh?'

She flexed her hands, a gesture I've seen her make when she's thinking about hitting somebody. 'If we're going to be a *we* again,' she said, unconsciously echoing my earlier thoughts, 'then we're missing something.'

'What's that?'

'We're missing a Daix.'

'Ah...' I may have paled a shade or two. 'Is that really going to be necessary?'

'Yes,' said Tai, decisively.

'Why?' I hoped the word didn't sound as plaintive to her as it did to me.

'Because nobody does details like Daix, and I'm *really* not interested in meticulous process of elimination. Are you?'

'Fair point,' I allowed.

'Besides,' said Tai, smiling rather grimly. 'She's our best friend.'

'Right,' I said, nodding. 'I was forgetting that.'

6

— · —

TAI

I left Fionn's studio in a disoriented frame of mind.

I felt... happy. Oddly so. Fionn hadn't been friendly, by any means — she hadn't been so chilly to me since the day we first met. But she hadn't extracted my eyeballs with a dessert spoon, either. I emerged intact, entrails safely on the inside where they're supposed to be, and Fionn hadn't looked more than vaguely tempted to rectify that situation.

In fact, for a moment or two here and there, we'd forgotten the weight of years and regrets and talked almost normally. The way we used to.

And now I had her number, and a reason to sometimes call it.

Mearil's continued absence was a fist around my heart, slowly tightening, and Fionn's news had made that much worse; but Fi herself... I stepped out of her building smiling.

And stopped, brought up short by the belated realisation I had no idea what to do next. I had talked of finding Daix with a breezy confidence I had no way of acting upon (I know, *so* unlike me).

Fi and I may not have talked in all these years, but I had always known what she was up to. I'd always had a way to find her, if I wanted.

Daix, however, had walked out of our lives and — vanished. Completely. I had not the first idea what she had been doing, or where she was. She might be in Bali for all I knew, or Chisinau. Mumbai. Anywhere.

I still recalled several of the aliases she used to use, but how did that help me? She wouldn't be using the same names now.

Wanted, ran the ad unfurling in my mind. *One imp, under five feet high. Known as Daix de Montfort, and sundry other monikers. Evil incarnate, approach with extreme caution.*

Sure, that'd work.

As I stood there, dithering, something caught my eye: some lightweight thing, wafting down from above, turning airily upon a stray breeze.

It fell neatly to the floor at my feet, and lay there. Waiting.

A card. An innocent, rectangular snippet of paper, with somebody's name printed on it in black Garamond.

My eyes narrowed. I looked up at the clouded skies, but saw nothing that might explain the card's appearance. No faces at the windows of Fionn's building, towering behind me.

I sighed, and stooped to pick the thing up.

Daix de Montfort, read the name.

I turned the card over. On the back, naught appeared save a string of numbers; meaningless, until I realised I was looking at a set of map co-ordinates.

I resisted the temptation to screw the card up and hurl it at something. At Daix, by preference, but that could wait for later. I settled for making a rude gesture at nothing in particular, satisfied that *this* would, by whatever method, relay itself to the lady in question, and shoved the card into a jacket pocket.

'Fine,' I sighed. 'We'll do it your way.'

Somewhere, Daix was smiling.

OF ALL PLACES I might have expected to find Daix, a library wouldn't have ranked high among them.

Not just any library, either. The Maughan Library, Chancery Lane. Frighteningly close to my house, in point of fact. Even closer to Fi's studio.

And incidentally, a research library associated with King's College, London. Mystified, I prepared myself for a surprise — knowing Daix, it would be of a highly unpleasant nature — and went there at once.

The building's spectacular, I'll give it that. It's ancient, it's elegant. Façade a mass of mullioned windows crowned with balustrades, miniature turrets — the lot. It wouldn't have disgraced a palace. But the whole picture left me cold as I approached, for somewhere under that classic roof was Daix, and what mischief she might be getting up to *here* proved an… occupying question.

Inside, I trekked through room after room, passing, no doubt, hundreds of thousands of books, and found no sign of her. Students aplenty bent over desks, charmingly illuminated by bright reading lights and working away furiously at who-knew-what; but no Daix. Endless, towering bookshelves crammed with every conceivable scrap of knowledge; but no Daix.

I was beginning to imagine myself sent on a goose chase, and visions of the exquisitely painful things I would do to Daix in consequence — whenever I finally found myself face-to-face with her — were floating, pleasantly, through my mind, when I tripped over her.

Quite literally.

As I endeavoured to halt my downward progress with a catch at the nearest desk, there came Daix's low, rather smoky voice, faintly accented with French. Or I suppose I mean, Frankish. 'Thetai Sarra Antha. You're eighty years late.'

I gripped the desk hard enough to produce a creak of protest from the abused wood, gritting my teeth. 'Only seventy-five, and I wasn't counting. Hello, Daix.'

'Hi!'

I straightened. There she sat, tucked into a corner wherein, somehow, the shadows roiled more deeply than they ought. I hadn't seen her, skulking there like an overgrown spider; I hadn't been meant to see her.

She had announced her presence by sticking out her foot to trip me. She made no attempt to disguise the fact, either, for her leg was still outstretched, dainty little foot clad in a polished burgundy boot.

The rest of her was clothed to match, all wine-red, but she was wearing some kind of suit, and that didn't look like the Daix I knew at all. She wore her hair — white-blonde today — swept up into a respectable-looking bun, and a pair of silver-framed glasses sat poised upon her nose.

If she was still wearing her horns, I couldn't see them.

'And if I'm late, so are you,' I said, glowering at her.

She sat back, shrugging. Her face disappeared into shadow again; I couldn't see her expression. 'I've been here.'

'*Here*?'

'Around. Perfectly accessible, if either of you ever thought to ask.'

'I had only to say the name, and Mary Poppins would appear.'

Daix's gesture was one of approval at the comparison. 'Lady has style,' she nodded. 'Knows how to make an entrance.'

'Uh huh. And you've had us under surveillance why?'

'You don't think I'd leave you two loose in London without someone to keep an eye on you?'

'An *eye*?'

'An eye, a camera...' Daix grinned. I saw the flash of white teeth, sharper than they ought to be.

'A whole legion of the latter, unless I miss my guess.'

'There are dangers everywhere,' said Daix gravely.

'What dangers?'

'You have no idea.' Daix picked up a stack of papers from the study-table at her elbow, and prissily tidied them. 'Which is the whole problem.'

'What.'

'You can thank me later.'

'*Thank you*? For spying on us?'

'Someone had to.'

I took a deep breath, meant to be calming, but ineffectual. 'All right, why did someone have to?'

'The very pair of you! Swanning around London with your heads full of clouds; faffing around with artsy nonsense — I tell you, you'd have been dead in a week if someone hadn't stepped in.'

'Artsy nonsense.'

'Yes.'

'And you're doing what, exactly?'

'Research fellowship.'

'Seriously.'

Daix set the papers down again. 'Forensic Science is the field, not that you asked. You don't want to hear about the dead-in-a-week thing?'

'I ignored that, with supreme grace and near total indifference.'

'Then you've got a death-wish,' said Daix, nodding wisely. 'It happens in beings of advanced age.'

'You're far older than I am.'

Daix leaned forward, her enchanting face emerging from shadow. She looked deep, deep into my eyes, her own glinting green, and said: '*Or am I?*'

'Okay, do we have to play games? Because one or two things are a bit more urgent right now.'

'All is not well with the selkies,' Daix nodded, releasing me from what was probably supposed to be a hypnotic stare.

'So you know about that?'

'Surveillance, remember?'

'Tell me you didn't hear every word of my conversation with Fionn.'

Daix carefully lined up the books on her table. 'Lying isn't an attractive quality, especially among friends.'

'Neither is covert surveillance.'

'*Fine,* I'm sorry about the spying thing.'

'Lying isn't an attractive quality, especially among friends.' I folded my arms.

'Okay, I'm not sorry. Is that better, or worse? You're confusing me.'

'How about we go someplace else, and you tell me how you're planning to help.'

Daix brightened at once. 'I do have some ideas—'

'Great,' I said, cutting her off. 'Because I've a small ocean of dull, detail-oriented paper-pushing with your name on it.'

Daix's fingers strayed towards the papers she'd already tidied once, and clutched possessively at them. 'You always did know how to make my day.'

'Yeah, I missed you too. Come on.'

'WHAT WAS WITH THE card?' I asked her a little later, having exited the Maughan Library. Daix had plunged immediately into the throngs of people abroad in the city, walking rapidly, and with an air of bustle; I found it oddly difficult to keep up, despite my superior height.

'What about the card?' said Daix without looking at me.

'Why'd you help? You could have let me flounder for days without finding you.'

'That *would* have been more like me, wouldn't it?' Daix agreed, a dimple appearing in one cheek.

'You could've sat back and watched the show,' I continued. 'Taken an inordinate and sadistic pleasure in my total failure to locate you. Tormented me about it *mercilessly* for years to come.'

Daix sighed, a wistful sound. 'Stop it. You're making me sad.'

'Heartbroken for what, now, can never be?'

Daix nodded, mournful. 'The thing with the card was, I was interested.'

'In me?' I said, in some surprise.

'Don't be ridiculous.'

'Right.'

'I was interested in the *case*. I haven't encountered so fair a prospect in *decades*.'

'Kidnapping, theft, murder,' I agreed. 'Possible enslavement. No selkie is safe, and who knows when the rest of us will be at risk of evisceration or dismemberment? Nothing could be better.'

'You're unduly preoccupied with evisceration,' said Daix. 'Might want to work on that.'

'Dismemberment, though, is always in style.'

'Gloriously.'

'Daix, this isn't a party. I've lost a friend, and so has Fi.'

'In point of fact, Fionn lost a temporary employee, not a friend. As for your *roommate*—' Why Daix pronounced the word with such emphasis, or such apparent disgust, I had no idea '—she we may yet recover.'

'So I'm hoping, which brings me to my next question: where the hell are we going?'

Daix had led us in a befuddling, criss-crossing route down several streets, not to mention one or two narrow alleyways that shouldn't have been there at all. I've lived in London long enough to be very familiar with it, but even I had lost track of where we were.

'The Puca,' she said. 'If we want to talk openly, that's the best place. No need for glamours or bemufflements.' She made a dismissive gesture, illustrative of throwing the entire class of enchantments out like garbage.

'Bemufflements,' I repeated.

'Yes. You know, the thing where anybody who's listening as shouldn't won't hear a word of interest.'

'You mean a muting charm.'

'That's what I said.' Daix nodded.

The Puca, or rather The Booted Puca. I hadn't been there in decades, but the name still had the power to cause a twinge of nostalgia — even, regret. It's an ancient pub situated... somewhere in London. The precise location changes; or rather, it's the route that changes. The pub's where it's been since Robin Hood's day, if not before, but you'll never reach it by the same road twice. That explained Daix's erratic navigation, not to mention the disappearing alleys. You don't so much walk to the Puca as track it down, like errant prey, and you'd better be tenacious about it, too.

We used to go there a lot, back in the day. I'd gone there a few times since, but without Fi and Sil and Daix, it wasn't the same.

I doubted Fi had gone much, either. Daix, though... Daix is the closest thing to indestructible I've ever met. Regret, heartbreak, grief, nostalgia — these things have no power over her whatsoever.

Sometimes I find that enviable.

Daix had led us in circles, I thought, for we entered a residential street full of grand-looking properties I was sure we had walked down only three minutes before. But then she took a sudden left turn down another improbable alley, and that was new — and then another left, into an impossible park of aged oaks; — she broke into a run, and so did I, and then there was the Puca, its rickety thatched roof emerging from among the trees like a mirage in the desert.

Daix ran like mad, and we didn't stop until she and I had planted both feet in the Puca's cobbled courtyard.

'Right,' she said, slightly out of breath. 'Good.' Somewhere en route her burgundy ensemble had altered; now she wore a fourteenth-century kirtle, lavishly embroidered, with a band of gold about her brow. Fitting.

My garments hadn't changed, which was also fitting. Daix learned long ago not to mess with me in *that* respect, if in few others.

The Puca's a humble building, viewed from the exterior. Stone-built, with cloudy, mullioned windows and an air of mild, tumble-down neglect, it doesn't look like much. The painted sign swinging over the heavy oak door depicts the Puca, in the shape of a cat, wearing the familiar tall, buccaneer's boots (there's more to the legend of puss-in-boots than most people know). Behind the Puca, though, another boot appears, apparently in the process of kicking the maddening creature into the middle of next week.

Sounds cruel, perhaps, but don't be fooled by the kitten-cute appearance of those things; they're ruthless mischief-makers.

So much for the outside of the pub. The inside... that's a whole other matter.

We went in, the trailing hem of Daix's ridiculous crimson kirtle dragging in quantities of dirt and dead leaves along with us. We were greeted with a blaze of music: something that sounded, to my practiced ear, like an escapee from Victorian musical theatre. Everything inside was dark oak and crimson velvet, with frankly unjustifiable quantities of gilding.

'Burlesque,' I muttered. 'Nice.'

'It *is*, isn't it?' said Daix, beaming, and throwing wide the door. 'Last time I came in they were doing that fifties American diner look, and I just can't admire it, can you?' Her kirtle, I perceived, had vanished again already. In its place she'd adopted a cropped black velvet jacket worn over an ivory corset, with skirt and boots to match.

Becoming aware of an abrupt tightening around my torso, I glanced down, with a sense of dread, to find myself similarly attired.

'Daix,' I said, through gritted teeth.

'What?' she said, glancing around. 'Oh. Yes, sorry. That colour isn't right for you at *all*, is it?' She waved a hand, and the gold-gilded absurdity of my new coat and skirt changed to silver and black. 'I'll save the gold for Fionn,' she murmured, turning away again. 'Much more her style, no?'

'*Daix*,' I began again, but she'd already wandered out of hearing. She began flirting shamelessly with the clurichaun keeping bar, and by the looks of them, they were old friends.

I abandoned the point, albeit with ill grace. We had more pressing problems than the state of my clothes, and besides, she'd had sense enough to leave my arms and hands more or less unencumbered. I'd have a little more trouble fighting in this get-up; corsets are *not good* for freedom of movement; but we were unlikely to encounter trouble at the Puca. It's ancient, neutral ground, and that status is both hard-won and fiercely protected. Anyone drawing weapons in *here* would find themselves swiftly eviscer— er, dismembered.

Possibly by me, and that prospect ought not to please me half so much as it did.

Apparently respectability doesn't altogether agree with me.

I left Daix to it, sliding into a seat in an appealingly darkened corner. I watched her for a little while, both awed and appalled by the facility with which she manipulated people. All her brittleness and sharp edges had vanished; she'd become an adorable, pint-sized little princess, winning over the poor bartender with dimpled smiles and an air of kittenish cluelessness.

I spared a moment's sympathetic reflection for all the hapless souls who had attracted Daix's notice over the last several years. Honestly, Fionn and I should probably have been keeping an eye on *her*.

Abandoning the bartender to his fate — it was clearly too late for him — I let my gaze wander around the pub. It was quiet at this hour, and most of the tables stood unused. On the opposite side to where I sat, a trio of sluagh slumped, desultorily drinking. It wasn't the hour for it, and they didn't look happy about it, either. Besides these three, and Daix, the only other patron was a feorin, seated a few tables away. She sat wrapped in thought and a green coat, periodically scrawling something in the notebook that lay before her.

Little of interest, then, to occupy me, but I had thoughts enough of my own for that. I should not have chosen this table. The décor might be altered, but this vantage-point I recalled only too well, for this had been my favourite seat. Fi used to sit on my right, Sil and Daix opposite; we'd whiled away many an hour with wine and song, in better days.

I shifted impatiently, and stood up. Daix was taking too long.

I took an inordinate amount of pleasure in looming over her as I approached the bar. She'd taken a seat on a high bar stool, but she was still tiny. 'Daix,' I growled.

She awarded me a bright, winsome smile. 'Tai! You know Tully, yes?'

'We're unacquainted,' I said, with a polite nod for Tully. 'And I daresay I'd be delighted to rectify that another time, but in case you've forgotten we've urgent business on hand.'

'Oops,' said Daix, with a giggle. 'Right. Tully darling, waft us a couple of King Goblins, will you?' She slipped off the stool without waiting for an answer, heading for the table I'd recently vacated.

I locked eyes with Tully. He wasn't a tall man himself, the top of his head only as high as my shoulder. He had an artfully disordered mop of reddish hair, a roguish smile, and a mobile face liberally creased with laugh lines. 'She's evil incarnate,' I told him. 'You *do* know that, right?'

He grinned. His green eyes developed an odd, gold flush as he did so. 'Ah, she's a darling. Tai, was it?' The enquiry seemed casual, but the way he was inspecting me was anything but. Somewhere behind his genial smile lurked something intent. Possibly calculating.

'Thetai,' I said.

'Thetai Sarra Antha.' He'd turned from me by then, reaching to retrieve a couple of black, silver-labelled bottles from behind the bar.

'How do you know that name?'

Tully tossed the bottles into the air, one by one. I heard Daix delightedly clapping her hands as they floated their way over to her. 'Used to run with the Fatales, no?' he said, nodding meaningfully in Daix's direction.

'That was a long time ago.'

'Not so very long.'

By faerie standards, I suppose he was right; eighty years was next to nothing. I couldn't tell if he approved of my history or not. Whatever his thoughts might be, they were well hidden behind his congenial bar-keep attitude.

'Happen faerie has missed you girls,' he offered, when I didn't speak. 'You working again?' He glanced around, as though he might see Fionn materialise at any moment.

That floored me; my eyebrows shot up into my hair. '*Missed* us?'

He shrugged, drumming his fingers on the polished surface of the bar. 'You had supporters.'

'And detractors.'

'That's life, love. 'Specially if you're the type to take a stand.'

I couldn't argue with that. 'We do have... business, again,' I said slowly. 'Heard anything about selkies going missing?'

He lifted his chin in Daix's direction. 'Your girl there's just been grilling me on that very subject.' He chuckled, the creases around his eyes deepening. 'Fancied herself very subtle.'

I revised my opinion of Tully. Obviously he was well up to Daix's tricks. 'Thanks,' I said, accepting the pair of glasses he offered me.

'Fionn coming in, or...?' He was glancing at the door.

I grinned. 'I daresay she will, once she knows she's got *fans* here.'

Tully smiled, and — I kid you not — tugged his actual fore-lock in my general direction. 'I'm a fan of yours, too, Thetai Sarra Antha. And not just of yer singing. Come back anytime.'

He turned away, and just as well, for he'd rendered me speech-less. A rare happenstance. I walked slowly back to our table, frowning.

'What was that about *urgent business*?' said Daix tartly as I sat down. 'You took your time.'

'I was...' I set the glasses down, sliding one to Daix. She swapped it for a dark bottle of hobgoblin beer. 'He's heard of us.'

Daix rolled her eyes. 'Just because you wandered off and for-got about us, doesn't mean everybody else did.'

'I didn't forget.' I dropped into my seat and took a long slug of beer.

'You tried pretty damned hard.'

'I'm not sure why you didn't.'

'I told you. Someone had to keep an eye on things. Or did you think the whole of faerie has just obligingly behaved itself while you and Fionn were off drowning in self-pity?'

'Harsh, Daix, even for you.'

She shrugged, and swallowed a huge mouthful of beer. 'If you think Sil would've wanted the three of us to abandon ship on her account, you're an idiot.'

I slammed the bottle down onto the table. 'Do *not* throw Sil's name in my face.'

'Why not? Isn't that what all this shit has been about?'

'We — failed her. All of us.'

'We did. Sil failed, too. None of that means we get to turn in our Fatales badges and fucking retire.'

Anger roiled through me like a dark cloud. Anger, grief and shame: a familiar mix. I wanted to grab Daix's enchanting little face and slam it against the table. Anything to make her *stop looking at me like that.*

But my mood shifted in the space of a breath, as it is sometimes wont to do, and instead I chuckled. 'Fatales badges,' I repeated. 'As if we'd ever had anything so fucking lame—'

I stopped, because Daix had shoved a hand into a pocket and retrieved something, which she proceeded to shove in my face.

A badge. More of a pin, actually, classy enough, with an embossed design: the letter *F,* shimmering in bejewelled colours, and inscribed inside a black triangle.

'The fuck,' I said.

Daix considered the pin with satisfaction. 'Looks good, doesn't it?'

'A triangle?'

She polished up the pin on her sleeve, admiring its shine. 'Like it or not, Tai,' she said without looking at me, 'there *are* three of us now.'

I took another long swallow of beer, thinking. 'How long have you had that thing?'

'Had 'em made in '52.' She dropped the pin onto the table before me. 'Thought you and Fi would get over yourselves a bit sooner.'

I rubbed at my stinging eyes, muttering something under my breath.

Daix grinned. 'I know I am.'

'It's a dumb name,' I said, flicking a finger at the pin. *Fatales.* We'd developed the nickname so long ago, I'd just... got used to it. Eventually.

'Hey,' said Daix. 'Nobody forced you to name your band after it.'

'Okay. Setting your little jewellery design project aside, perhaps we could focus.'

Daix toasted me with her half-empty bottle of King Goblin. '*That's* what I'm talking about.'

'Yeah, shut up. What did Tully tell you?'

'He hasn't heard of any more mysterious absences,' she said.

'Right.'

'*But.*'

I waited.

Daix grinned, one of her more fiendish smiles. 'The Puca's had some new customers lately. Tully doesn't like the look of them at *all*. Said one or two patrons overheard the kind of chatter that might interest us a bit.'

Daix paused for effect.

'You can spit it out, or I can beat it out of you,' I said, agreeably. 'Your choice.'

She rolled her eyes. 'Fine. Tully couldn't absolutely confirm this, but he *heard* that one or two of these guys have been enquiring about selkie pelts.'

I sat up. 'What? As in — buying?'

'Or selling. Maybe both.'

'Neutral ground,' I said with a sigh.

Daix nodded. 'Only place in London all parties could meet without starting a war.'

The Puca had an unsavoury reputation with some, for precisely that reason. Tully may have applauded me for taking a stand — in a way — but the Puca specialised in the opposite. Everyone was welcome over the threshold, whoever they were, whatever they'd done — provided they left their personal conflicts at the door.

That made it the perfect place for the transaction of shady business.

'Good call,' I said to Daix. 'I should have thought to come here myself.'

'I'm pretty sure you're still capable of rational thought, once in a while,' said Daix kindly.

'Thanks. Did Tully say anything else about these people?'

'They're sluagh.'

'Just once, I'd like it if those fuckers could surprise me.'

'You mean like Phélan?'

'Right, we *really* aren't going to talk about Phélan.'

'Then why'd you call him?'

'Daix. You need to get those cameras out of my *everywhere*.'
'But—'
'Or I'll be shoving them down your throat.'
'You've turned violent. I like it.'
'Just repressed. I haven't gutted anyone in *way* too long.'
'You're in luck. We've a troupe of sluagh who seem to be asking for it.'
I smiled. 'My birthday's come early.'

7

— · —

FIONN

Tai's departure from my studio had the most curious effect on me. As the door closed behind her and the sound of her last words faded from the air, she seemed to leave a vast emptiness behind her; a void, where something precious ought to be.

I quickly realised that this was not new. The void had been there for seventy-five years; I'd just grown so used to pretending it wasn't, so adept at navigating around it, that I had stopped noticing it.

Tai only needed to reappear for fifteen minutes, and that was enough to rip all my careful defences to ribbons. Her absence advertised itself by every possible method, and all my old fears came back new.

What if this was just a temporary reprieve? Her interest here was on Mearil's account, not mine. Once that business was resolved, she could disappear again in a heartbeat. Probably she would.

And we'd go right back to never seeing each other again.

Daix. Tai was gone in order to fetch *Daix*. My feelings there were much more complex. Tai wasn't wrong when she had called Daix our best friend. She and Silise had been exactly that, once, though one rather *chose* to love Daix than anything else. Maintaining a close relationship with Daix de Montfort is the emotional equivalent of cuddling up to a polar bear: apparent fluffy harmlessness followed by a swift and bloody death, probably in short order.

I'd missed her, too.

I had to physically shake myself to disrupt so unhelpful a train of thought. *My* interest here should be focused on Mearil, too, and Narasel. Permitting myself to become too distracted by personal matters would help no one, not even me.

I hauled myself out of my chair, feeling intensely wearied. A long night of deep, uninterrupted slumber ought to have refreshed me more. But then, quite a lot had happened since.

'Jane?' I called, when I opened my door. I knew she would be hovering nearby; the moment she'd seen Tai leave she would have made a beeline for my office.

'Yes!' said she, and bustled over. I opened the door wider to admit her, and closed it after her.

'Everything's moving very well,' she was saying, already talking before she'd even sat down. 'We have Harrods and Selfridges already on board, I *knew* they would love this one. Oh, and Liberty's expressed an interest in the sea-foam silks, didn't I tell you it was smart to run production on those? There's a future in textiles for Serenity, I'm telling you, we should run with this—'

'Jane,' I interjected.

'Mm?' She paused, mid-sentence, though she wasn't looking at me: she was riffling through a stack of papers and notebooks she'd brought in with her.

'All fantastic,' I said, ruthlessly dismissing the whole of her report in two words. 'Thank you. But I need to talk to you about Narasel.'

She did look up at that, blankly confused. 'Narasel?'

'Model number twelve.'

By lineage, Jane is half hob, which makes her diminutive. She's also determined and highly organised. I value her extremely for these traits, but she cannot remember names. At all. Or faces, either. She wouldn't remember who Narasel was — not until I'd identified exactly where the selkie model had fitted in during the show.

Understanding dawned.

'Twelve,' said Jane, her hair bouncing as she nodded. 'Absent at the eleventh hour, which I'll be speaking to her about — *if* you want to hire her again, Fionn, and I wouldn't blame you if you wanted to drop her. It's unacceptable. Not that you didn't do a fantastic job in her stead, so much so that another time, maybe we could use you again—'

'There'll be neither need nor opportunity to speak to her, Jane,' I said, cutting in on this flow of ideas. 'She is dead.'

Jane stopped abruptly. 'Dead?'

'Her body was pulled out of the Thames this morning.'

'The *Thames*? But she's — was —'

'Selkie. Yes, I know.'

I didn't have to explain what that meant. Jane knew. Her face registered horror; she stared at me.

'As I recall,' I said, after a moment. 'She was last seen about half an hour before show time. You said she'd been spotted heading for the ladies — at a run. Is that right?'

Jane sat in frowning thought for a moment, no longer looking at me. Her eyes were blank, her thoughts turned inward, into memory. 'I didn't see her myself,' she said, slowly. 'It was — one of the other girls reported it to me.'

'Her name?' I asked, without much hope.

Jane was already shaking her head. 'Model number seventeen,' she said, and dived back into the pile of papers she'd dropped into her lap. 'Hang on — think I still have the schedule — yes.' She withdrew a single sheet, much covered in sketches and text, and consulted it. 'Seventeen. Melly, that was it.'

My turn for a moment's deep thought. I knew that name. Not well, because we'd never used her before; last week's show had been her first with us. But there was something...

Ah. 'Selkie,' I said. 'I think? Isn't she?'

Jane shrugged. 'Isn't on the schedule.'

No, it wouldn't be. The heritage of each model was of no particular relevance to the orderly workings of the show, so Jane would have no interest in that subject. If I tended to display a bias towards selkies when we were hiring, that was my own problem.

But I was fairly sure I was right, which cost me another surge of alarm. We'd had two selkies among the models that night, and one of them was dead. Tai's selkie roommate was missing.

Had anyone checked on Melly?

'I should have *thought*,' I said, reaching for my phone. I'd been musing, not long before, about how to reach — and warn — other selkies in London, and I still hadn't happened to remember Melly.

'Thought what?' said Jane. 'I'm appalled at what's happened to Narasel, but it's just one incident, right? Even if her skin—'

Was stolen. I heard the rest of the sentence as clearly as though she'd uttered it herself, and I knew she'd stopped out of a misguided attempt at sensitivity. It didn't help. Why did people think that never bringing certain things up in my hearing would somehow protect me from the reality of them? Nothing could do that.

'It isn't just one incident,' I said. 'Tai was here just now because her selkie roommate has disappeared. I need you to get me

Melly's contact details, please. Phone, home address, anything you've got.'

Jane set to, and I waited while she fumbled through papers, maintaining an enforced stillness as I sat. Fidgeting, or pacing, were distracting; only calm could help.

'Got it,' she said, but instead of handing it to me, she pulled out her own phone and began immediately to dial.

I waited, my eyes locked with Jane's as we listened to the ringing of her phone.

It rang and rang — and then the ringing stopped.

Hope leapt in my heart.

But Jane was shaking her head. 'Voicemail,' she mouthed, then spoke into the phone. 'Melly, this is Jane Ashen of Serenity. You left one or two possessions behind at the show last week and we'd like to restore them to you. Please get in touch.'

She shut off the call, her lips tightening. 'Someone had better go over there. I'll deal with it.'

I wished, again, for some kind of police force associated with Faerie. This was just the sort of time when it would be nice to have someone to call. 'I'd better go,' I said. 'I don't know — what we might find.' Worst case scenario would be Melly's body, if we were already too late, though given the patterns emerging, she probably wouldn't have been killed at home. Otherwise, who knew? Some manner of clue as to her absence: that would be my hope. Some kind of danger... not likely, but possible.

Jane nodded, but she was not convinced. I caught her studying me, frowning slightly, her thoughts obvious. What was it about me that made me a better candidate for this assignment than anyone else? To her, I was a designer, a CEO, a model. She had no way of knowing what else I'd once been.

'It will be fine,' I said crisply, rising.

'I had better go with you,' said Jane.

'I've another task for you, if you please. Get in touch with all the other models that were at the show that night — not just models, actually, but everybody you can get hold of. Ask them if they talked to Narasel that night, or saw anything that might be relevant. Anything that might tell us where she went.'

'I can do that,' said Jane. 'Or I can get Sunny to do it and I'll go with you.'

I regarded her with a disapproving frown. 'I've no need of you for this, Jane.'

She put her hands on her hips, and stared me down. 'Fionn. If you weren't so brilliant about *some* things, I'd be tempted to call you an idiot.'

I blinked. 'I beg your pardon?'

'We have two, possibly three selkies missing. Two out of those three were associated with the show, and one of those two is already dead. But Narasel and Melly weren't the only selkies at the garden that night, and they certainly aren't the only selkies in London. Does it not occur to you that *you* might be in some danger?'

I felt like I'd been punched. For a long moment I couldn't breathe, let alone speak.

The idea had occurred to me, and yet, it hadn't. I wasn't used to thinking of myself as vulnerable anymore, and there was good reason for that. Vulnerability had broken me; since then, I'd devoted everything I had to erasing every weakness I could be said to possess. I'd become the kind of person people *feared*, not the kind of person they preyed upon.

But all that had been a very long time ago. What was I now?

A designer. A model. A CEO.

If anything could protect me from being targeted like Narasel, or Mearil, it was my prominence: it wouldn't be a low-key crime, disappearing me. But nothing else would protect me. I wasn't Fionn of Cuath-Tor, fearsome fatale, anymore. I was just Fionn.

'All right,' I said, though I wondered, as I spoke, what Jane thought she was going to do either. Still, she had a point. Having company — any company — was better than going alone.

And soon... perhaps I'd have Tai or Daix with me for errands like this.

Melly's address was on the outskirts of the city, far from the centre: a cheap situation. I was not surprised, when we knocked upon her front door, to find its green paint peeling, and the sash windows dingy with grime. Nor was I surprised to find, upon its being answered, that she did not live there alone. The girl who opened the door looked human, at first, but upon beholding her visitors she let the glamour fade away. Underneath, she was full-blooded hob, but rather young. She was slight and thin, her curly hair unbrushed, her face set in a sulky expression. She said nothing, only stared at us.

'Is Melly in?' I said.

'She's not here.' The hob girl made as though to shut the door in my face.

'Wait,' I said, and stepped forward, shoving the door wider. 'This is important. When did she go out?'

'Who are you?' A belligerent question, accompanied by a glower.

'Fionn of Cuath-Tor,' I said. 'Your friend Melly was employed for my show recently, and I need to talk to her.'

'The Serenity show?' The sulk vanished. 'She was so excited about that.'

'And she did a great job, but—'

'*So* great,' interrupted Jane, 'that we'd like to talk to her about an upcoming show. In person. We can really see her taking a regular slot on our catwalks.'

'She isn't here,' repeated the hob girl. 'But, like, shouldn't you talk to her agency about that? I can get you their number—'

'We've done that,' said Jane. 'We really want to talk to Melly in person. Can you let us know where to get hold of her?'

A shrug. 'She hasn't come in yet today. Try calling.'

'We've tried,' I said. 'Is it common for Melly to stay out all night?'

'What's it to you? She's reliable, if that's what you're worried about. She'd never miss a show.'

I exchanged a look with Jane. Subterfuge wasn't helping. It would have to be truth, whether it alarmed this girl or not. 'Can we come in?' I said. 'Please. There is more afoot here than I would like to explain to you from the doorstep.'

The wariness was back, but the girl opened the door wider for us, albeit with ill grace. We followed her into a tiny, and untidy, kitchen, with a single dingy window overlooking a ragged patch of garden. 'I can't offer you tea,' she said. 'Kettle's broken.'

'What's your name?' I asked, taking a seat at a cheap IKEA table.

'Tanna.'

'Tanna, one of the models contracted for my show was murdered last night.' I gave that a second to sink in. 'Melly was the last person known to have talked with her. Five minutes later, Narasel left, and we don't know where she was going, or why. As I'm sure you can imagine, it is important that we find out whether Melly knew anything that might help us.'

'Narasel's dead.' Tanna said it flatly, perhaps in disbelief.

'Did you know her?'

'Not really. Melly brought her round a couple of times.' She ran thin hands through her mass of hair, and sighed. 'I wasn't worried when Melly didn't come home last night. She does that, sometimes. But *now* I'm worried.'

'So are we,' said Jane.

I debated whether to tell Tanna about Mearil, but decided against it. Rattling her further wouldn't be of use, provided she was disposed to help. And she looked it. She'd taken a phone from somewhere and was scrolling through it, already shaking her head. 'Nothing from her, but she can be a total flake.'

'When did she leave?'

'Late. She was meeting somebody...' Tanna's eyes strayed to mine, registering horror. 'Shit. You don't think she — that whoever she met might have—'

'You don't know who she was meeting?' I persisted.

Tanna shook her head. 'Someone she met at a bar,' she said, looking miserable. 'She seemed excited, but, I never thought—'

'Never mind that,' I said. 'Self-recriminations help no one. Which bar was it? Do you know anything else about this person?'

'Eventide,' said Tanna. 'I don't know anything about them, she wouldn't tell me. Acted like it was a big secret, like... she knew she shouldn't be going there, and was, kind of, thrilled about it.'

'Eventide?' I echoed, momentarily stunned. 'But that's crazy.' Eventide was a popular fae carousing spot in central London. Classy, expensive, elite... a girl who lived in a house like this had no business in a bar like *that*. They were sticklers for their reputation, to the point of blatant snobbery. How had she even got in?

The look on Jane's face reflected similar thoughts to mine. If someone had taken Melly to Eventide, and that someone had something to do with her disappearance — and Narasel's, and Mearil's — then we were dealing with someone who had clout. Someone with means and connections. Conceivably someone respected.

'Seems I'm paying a visit to Eventide tonight,' I said.

Jane grimaced. 'They aren't going to let *me* in there.'

'They might, if I took you with me. But... I think I've another idea.' Jane might pass as part of my entourage, but Tai had the clout to get in on her own account. And if it came to trouble, I knew who I'd rather have at my back.

'I'll make some calls,' said Jane. 'See if any of the other girls knew who Melly was seeing.'

I nodded. I doubted she would find much; if Melly had kept her date's identity a secret from Tanna, I couldn't see why she would have bragged about it to her fellow models. But it was worth a try. Everything was worth a try.

'What should I do?' asked Tanna, sounding a little plaintive.

'See if she comes home,' I said. 'I'll leave you my number. If you see her or hear from her, call me. If you know of anybody else who might know more, call *them*, and then call me. If you find anything in this house that seems relevant, call me.'

Tanna nodded. 'I can do that.'

'And,' I added. 'If you know any other selkies in London, warn them.'

'Warn them about what?' said Tanna, not unreasonably.

I sighed. 'Warn them to keep a closer than usual eye on their skins.'

ANYONE WHO'D BEEN SLAVE-TAKEN before needed no such warning, of course. I felt no more than a faint impulse to go and check on mine. It needed no such oversight; it would probably be easier to get into Alcatraz than to steal my sealskin. Still, most selkies were more fortunate than I, and had no reason to be so paranoid. Yet. I wondered how many were blithely wandering the city with their skins somewhere about their person, perhaps in the naïve belief that it was safer to keep the thing with them, under their own eye.

Only in the same way that it's safer to wear all your priceless diamonds than to lock them up in a vault.

Jane and I left Melly's house in a sombre mood. So many selkies had already gone missing, in the space of a mere couple of days. As prompt as we were to investigate, we were nonetheless too late, or so I feared. I had begun to live in dread of the next report: another drowned selkie adrift in the river, sealskin unaccounted for.

'I want to take a closer look at Eventide,' I said, after we had gone some way in silence. 'It seems... wrong, that such a place should be involved.'

'Perhaps it isn't,' Jane cautioned. 'Whoever Melly met there might have had nothing to do with her disappearance.'

'True,' I agreed. 'But do you believe that?'

She sighed. 'Not really.'

'There was no good reason for Melly to be there.' Part of me wanted to believe that the girl had just been lucky enough to meet someone of status who genuinely appreciated her. But I knew the clientele at Eventide. I had frequented the place myself, years before; it wasn't so elitist, back then. When that tide had turned, I had stopped going. I knew too well how its regulars would have viewed a girl like Melly. Anyone who had invited her *there* could have few good intentions.

'Who even owns it now?' asked Jane.

A question I could not answer. It used to be the property of a wonderful kitsune lady, Ayaka. She was as old as the hills, and some kind of genuine noblewoman, if report was to be believed. She had owned the site for two hundred years, and taken it through various names and incarnations, Eventide being the most recent of them. But she had retired, and sold it. Whoever had taken it over had very different ideas about its management, and I had never heard who that was.

'I'll find out,' I said. Another thought occurred to me, and I reached immediately for my phone. 'I want to know,' I said as it rang, 'if Narasel had any connection with Eventide recently — or if Mearil did.'

The phone rang and rang, and I'd almost given up on its being answered when Tai's voice spoke. 'Fi? You found something?'

I'd only spoken to her a couple of hours before, but it was still good to hear her voice again. 'Maybe,' I said, neutrally. 'Another missing selkie, for a start.'

'Shit. Who is it?'

'Another model from my show. We had two selkies there, as it turns out. The second, Melly, was accounted for up until the show, or shortly after, but she hasn't come home.'

'Uh huh.'

'Her roommate says she went out with someone she met at Eventide.'

'Eventide.' Tai repeated the word thoughtfully. 'That seems... odd.'

'Highly. I have no idea yet whether Narasel ever went there, but I thought you might know if Mearil had.'

'I don't,' said Tai. 'But I haven't been home a lot lately, on account of the tour. And to be honest with you I've been completely oblivious, also on account of the tour, and *now* I feel bad. I'll find out though. Coronis might know.'

'Do you happen to know who owns that place now?'

'No, but Daix is threatening to set me on fire if I don't give her the phone, so—'

'Daix?' I said, startled. 'You already found her?'

'Nope,' said Tai sourly. 'She found *me*. Or rather, us.' Her tone turned suspiciously sweet. 'Why don't I let her tell you allll about it?'

'I—' I began, but too late. Daix's voice cut in.

'Fionn of Cuath-Tor. *What* have you got yourself into now?'

'Hello, Daix.'

'That's it? *Hello, Daix?*'

'I trust you've been well.'

She snorted. 'Better than you, I'd say.'

'I won't ask how you know that.'

'Fine, but Tai says I have to tell you allll about it.'

'Since when do you do what Tai says?'

'When it happens to coincide with my own interests. I've been keeping a close eye on everything, Fi. *Everything.* Including you, including Tai, and including Eventide, and you can thank me later. It's owned by the Quinn-Diamhors now.'

'I know that name,' I said slowly.

'I would hope so.'

The Quinn-Diamhor family are leannan sith. At their best, the leannan are sensitive aesthetes and devoted patrons of the arts, and the Quinn-Diamhors are certainly known for associating with artists by preference. Wealthy, successful artists. Their purchase of Eventide made sense from that perspective.

The leannan are also known for being dangerously seductive, and they are terrifyingly beautiful. The kind of beauty that's hard to resist; the kind that could persuade you into almost anything. In fairness, the same can be said of many of the fae, including selkies; it's just that the leannan have it in buckets *and* spades. Those old stories about mortal girls, seduced by the Fair Folk and disappearing under the mounds? It's often the leannan sith they are talking about. Not always, but often enough. Anyone with their wits about them treads very carefully around the leannan.

Tanna's words floated through my mind. *Acted like it was a big secret. She knew she shouldn't be going there. Thrilled about it.*

If she had run into the leannan, that might explain the secrecy — and the thrill.

I groaned. '*Why* are girls so attracted to bad boys?'

I could practically hear Daix smirking. 'They're a hell of a ride.'

'You would know,' I heard Tai saying in the background.

'Like you wouldn't,' Daix said tartly. She didn't speak the name of Phélan, but it hung there, all the louder for being unspoken.

'Low blow,' said Tai.

'Harsh but fair,' said Daix.

'Look,' I said, cutting in. 'We need to look around Eventide. Tai and I will go there tonight. Daix, can you employ whatever connections you have no doubt cultivated and try to find out more?'

'You don't want me with you at Eventide?'

'No.'

'I'm offended.'

'A great pity.'

She snickered. 'All right. You and Tai can dress up to the nines and go hobnob with the rich and powerful all night. I'll sit alone in my bunker, trawling the underworld for word on the Quinn-Diamhors, on Eventide, and on anything sticky the leannan are known to have their fingers in lately.'

'Your bunker,' I repeated.

'It's cosy. Everyone should have one. Oh, we should probably tell you—'

'Fi,' came Tai's voice, cutting Daix off.

'*Hey*,' Daix objected, distantly.

Tai ignored that. 'We've been to the Puca,' she said. 'There are rumours of some kind of shady selkie-skin-dealing crap going on in there. Sluagh.'

My stomach performed a slow turn. 'Ah,' I said, mouth dry.

'I know. We don't know who they are yet, but Tully's going to let us know if they show up again.'

Ah, the sluagh. Fine folk, in many cases; I'd be the last person to throw shade on the entire race. But they have... quirks. They are merciless warriors, and unquestionably the fiercest and most bloodthirsty of the fae. When they troop, they make up the Wild Hunt — together with the coin-sith, what might colloquially be termed hell hounds. To look upon the Wild Hunt is to go mad, certainly if one is a mortal, but even the fae are not impervious to the combined effects of many sluagh in one place. Individually, they aren't so dangerous, though they have an ease with the souls of the departed which is, frankly, creepy — especially since some are known, or at least *said*, to devour them. Short of that, they can mess with your head in ways that are... not pretty. Tai can testify to that.

When the sluagh turn to crime, the results are not pretty either.

A picture was beginning to form, and it was making me uneasy. If we had sluagh and leannan sith involved in the same scheme, that made for too many dangerous powers, working together in troubling ways. If some of those folk also had the backing of rich and powerful people — possibly the Quinn-Diamhors, even — then this problem was bigger than a couple of unfortunate selkie-girls who'd been in the wrong place at the wrong time.

'Meet me at Eventide,' I told Tai. 'Eight o'clock.'

'I'll be there.'

I hung up, and relayed the news to Jane.

'Right,' she said, her mouth forming a grim line. 'I'm going back to the studio. I'll get in touch with everyone I can think of, see if anybody else has received an unexpected invitation to Eventide lately.'

'Ask if anyone knows who Melly was seeing,' I said. 'And Narasel. I wouldn't be surprised to find that there was a mysterious stranger in *her* life lately, too.'

8

— · —

TAI

STRANGE, GOING BACK TO Eventide in Fionn's company. Bittersweet, because it was just like old times — and yet nothing like that at all.

Strange going back under any circumstances, to be fair. I don't mix with the type who go there now, not if I can help it. It was a sad day when Ayaka retired. No one with any sense could approve of what's been done with the place since.

The staff used to be merely friendly. Now they're downright creepy — *if* you've eminence enough to pull your weight in there. As successful artists with a modicum of fame, Fi and I do, more's the pity.

Eventide's front doors are just for show. And *what* a show: clear glass lit with its own golden radiance, like afternoon sun on the water. Beyond that, a swirl of drifting mist, moon-silver, opaque; peering into that golden world is like catching a glimpse of heaven. Tantalising, provocative, out of reach.

Pretty, manipulative shit.

You can tell who's new to Eventide, because they're trying to get in that way. They don't get far. The real entrance is around the back, and *that* is like wandering into the garden of paradise. Roses rambling everywhere, whatever the season; water features; thick carpets of golden moss, bejewelled with diamantine dew; and somewhere in there, a door, discreet compared to the front ones. It's guarded by a couple of bouncers, typically drawn from the troll clans.

Tonight was no different.

'Ladies,' said bouncer number one, as Fi and I approached. Seven foot tall and stacked, the guy made for an intimidating door-guard. Nobody much wants to tangle with *one* mountain-troll, let alone two, although if the pair of them couldn't keep their eyes where they belonged I'd be reconsidering my stance on that.

I clenched my fists, running my thumbs over the stones adorning my knuckles. I'd left the gloves at home. The jewels are decorative enough, in their way, and if their presence gives anybody pause before they think about getting too close to me, all the better.

Fionn stepped past me, nudging me none too gently as she did so.

Right. I was scowling. I replaced my thunderous expression with a smile; it felt badly pasted on, but it passed muster. Whatever Fi said to the tossers on the door produced a chuckle, and with a gracious inclination of her elegant head she was sashaying inside.

I followed, receiving an obsequious hat-tip as I passed.

So far so good. I paused inside the door to take a breath, and unclench my fists.

Fionn gave me a cool look. 'You used to be better at this.'

'Out of practice,' I said shortly.

That might have been a flicker of sympathy somewhere at the back of her eyes, but I couldn't be sure. Maybe it was just a trick of that silvery mist. *She* looked incredible, of course, in all her supermodel glory. Her shimmery satin gown looked like a sheath made of water itself, its style evoking the best of 1930s glamour. She wore pearls in her upswept hair, and her eye make-up was fabulously over the top. Perfect.

I'd gone for a more severe style. Black velvet: floor-length, long-sleeved and backless. Fi had lent me a pair of her skyscraper heels, which I had accepted only reluctantly, expecting to resent their spectacular lack of practicality. Actually, I didn't. I liked the way they made me feel. Taller, for one, which is important anytime I have to stand next to Fionn.

Eventide wasn't busy yet; the fashionable hour wouldn't hit until nearer midnight. We had time to settle in, get our bearings, grab a drink or two, and try to remember what the fuck we were supposed to do in there.

I wasn't kidding when I said I was out of practice. My old instincts aren't entirely gone, but close enough. I could have walked up to the music stage and rocked the joint without a moment's hesitation, but to mingle and hobnob and angle for information? These days, I'm more inclined to punch people than make nice to them.

Fi catwalked her way to a table and slid into a silk-brocaded chair, somehow managing to look coolly unconcerned and oblivious to those around her. I, though, recognised the signs: the way her gaze flicked from face to face, taking note of who was there, observing who sat with whom. The way she positioned herself so as to have a view of as much of the room as possible, her back to the wall. *She* wasn't out of practice.

I strutted over to join her. Wasn't even intentional, but you can't wear four-inch heels without strutting about like a damned peacock. It's sort of the basis of their appeal. 'One might ask what you've been up to all this time,' I said to Fi, 'besides staging a takeover of the world of haute couture.'

Her gaze settled on me, more or less expressionless. 'That's more than enough to keep a person busy, I assure you.'

To which attempt at side-stepping my question, I merely raised an eyebrow.

'What?' she murmured, cool as ever.

'Been taking a side job or two?' I persevered.

'You mean, do I secretly run an underground detective agency in some dingy back street?'

'By day, she decks the city in silks, satins and pearls,' I said. 'By night, she champions the down-trodden masses from her secret lair.'

'Nonsense.'

'Come on, Fi. Once a Fatale, always a Fatale.'

'Really? Where then is your secret lair?'

'If I told you, it wouldn't be much of a secret.'

Fionn bestowed upon me a withering look, and signalled a waiter. 'Bring me a strawberry gin fizz,' she murmured.

'I'll be needing something stronger,' I said, flashing the waiter a smile. 'Pray get me a love potion.'

'Which is what?' said Fionn.

'Fruit juice and vodka, emphasis on the vodka.'

'You're nervous.'

'I'm never nervous.'

'And you never lie.'

The waiter had gone; I permitted myself a grin. 'The truth should never be allowed to get in the way of a good joke.'

'Of course,' said Fionn, gracefully inclining her head. 'Protecting the sanctity of the joke. Nothing whatsoever to do with protecting your pride, resisting perceived pressure, or stubborn bravado.'

'See, this is why I stopped having friends,' I said. 'Too much self-knowledge is bad for a girl.'

'You prefer self-deception.'

'Who doesn't.'

Fionn, bless her, actually considered that question, and finally awarded me the point. 'I can't say that you're wrong.'

'Thank you.'

'Only you need not actively cultivate it, surely.'

'I do indeed need, if it gets me through the damned day. Also, starry-eyed dilettante to your left.'

Fionn did that thing where she looked without seeming to. I... tried. We observed, more or less covertly, as a frighteningly young-looking girl came in, dressed up to the nines in too much make-up and too little satin, her eyes everywhere as she took in the scene. She'd gushed and stammered her way past the door guards, and as Fi and I watched, she tripped over to the bar and repeated the trick with the bartender. She walked like she was taking an exam in nonchalant elegance, and expected to fail.

'Never been here before in her life, I'd wager,' I murmured.

Fionn nodded. 'Never expected to be, either.'

'Does she look selkie?'

Fionn gave a tiny shrug of one shoulder. 'I can't always tell at a glance.'

Neither could I. The girl was certainly beautiful, in a gauche way, and just as clearly fae. Eventide was still close to empty; we'd arrived early on purpose, wanting to watch as the clientele came in. The newcomer took a seat alone, and sat with an air of suppressed anticipation, eyes everywhere.

Our drinks had arrived. I took a larger-than-advisable mouthful of raspberry and searingly-strong vodka, and felt steadied by it.

'She's meeting someone,' said Fionn.

'Someone with clout, if they got her name added,' I agreed. It was one thing to finagle an unusual guest past the door guards if you were present to talk them into it; another to contrive admittance for them on their own account, unescorted, at any time they chose. There was a list somewhere, by repute a short one, of people welcome to frequent Eventide — the sort who lacked the eminence or connections to score an invitation on their own. I didn't know who might have the power to get a name added to that list — besides, of course, the club's owners.

'We should go talk to her,' I said.

'No,' said Fionn immediately. 'We shouldn't show ourselves yet.'

'What do you mean, show ourselves? We're just patrons here, enjoying a drink, mingling with the other guests. And that girl looks ready to faint with joy at meeting a certain name in fashion design. Unless I miss my guess, that's one of your pieces she's wearing.'

'You have been paying attention,' Fionn murmured, with a fleeting smile.

'Come on, we're going over.'

'Tai, show a little caution. People may still remember—'

'*Very* few people remember, Fi, and she isn't going to be one of them. I doubt she was born the last time you and I spoke.' So saying, I got up, collected my drink, and made my way over to the starry-eyed girl's table. 'Serenity,' I said, nodding towards her gown. Like many of Fi's designs, it was pure silk and had the fluidity of running water. Fionn is the king *and* queen of fabric drape. 'I think I detect a fan.'

'Oh my gosh, yes,' gushed the girl. 'I've never had a real Serenity gown before. They always look so *beautiful* in the shows, but wearing them is even better, isn't it? It's like wearing a waterfall, or a cloud—'

'The waterfall was, in fact, some part of the inspiration for that gown,' said Fionn, quietly joining us, and flowing into a seat. 'You were lucky to get hold of that piece. We didn't make many.'

The poor girl looked ready to explode, though not so much with joy. She'd clammed up, capable only of staring at Fionn with a kind of appalled wonder.

Which unfortunately meant she wasn't responding to Fionn's prompt. I saw the direction Fi was trying to go in: she *had* been lucky to get hold of that gown, and the thing was likely to be eye-bleedingly expensive. Her artless chatter reinforced the idea that she wasn't normally in a position to own such things; she lacked the wherewithal, then. So how had she got the dress — or more likely, who had given it to her?

When in doubt, try being direct. 'I'm jealous,' I said, toasting her with my somewhat depleted love potion. 'Where did you get it?'

The girl's gaze travelled back to my face, eventually. 'I— well, the truth is,' she said, her eyes going wider. 'The truth is, I don't know. I mean, I didn't exactly choose it, I...' She trailed off, looking from one of us to the other, hesitating.

Silence from Fionn.

'Curious,' I said, laughing. 'What, you found it in the street? I wish *my* lucky stars were so generous.'

'Of course not.' She gave an awkward laugh.

'No, that would have been too good to be true,' I agreed.

'I, um, found it on my doorstep.'

I blinked. 'What?'

'Yesterday,' she said. 'With a note, inviting me to — to come here, tonight.'

'Lucky girl,' put in Fionn. 'You've an important admirer.'

That observation was productive of a rosy blush, and the poor fool visibly preened. 'I don't know who it is, yet,' she confided. 'Though I have an idea...'

She had a wish list, in other words, and a head full of daydreams. I doubted any of those dreams were about to come true. Though, one question preoccupied me: did whoever had given her the dress know that she was a fan of Fionn's, or had it been a coincidence? If the former, perhaps her mysterious admirer was someone she knew.

The mystery of it all made me uneasy.

'You're Fionn of Cuath-Tor, aren't you?' said the girl, and she had probably been dying to say that for some minutes. 'You designed this dress! You're so amazing. I applied to walk for your shows, but, no luck yet. I'm still trying.' She gazed at Fionn with a trusting hopefulness I found rather heart-breaking. Innocence. It's *so* easy to take advantage of.

'You're a model?' said Fionn, sipping her gin fizz.

'Just getting started, yet,' came the answer, with another blush. 'My agent says I have potential — ah, my name's Cellann, by the way, Cellann of Indra-Tath, I'm with the Anna Sant Agency—'

Cellann of Indra-Tath rambled on, clearly hoping to impress Fi with her credentials. I let my attention wander. More people were coming in at the door, a few I vaguely recognised: a half ban sith brunette who was somebody in television; a tall, moody-looking sluagh I'd bumped into backstage once or twice. The rest were unfamiliar, as yet, and so far nobody showed any signs of wanting to approach Cellann's table.

Fionn was excusing herself. Apparently she was tired of the chatter, as was I; I toasted Cellann with the dregs of my love potion and followed Fi, though we did not return to our table.

'Perimeter prowl?' I said, falling into step beside Fionn.

'Eavesdropping circuit,' said she, flashing a glamorous smile at a passing rakshasa. 'Were you really jealous?'

'Of the dress?' I cast a fleeting glance at Cellann's gown. 'No. Not my style.'

'You lied to an impressionable youngster? Deplorable.'

'I will lie to that impressionable youngster all night if it will keep her from turning up face-down in the river.'

'Or Mearil, either.'

'Right. If someone's luring girls like her to Eventide, I'm not leaving until we find out who it is. By the by, if you're heading for Rudy with intent, you're on the wrong track. I know him. He's okay.'

'Rudy?'

'The sluagh I suspect you're trying to eavesdrop on. He's the type of dangerous-looking that wouldn't hurt a fly.'

'*Rudy*? Really?'

I grinned. 'Full name's Rudlund Mathis. He's the drummer with Tormented Wraith.'

'Tormented. Wraith.'

'Death metal.'

Fionn's look might best be described as indecipherable, with a side of appalled. 'On which topic. Why power metal, Tai?'

'Because it makes me feel powerful, Fi. Why else.'

'Like you ever needed help there.'

'I might also have been a bit angry about a few things.'

'Farewell Fatales.'

'Exactly.'

'If you're finished being angry,' Fionn said, letting this pass, 'You've the voice to do anything you want.'

'Which I can't take much actual credit for, but that aside, what I want to do is power metal.'

'I see.'

'And I do it very well, for your information.'

She inclined her head. 'Pheriko and Orandine aren't bad either.'

'And you know the names of my bandmates how exactly?'

'Same way you're able to recognise my gowns at a glance, I expect.'

'I love them,' I said, not referring to the gowns. 'But they're no substitute.'

'Were they supposed to be?'

I had to think about that one for a second. 'How much honesty do you want?'

'All of it.'

'Then yes.'

She nodded.

'If you were Daix,' I went on, 'you'd have something acidic to say about people who try to replace their best friends instead of mending fences with them.'

'Let's all be thankful that I am not Daix.'

'But—'

She elbowed me. 'Hush. I do believe Rudy's coming over.'

He was, too. He'd been trying to catch my eye for a few minutes, an effort I had steadily resisted, but the man was persistent. He approached with that manly, rolling-the-shoulders walk he likes to affect, grinning what was doubtless supposed to be a knee-weakening grin. 'It's my favourite Fatale,' he said.

'Hi, Rudy,' I said, suppressing an urge to roll my eyes. 'Have you met Fionn?'

He did her the honour of a slow looking-over, which Fionn bore with her usual grace. 'Ma'am,' he said at last.

'Ma'am?' I echoed. 'Since when are you so polite?'

'I'm scrupulously polite to anyone I haven't seen roaring drunk.' He had the cheek to wink at me.

'Drunk, hm?' said Fionn, raising a brow.

'Rudy's going to go away now, and take story-time away with him.' I directed at Rudy a mega-watt smile, liberally laced with venom.

He chuckled. 'But seriously, Tai, I didn't know you were an Eventide girl.'

'One of my better achievements, clearly.'

'Ma'am. Permit me to provide you with a drink.' He actually bowed.

'Perfect,' I said. 'I'm all out of love potion. But, Rudy, before you do that, tell me something. Do you come here a lot?'

His eyebrows climbed into his hair.

'It's not a pick-up line,' I said, suppressing an urge to kick him with my delightfully pointy-toed shoes. 'Real question.'

'Uh, I suppose?' he said, looking from me to Fionn in confusion. 'Once a week, sometimes more.'

'Okay. So. Have you noticed anyone unusual hanging around here of late?'

He turned his head, and looked straight at Cellann, who was still sitting alone. 'You mean like her?'

'Like her, and whoever the hell is getting people like her in here.'

'I didn't think you cared about stuff like that.'

'Rudy, I'm not asking because I've turned into a giant snob overnight. It's important.'

Fionn spoke up. She never raises her voice, but somehow she's always heard. 'Tai's roommate is missing,' she said. 'And we fear she may have met somebody here who had something to do with it.'

My turn to raise an eyebrow at Fi. She gave me that eye-flick that functions as a dismissive shrug.

Fine, if we were going to do honesty and hope for the best...

'Fi's also short a couple of models from her shows,' I said. 'One of them's dead. And that innocent little girl right there is exactly the type.'

Rudy's gaze sharpened, all traces of humour vanishing from his face. 'Selkie they pulled out of the river. That's what you're talking about?'

'You heard about that?'

'Everyone's heard about it.' Rudy was looking dead serious now, which is unusual for him, for all his death metal glory. 'Tai, you want to be careful who you're asking about that.'

'I'm not running around asking people questions at random, if that's what you mean.'

'So you had some bullet-proof reason to think I couldn't possibly be involved?'

I folded my arms. 'Haven't seen anything about you that might suggest you're a crazed killer.'

'What does that matter?'

He did have a point.

Too bad. 'Got to take risks sometimes, Rudy. We can't make progress on this case if we're too cautious to actually investigate.'

He shrugged. 'You've got that siren voice going for you, I suppose. Might get you out of a tight spot.'

It might indeed; had, in fact, on many occasions. I don't use it lightly. I mean, there's singing, which I will cheerfully do all day, and then there's *siren*-singing, which is different. If you're caught off guard by a siren song, you'll do anything. Anything at all. And you may or may not remember it afterwards. It's sort of like drunkenness that way, only without the long lead-up of knocking back shots.

Some people like that about a girl.

Some don't so much.

It really depends on how much the siren happens to like *you*.

Anyway. Unlike Coronis, Rudy either hadn't heard the old stories about the *fatales*, or he hadn't made the connections between those same old stories and the name I'd somewhat unwisely chosen for my band. He thought I might get hurt.

Sweet, really.

I lifted my hands and showed him my diamond-studded knuckles. 'I'll be fine, Rudy.'

'And your friend?' He looked again at Fionn, who certainly appeared delicate with her silk-clad slenderness and bejewelled elegance. All lady-like and dainty.

'Pray you never catch Fi with a couple of knives in her hands,' I said.

Rudy's brows went up. 'There's a story somewhere behind that.'

'There is, and we're not getting into it,' I said, Fionn having opted merely to return Rudy's gaze with an amused expression.

'Pity,' said Rudy, and grinned. At Fi.

'Right, when you're done flirting with my friends, feel free to go back to your life,' I said. 'And if you hear anything else, Rudy, let me know.'

He tugged his forelock at me, the cheeky grin I was more used to restored to his face. 'We'll do that drink,' he said, 'but maybe another time.' Back he went to his table.

'Interesting,' said Fionn.

'You two can hook up later, but for now, focus,' I said. 'Unless I miss my guess, our baby model there is expecting imminent company.' Cellann had lost the increasingly listless look she had worn for the past half-hour or so, as time went by and nobody came for her. Now she was sitting bolt upright, eagerly scanning the new arrivals as they came in. What had led her to believe her rendezvous was imminent I couldn't say.

We couldn't stand there and openly watch; Rudy's warning might have annoyed me, but he wasn't wrong. Fi and I strolled over to the bar to pick up fresh drinks, then wandered back to our table. By the time I felt at leisure to cast another covert glance at Cellann, she had company.

Female company.

'That's... unexpected,' I said.

'Why?' murmured Fionn, taking a sip of champagne cocktail.

'I mean, I know women can be assholes, too. But Tanna definitely implied Melly had been meeting a man.'

'They don't have to be the same person,' Fionn pointed out. 'We probably are dealing with a gang. Anyway, Tanna never actually said Melly's date was male. We don't know that Melly herself ever said that.'

'Good points all.' I paused to be certain, for Cellann's date was wearing heavy make-up, and she'd had a change of hair-colour and style since the last time I had seen her. But... no, it had to be the same person. 'I know her,' I said.

Fionn looked at me.

'You know her, too,' I said. 'She used to frequent this place about a century ago, back when it was still Blue Havens.'

Fionn sat up a bit. 'Red hair back then?'

'Red hair, green gowns, never seen without a cigarette holder in hand.'

'Brianne Lamarre.'

'That's it.' She'd ditched the smoking affectation, swapped her red hair for what I suspected was her natural green, and she was wearing a gown of the sumptuous gold Fionn favoured. But that wide, cat-like smile was all Brianne, as was the air of calculated sensuality with which she was dazzling poor Cellann.

Brianne is a morgan. In shorthand terms, picture a cross between Fionn and me and you wouldn't be too far off. They live undersea; they've a taste for jewels and finery to give Fionn a run for her money; they've all the seductive beauty of the selkie but with something of the mesmerising voice of a siren.

That makes Brianne Lamarre as dangerous as Fionn and I put together — and Daix, too, for I never knew this lady to possess much in the way of moral fibre.

She's among the few who could out-fatale all three of us. Despite all this — or, hell, *because* of it — she was a friend, once. I'd suspected her of all kinds of shady dealings at one time or another, but by accident or design, her path and ours had never really crossed in the business way of things.

I'd liked her, even if we'd never been close. She had qualities I could respect. As with so many things, I'd lost touch with her since the Fatales had broken apart; it came as a jolt to see her sitting in Eventide, so different, and so much the same. Like a piece of the past had suddenly come to life, and wandered in to say hello.

Regardless. However dazzling she may be, she's still a shark. A naïve girl like Cellann of Indra-Tath is far out of her depth with Brianne Lamarre.

'So that's a problem,' I said after a while.

Fionn had developed a stony look. 'You were right,' she said. 'We are going to need Daix.'

'*Hell,* yes.'

Fionn finished up her drink, and pushed back her chair. 'Well, then.'

'Right,' I said, rising from my chair. 'No further point in caution.' If we remembered Brianne, she'd remember us, too. She might not be showing any sign of it now, but she'd have seen us the moment she walked in, and it was of no use hoping she'd think we were just catching up.

Time for the more direct approach.

9

—·—

FIONN

THERE WAS A TIME when I held Brianne Lamarre in high esteem.

She has class, no doubt about that. She also has conversation, wit and humour, and a personal style I admire. She's exactly the type of person I'd want for a friend, in short, were it not for the incidental fact that she has no morals whatsoever.

We found that out a long time ago.

I haven't seen or heard from her for many years. Presumably she went back to that undersea palace she's so proud of, and has contented herself with draining (and drowning) an occasional mortal ever since.

Her turning up at Eventide tonight of all nights might be a coincidence, but her making a beeline straight for Cellann's table could not be.

I smiled as I strolled up to join them. 'Ah, have we discovered the identity of the secret gown donor? How generous of you, Brianne. But you always did have excellent taste.'

'As do you, love,' she said, casting my attire a look of decided approval. 'Naturally I couldn't think of patronising anybody *else*.'

Cellann appeared flustered, as well she might. Brianne was stunning, her sleek, jade-green hair coiffed in sculpted waves, her mouth a perfect crimson pout. Eyes to drown in; a calculated effect. But it's more the glamour of her that seduces people. She has an enviable magnetism, an effortless confidence and poise that cannot help but cast others into her shadow.

Most others, anyway.

'Did you *really* send me this gown?' Cellann was saying, pink with pleasure. 'How, how can I thank you—'

Tai took a seat, and propped her splendidly heeled feet upon another chair. The lounging, casual pose was deceptive; I knew she was anything but unthreatening. Brianne probably knew it, too. 'One rule to remember in life, Cellann,' she said. 'Never say thank you until you understand the angle.'

Cellann blinked at her.

'Ulterior motive,' Tai elaborated. 'Why would someone you've barely met make you an expensive present, do you think?' She smiled at Brianne. 'What *is* the angle, Bri?'

'Ah, and sweet Tai,' answered Brianne, her slow smile containing more actual warmth than I'd expected to see. 'Charming to see you lovelies together again. Shall we be expecting the wonderful Daix de Montfort as well?' She glanced around the club. 'Perhaps she's here already. I hope she wouldn't think it necessary to *avoid* me.'

'Games afoot, Bri?' said Tai.

'Just contributing my mite to the deserving, sweetheart.'

'Been doing a lot of that, have you?'

'Generosity is a virtue, in case nobody's told you.'

'I thought I'd already called bullshit on that.'

'How cynical of you.'

'The product of long experience.'

'Let us be clear,' I interjected. 'I have taken an interest in this *deserving* soul myself. I'd like her for my next show, and it would be a great pity were anybody to interfere with that.'

Brianne's smile faded. 'It *would* be a great pity, would it not? To lose one model might be considered misfortune. To lose two — or, we may say, *three* — looks more like carelessness, doesn't it?'

Curse the woman for quoting Wilde even as she needled me. 'I won't lose three,' I said calmly.

'Let us hope not, hm? For this charming young person's sake.' She turned her feline smile on Cellann again as she rose from her chair. 'Any problems, darling, call me,' she said, and left without another word to Tai or to me.

'Three,' murmured Tai.

'Yes,' I said. If Rudy was right, everyone knew about Narasel's demise; it wasn't too much of a stretch to imagine that word of her profession, and her connection to me, might have got about also.

But Brianne had heavily implied she knew about Melly, too.

We lingered at Eventide for a few hours more, to minimal effect. If any other rendezvous had been planned for the night, our presence had probably put paid to that. We had warned Brianne we were paying attention, which had ruined all possibility of further covert observations — at least for one day — but I hoped that it would be enough to protect Cellann.

That Brianne was involved somehow seemed beyond question; I couldn't see how else she could be aware of Melly's disappearance otherwise. But what was she? Was this her scheme, or was she merely acting as bait?

Either way, what was it for? Cellann's precise heritage still eluded me, but I was fairly sure she was half selkie, if not more. Most modelling agencies have at least a couple of selkies on their books, whether they know it or not. The inherent beauty that makes our skins so widely desired can also serve us well, in certain professions.

It begged a number of questions, though. What would Brianne, of all people, want with either selkies or their sealskins? Why would she lend herself to such a scheme?

'Bitch is slippery,' muttered Tai as we left Eventide at last, disappointed of our hope of discerning anything useful about Brianne's actions. She had lingered hour after hour, charming her way through various of the club's patrons, and ostensibly ignoring the both of us. She'd drunk a lot, danced a lot and laughed a lot, and nothing else that she'd done had given us the least clue as to what she might be up to.

'I don't like her involvement, either,' I agreed, drawing my gauzy wrap closer about my shoulders. The night was moonless and dark, and the midnight air held a dank chill to it. 'It makes no sense.' From what I remember of Brianne's tastes, while she's certainly capable of predatory and deadly behaviour she tends to prefer the human male. Selkie girls like Cellann, no.

'If she knows where Mea is...' Tai left the sentence unfinished, but I knew where she was going with the idea. The consequences were likely to involve a certain set of diamond-knuckled fists applied, repeatedly, to Brianne's smiling face.

I hope I get to be present when that day comes.

'I'd like to have her tailed,' I said. 'But I don't have those resources anymore. I haven't had to think about shadowing anybody in years.'

'Nor I,' said Tai. 'But Daix hasn't been nearly so lax.' She was already calling Daix, her phone casting an eerie glow over her face in the darkness.

I stepped closer, and tilted my head towards Tai's to hear the conversation.

'Yes, darlings?' came Daix's voice, tinny and distant through the phone. 'You have something juicy for me?'

'Darlings?' said Tai. 'Now you sound like Brianne.'

'Brianne?' said Daix sharply. 'Brianne Lamarre?'

'Who else?'

'*She* was at Eventide? Tell me quick.'

I stood shivering as Tai filled her in. Daix listened in near silence, interjecting an occasional 'Okay, yes,' and, once, a low whistle. 'Bitch,' she said when Tai had finished, but her tone wasn't condemning. It was... admiring.

'Still got that crush going on, hm?' said Tai.

'Badly,' said Daix cheerfully. 'But I love you *much* more.'

'Thanks.'

'You too, Fionn. You *are* listening, aren't you?'

I rolled my eyes. 'Yes, Daix,' I said, when Tai held out the phone for me.

'Quit flirting and focus,' said Tai, echoing what she'd said, a little earlier, to me. 'We need to find out what the lady's up to. Can you turn some of those surveillance operations of yours to good effect?'

'I'll ignore the suggestion that keeping tabs on the two of you doesn't qualify as *good effect*,' said Daix. 'I'll be delighted to find out *everything* about the luscious Brianne's doings.'

'Not loving that tone of gloating satisfaction,' said Tai.

'Live with it.'

'This is Daix,' I said. 'We let it pass—'

'—or we live to regret it,' Tai finished. 'Right. I'll get the hang of this thing again, I swear.'

I heard a distant cackling from the phone.

'Anyway,' Tai said, 'the model, Cellann. I'm hoping Brianne or whoever won't be dumb — or brazen — enough to make a target of her now that they know we're aware, but I can't be sure. I've asked Rudy to watch her—'

'Rudy?' spluttered Daix.

'If you're under the impression that Rudy's ineffectual, get over it.'

'Fine, fine. Rudy's a god. But you were going to ask me to watch her, too, weren't you?'

'I was.'

Daix gave a deep, theatrical sigh. 'What would you two do without me.'

'Beat information out of Brianne,' said Tai.

That prompted a gasp. 'Break that perfect face? Tai, you wouldn't.'

'Not today. Probably tomorrow. So if you were planning to make *use* of that perfect face, make it fast.'

Daix sighed again, a more mournful sound. 'Too late for that. We've already been rumbled.'

'It'll have to be stealth, then.'

'Shame.'

'It is,' Tai agreed. 'Seduction is way more fun.'

'*Way.*'

'Did you turn up anything useful for us while we were hob-nobbing?'

'Ooh!' said Daix. 'I did!'

'Great. Floor us with your brilliance.'

'The Quinn-Diamhors,' said Daix. 'Just bought another club in the city. Sale went through two months ago. *Not* like Eventide, this one. It's on the other side of town. Used to be a bit of a dive by all accounts, though they've fixed it up.'

'Not their usual,' I said.

'Not at all their usual. They weren't interested in advertising the purchase, either. They acquired it via a puppet company called Greenacre, and it wasn't easy to trace that one back to them.'

'What's the place called?' said Tai.

'Used to be called Moondance, but it reopened three weeks ago under a new name.'

I waited.

'*And*?' Tai prompted. 'Suspense successfully heightened, spit it out.'

'Remind me to talk to Fionn next time. Woman has patience.'

Tai handed the phone to me without another word.

'Hello, Daix,' I said.

She squealed. 'Fi!'

'I love you too. What's the new name?'

'You won't like it.'

'Intriguing.'

'Selkie's Pearls.'

For a second, my heart froze. 'Selkie's Pearls,' I repeated.

'Suggestive, hm?'

'Highly.'

'That's it,' Tai said. 'That's a clear link. Those fuckers are in on it.'

'Far be it from me to be the person advising caution,' Daix began. Then she paused. 'Nah, fuck it, you're right. Take them down, Tai.'

'Right, *I'll* have to be the person advising caution then,' I said, with a calmness I didn't at all feel. My heart was hammering and I felt sick. *Selkie's Pearls.* 'The Quinn-Diamhors aren't people we can accuse without proof, and no, a highly suggestive name for their new club doesn't count.'

Tai was looking at me. 'You okay?'

I inclined my head, not wanting to get into how much less than okay I suddenly felt, or why. My own pearls, draped in their customary spot around my left wrist, felt suddenly heavy as lead.

'Two of your models,' said Tai. 'My roommate. Brianne Lamarre luring girls to Eventide with *your* gowns. And Selkie's Pearls. Is it me, or is all this starting to seem rather personal?'

'Completely,' said Daix, with relish. 'Ladies, we appear to be facing a vendetta.'

'Who the fuck did we piss off that much?' said Tai.

'Tai? Darling? *Everyone.*'

'Thanks for that.'

'We're — going to have to go to this club,' I said, forcing the words out. I had some horrible feelings about what we were likely to find there, but no matter. I'd have to face it. 'Where is it?'

Daix named a street I wasn't familiar with, but Tai frowned. 'That's not far from the Thames Barrier Park,' she said.

'Where Narasel's body was found,' I said, nodding.

'Shit.'

'It's also in Faerd's territory,' I said. 'I wonder that he didn't know about it?'

'Might not have heard,' said Tai. 'There's no obvious link to the waters.' She spoke rapidly, abstractedly; I could feel the tension in her. 'We're going. Now.'

'We're not prepared—' I began.

'*Mea* could be there.'

'Right. Daix, can you—'

Tai cut me off. 'Daix, be there in ten minutes or you get to haul our lifeless corpses out of the river.'

'That's what I call leadership,' said Daix, and hung up.

I handed the phone back to Tai. 'It's two in the morning, we are dressed in evening wear, and we are unarmed.'

Tai folded her arms and stared at me.

'All right, not entirely unarmed.' I could feel the comforting weight of the knife-sheath strapped to my thigh.

'Yeah, also?' she said. 'We have *me*.'

Tai, with her bejewelled fists and her siren songs. 'It isn't always enough,' I said. 'It can't always be enough.'

'It will be today,' said Tai. 'Besides, when *isn't* Daix dying to set someone on fire?'

It was still risky. I didn't like it, but I could argue with Tai's logic only so far. Mearil might be there. So might Melly. And if we could eliminate the place right now, we could ensure Cellann's safety, and that of every other selkie in London.

Tai stood in silence, watching me decide.

I stepped out of my heels and slung the straps around one wrist. 'You going to run in those?'

Tai grinned, and kicked off her borrowed shoes. 'Race you,' she said. 'Loser has to fight in this shit.' She waved her four-inch, spike-heeled shoes at me.

'Challenge accepted,' I said, took a deep breath, and ran.

Selkie's Pearls. The name shone down upon me from its position of honour over the door of the new club, lit up in ocean-blue. Seeing it there stopped me cold. I did not want to know what awaited us inside.

We'd run part of the way, then found a taxi to bring us almost to the doorstep. Now we stood, Tai and I, side by side, taking stock of the challenge.

The club looked innocuous enough. If it used to be a dive, it wasn't now, though it presented a modest appearance compared to Eventide. The frontage was relatively narrow, but the building rose a few storeys high. The windows were smoke-tinted, and curiously shiny; nothing could be seen through them of whatever might be occurring inside. The architectural equivalent of talking to a person wearing mirror shades, I supposed. Faintly unsettling.

Well insulated, too, for not a hint of music could be heard. Not even when the door opened, and somebody came out. Human, by appearance: a young blonde, very drunk. She might *be* human, though she was more likely fae, and heavily glamoured.

'I knew it was possible to *get* heels more outrageous than yours,' Tai muttered. 'I didn't know it was possible to *walk* in them.'

'It isn't,' I answered.

Tai's head tilted, watching the hapless club patron's progress down the street in silent consideration. 'No,' she agreed. 'It isn't.'

'Well,' I said.

'Well.' Tai squared her shoulders. 'I'll go first.'

She sauntered off. Nobody was on the door, by the look of it: no bouncers, no guard. Nothing. That was unusual.

Fae-owned and fae-patroned establishments tend to have measures in place to deter any humans that might wander in. Selkie's Pearls, like Eventide, was drenched top-to-bottom in gramarye. Anyone non-fae walking by would probably see an apartment building instead of a club, or perhaps an office block. That's customary. Once in a while, though, you get a human with enough fae blood — or enough of a way with gramarye, by whatever means — to see through the disguise, and that's when you need your bouncers.

Selkie's Pearls had nothing.

'Unusual,' said Tai, reaching for the door.

She never touched the door's handle. She did not need to. 'Thetai Sarra Antha,' announced a smoky voice from somewhere indeterminate, and the door swung open.

Tai halted. 'What.'

Two steps caught me up with her. 'Fionn of Cuath-Tor,' said the same voice.

The door remained open.

'Fi,' said Tai, glancing down.

'Yes?'

'Your pearls are... doing something.'

I lifted my wrist. My bracelet of lustrous, moon-pale pearls was glowing. This is not so very out of the ordinary for them; they do glow, once in a while. But it's a clear glow, like starlight on the water, and it happens when I am using them for something.

I wasn't using them now, and this glow was faintly sea-green.

'Selkie's Pearls,' said Tai.

'Not liking this.'

'Hey,' said Tai, stepping forward. 'It's not boring.' She vanished through the doors — vanished indeed, for a haze of pearly light waited beyond, curiously opaque; I couldn't see what had become of Tai after she passed through it.

I thought, with a moment's wistful longing, of last week, when the greatest worry on my mind was the upcoming show. How trivial it suddenly appeared.

I walked forward.

The light felt cool, which of course it should not. Light shouldn't *feel* anything, so it might rather be termed a mist; only there was no moisture in it. Whatever it was, it washed gently over my skin, leaving me feeling curiously cleansed.

Tai waited for me in a cool hallway, white-walled, its floor covered with a mosaic tile patterned with roiling ocean waves. A mother-of-pearl fountain occupied the centre of the floor, filling the otherwise silent space with the soft sound of trickling water.

'What kind of a club is this, again?' I asked.

'At this point, fuck knows,' said Tai, heading for the nearest door. 'Let's find out.'

This door opened for her, too, though without announcing her name. I followed her into a much larger room, every feature of which echoed the sea-theme of the hallway; but before we had taken more than two steps, the smoky voice spoke again.

'Daix de Montfort.'

'Bitches didn't wait for me?' snarled Daix. I turned to see her marching through the pale curtain of mist like it was nothing. She paused for three seconds to observe the fountain and the mosaic, then turned her glare on me.

'You were late,' I said.

'Seriously?' said Daix. 'Two minutes late and you ditch me? So much for being a *team*.'

'We aren't a team,' said Tai. 'We stopped being a team eighty years ago. Get in here.'

Daix stamped past me. She'd omitted to dress for the occasion — whatever that might be — and wore dark jeans and a hoodie, with the hood pulled up to cover her platinum-blonde hair. I might have termed it stealth attire, save that she'd chosen to wear a set of Demonia boots with electric-pink platform heels. The enhanced stomping effect clearly pleased her, for she made the most of it as she strode past me.

'What is this crap,' she said, surveying the room.

It dripped luxury, for one thing. More tile mosaic covered the floor, and spread up the walls; gilded here and there in silver and gold, it dazzled the eye. There were fountains; there were pools of cool, serene water in dreamy colours; there was a bar, pearl-painted and shimmering, and well stocked with bottled liquors, all of them clear, or in shades of green or blue.

'Forget *what* it is,' said Tai. '*Why* is it empty? Didn't you say this place re-opened weeks ago?'

'So claimed my sources,' said Daix, advancing into the room.

Tai went forward, too. I hung back near the door. The pearls on my wrist were still glowing, and they'd grown noticeably cool against my skin, as though I had dipped them in ice-water.

When I moved, the calm waters in the nearest pool rippled. Interesting.

I took a few steps nearer, and the ripples increased, turned into waves to greet me.

'While I'm at it,' I heard Daix saying, 'how the fuck does it know who we are?'

'That would be the part I like *least*,' Tai agreed.

'Does any of this scream "bad news" to you at all?'

'Loudly.'

'Tai,' I called. 'Daix.'

Their voices halted abruptly. I heard the click of Tai's heels and the *stamp-stamp* of Daix's boots as they approached.

Both sets of footsteps came to a sudden stop a few feet from me. 'The *fuck*?' said Tai.

I'd stationed myself in between three of the pools. Then, I'd dropped pretty much all of the gramarye that hid who I was. All trace of humanity was gone from me: I stood wreathed in sea-mists, the tang of salt in the air and my hair heavy with pearls.

The waters had responded with — rapture, somewhere between joy and greed; *hunger*, perhaps. The pools roiled with waves, waist-high; when I walked, the water formed for me a glimmering train, frothing with sea-spray and awash with colour.

'Ooookay,' said Daix.

'Uh, Fi?' said Tai. 'You all right there?'

'Fine,' I said.

'Uh huh.'

'I mean, I feel... amazing.'

That silenced them. I felt the weight of their joint attention on me: Tai's assessing, Daix's suspicious.

'Fi,' said Tai after a moment. 'You're enjoying this way too much.'

'I know.'

'Screw that,' said Daix. 'It's enjoying *you* way too much.'

She was right. The waters and I, we understood each other.

I never wanted to leave.

I was up to my thighs in water before Tai got to me. 'Nope,' she said, grabbing me in a painful grip. She hauled me bodily out of the pool and I am ashamed to say I fought her every step of the way.

We stood together on the edge, dripping and dazed.

'What the hell,' said Tai.

When I looked round, I saw Daix standing up to her waist in one of the other pools. Arms folded, jaw set, she was staring at me. 'I don't see what the fuss is about,' she said.

'It's like... paradise,' I said, my gaze drifting back to those clear, still waters. 'Perfect. Everything about it is perfect.'

'It's cold,' said Daix, and waded out again.

'Isn't it lovely?' I said dreamily.

Tai looked at me, her fingers twitching.

'Don't slap me,' I said. 'I'm lucid.'

'You sure about that?' Tai took hold of my arm — more gently this time — and pulled me a step or two farther away from the water.

'Not entirely,' I admitted.

'Okay. So we're in a club that's empty when it shouldn't be, it somehow knows our names, and there's a pool of water with a crush on you.' Tai raised a brow. 'Did I miss anything?'

I shivered, cold now that I'd left the water behind. 'Don't... don't let me drink any of it.'

'Were you planning to?'

'Yes,' I said tightly.

'Right,' said Tai, and towed me back towards the door. 'How much do you trust me?'

I focused on her face, but with some difficulty. All I wanted was the water. 'What?'

'Would you trust me with your life?'

'What? Why?'

'How about a limb?'

'Could you get to the point?'

Tai took my wrist, and stripped the bracelet of pearls from it. 'I'll keep these safe,' she promised, quickly stashing them out of sight in a pocket somewhere.

I almost punched her. 'Tai, you can't—'

'I can.'

'*I* can't—'

'You can, and you will. This combination of things is giving me a seriously bad feeling, and I've learned to pay close attention to those.'

I would have remonstrated further — going without those pearls is easier than going without my left arm, if not by much — but something else caught my attention. 'Where's Daix?'

'What.' Tai's head whipped around. 'She was just here—' Her hand closed around my wrist in a vice-like grip, hauling me mercilessly after her. 'Daix!' she yelled.

Daix answered, but not before I'd detected sounds of a scuffle. 'Back here!' she shouted.

Tai adjusted her trajectory, heading for the sound of Daix's voice. We ran past the glorious pools — I had time only for a brief glance of painful regret before they were out of sight. At the back of the room, past the bar, there yawned an open door, and beyond the door we found Daix.

Tai stopped dead on the threshold, so suddenly I collided with her back. 'What?' I said. When she didn't move, I unceremoniously shoved her out of the way.

The chamber behind the bar looked nothing like the sea-themed glory we'd just left. Some kind of intimate lounge area, I judged, with low sofas and chairs arranged around a glass table. Everything was black lacquer, polished wood and bronze fittings, and *everything* was Art Deco; the room could have come straight out of the 1930s. Or someone's studied idea of what the 1930s looked like.

Daix was there, clinging to the back of a tall figure clad in dark, nondescript attire. A fair tackle: she had both hands wrapped tightly around the man's throat, and judging from the expression on her enchanting face she'd throttle the life out of him without a second thought.

'What—*is*—this—' she was saying, face darkened with rage. '*Did you do this?*'

'It's not—*me*,' gasped the man she was gamely trying to kill, clawing at the hands around his throat. He spared no attention for me, and no wonder, because this was Phélan and he'd only ever had eyes for Tai.

She stood like a rock. I didn't dare look at her face. I've seen that heart break before; I didn't want to watch it happen again.

'Phélan?' she said at last, and faintly.

'Tai,' he choked. 'Good to—see you.'

'*You're* behind this?' Tai's voice grew stronger by the word; it never did take her long to get a grip on herself.

Daix had throttled him past the power of speech; he could only *look* at Tai, and I thought I read a negative there.

I *felt* it when Tai snapped. 'You—fucking—*shit*,' she gasped.

'Moment,' I said. Phélan was barely fighting Daix; why wasn't he trying harder? 'Tai, hold it together. Daix, could you maybe not—'

Too late. Where the hell Daix had conjured a knife from without releasing her hold on Phélan's neck, I have no idea, but suddenly the gleam of naked metal caught my eye.

And Phélan acted at last. The knife was gone from Daix's fingers in a trice; but rather than turn it on Daix, or on either of us, Phélan dropped it.

'No you fucking don't,' growled Daix. Tendrils of fire laced her fingers, and spread — and Daix lit up like a torch.

Phélan screamed.

Tai shouted something. I didn't hear what; all my attention was on the waters I'd left behind moments earlier. It waited for me there, so close, so receptive. I called to it, and it answered.

A deluge of damping water surged through the door, drenching Tai and me, aiming for Daix and Phélan.

But as quick as I had been, Tai was faster. Before the waters had travelled half the distance, Tai had opened her painted lips and voiced a *shriek*. Less siren-song, more ban sith howl; she screamed in three voices at once, a trio of discordant parts in a cacophonic wail that raised every hair on my body.

Daix stopped dead. So did Phélan. The flames around them vanished in a puff of smoke, seconds before the wall of my waters hit them both.

Phélan fell, and Daix with him.

And Tai was on her knees beside them, heedless of the water soaking through her gown. She stared dead into Phélan's eyes, and spoke. 'Did. You. Do. This?' Every word hit him like a bullet; he visibly flinched.

'No,' he gasped, a syllable raw with pain.

Tai let him go. I knew the moment she took her song off him, for he came to life again in an instant, and hurled Daix away from him. Daix hadn't had time to do much damage, but she'd achieved some: his throat was striped with livid red burns.

I expected him to bomb right out of there, but he didn't. He retreated a safe distance from Daix (if there is such a thing) and stood, chest heaving, dark eyes roiling with anger.

Tai picked herself up off the floor, and stared the sluagh down.

'Lovely,' growled Daix. 'We're really getting the whole gang back together.'

10

— · —

Tai

I don't know what possessed me to imagine I could handle having Phélan around again.

I stood in that messed up excuse for a club, a messed up excuse for a siren staring at *bad news incarnate* and wondering how the hell I got there.

Fi was a staunch presence at my elbow, somehow managing to be calming despite the state *she* was in. And I barely resisted the urge to launch myself at Phélan.

Not sure if I was planning to kiss him or slaughter him where he stood.

He looked... unchanged. Tall; some would say intimidatingly so. Longish dark hair rather mussed, thanks to Daix's tender ministrations. He's not handsome, precisely, but he might as well be; all that catlike, predatory grace is dangerously attractive, not to mention that *smile*—

'You cannot seriously have the fucking cheek to *smoulder* at me,' I said, and he was, the bastard. Cross between a brooding, Byronic stare and some kind of puppy eyes routine. Deeply unfair.

I threw my shoes at him.

He blinked. 'What?'

'What. Are. You. Doing here?'

'You *called me.*'

'And I expected you to show up at my house! What are you doing *here?*'

'I followed you. What are *you* doing here?'

'Our investigations led us here,' I said with infinite dignity. Then I began to laugh, because he looked so hang-dog, and my knees were weak with tension and possibly relief, and I never have managed to hang onto my dignity for very long anyway.

Phélan merely looked more confused. He glanced at Fionn, who sighed.

'Do you know anything about this place?' said Fi, with re-markable presence of mind.

'Nothing whatsoever.'

The silence stretched. Fi would be giving him the intense stare, the one that promises to vivisect the man if he proved himself a liar.

I caught my breath and stopped laughing, assisted by the sobering sensation of cold water soaking through my gown. 'I'll say this right now,' I said. 'If you turn out to be mixed up with this shit, I will personally remove your delicates one at a time and feed them to you.'

Phélan's brows rose towards his hairline. 'My *delicates?*'

I pointed a finger at his face. 'Eyeballs.' I pointed lower. 'Spleen. One kidney, perhaps both. Testicles—'

'*Okay*. Stop. I get the picture.'

'Lovely.'

He sighed, and ran a hand through his already tousled hair. 'Why did you call me?'

Daix moved behind him, and his eyes flicked to follow her progress. She grinned. 'Don't worry, pretty. I won't hurt you again... yet.'

'Daix,' I snarled. 'Knock it off.'

Phélan rolled his eyes. I had to give him credit for not wiping the floor with her face; he could have. He returned his gaze to my face instead, and waited.

'We need help,' I said, bluntly. 'We're over our heads in trou-ble.'

Phélan stared at me. 'Did you just say you *need help?*'

'Correct.'

'Thetai Sarra Antha? Asking for help?'

'We're eighty years out of practice and fae are getting killed. Get over it.'

His gaze sharpened. 'This is about that selkie.'

'Narasel,' said Fionn. 'She was one of my models. We've got two more selkies known to be missing, there may be more—'

'We were hoping to find them here,' I said. 'Fat chance I guess.'

'There's no one here,' Phélan agreed. 'I've looked around.'

'Someone came out,' I said, frowning. 'As we arrived. Drunk chick. Could've been human.'

'Possibly an illusion,' said Fionn.

'*Obviously* an illusion,' said Daix in disgust. 'Look, this whole thing has patently been set up for our benefit.'

'A trap,' I agreed. 'Considering our *names* were announced when we came in, though I don't remember hearing *yours*.' This last I directed at Phélan, who gave the faintest of smiles.

'I didn't exactly walk openly through the front door,' he said.

'You sneaked.'

'Effortlessly.'

'Even so,' said Fionn. 'The question remains: why the trap? What are we here *for*?'

'In case you were wondering,' said Daix. 'The front door locked behind me when I came in.'

'What?' I said, whirling around. Too damned *late*.

It took us a few moments to establish that there were no other doors into or out of the place, and no windows either; the ones we'd seen on the outer façade were bricked up on the inside. And the front door, through which we had so casually strolled a half-hour or so ago, was completely impenetrable.

'Well, then,' said Fionn, and began to strip off her gown.

'Fi,' I said, eyeing this procedure with grave misgiving. 'What are you doing?'

'I'm not sure what you or Daix are supposed to be here for,' said Fionn serenely, dropping her gown in a heap on the floor. 'But I clearly have a date with that pool of water.'

'You're not going back in?'

'How else would you like to proceed?'

'Search,' I said, groping for a sensible answer. 'There must be something else here—'

Fionn just looked at Phélan, whose negative came swiftly and with certainty.

'And we're just going to trust him, are we?' I snapped.

'You tell us,' said Fionn.

Phélan gave me a long look, mostly inscrutable, but I read a trace of interest in that gaze. Was I going to trust him? Even now?

'Damnit,' I muttered. 'Fi, you are not doing this alone.'

She merely shrugged one shoulder, already leaving us, heading back to that scummy pool of water. The thing was too pretty by far; nothing but disaster could come of this.

'Wait,' I called. 'Fi.'

She paused, but barely. The water had some kind of hold on her, and she was losing the battle.

I divested myself of my layers of velvet, and followed after. 'Daix, hold the fort?' I called back.

'Yeah,' Daix muttered. 'By all means, give me the fun job.'

'Tai?'

That was Phélan. I stopped, and turned back.

He held my gaze, his stare dark and intense. 'Be careful.'

'*Really* can't promise,' I said, and turned my back on him. Fionn was wading into the pool and I couldn't let her get too far ahead of me.

'Fi,' I called, and broke into a trot. 'Wait.'

She didn't. The waters rose up to welcome her; she walked until she hit the very centre of the pool; then, in a flurry of ocean-scented spray and moon-pale foam, she was gone.

'Shit,' I spat, and ran.

I wasn't sure if the waters would take me the way they did her; they had left Daix untouched, after all. But I wasn't Daix, and besides... I had Fionn's pearls.

I never did quite grasp what those things do for her. She doesn't talk about it, and I haven't asked. That they have some deep link to her selkie magics seems clear enough; beyond that, I haven't a clue.

The waters wanted them, though. The pearls lit up again the instant I stepped into the pool, glowing that eerie sea-green, and I felt a coolness emanating from them, a deep and foreboding chill. I kept a tight grip on them as I waded farther into the water, willing it to take me as it had Fionn.

Ocean spray flew up, filling my nose with sea air. An arctic chill seeped through to my bones, and I began to shiver so hard my teeth clattered together. I heard Daix shout something unintelligible behind me, just as my vision blurred; then ice-water filled up my lungs and I began to choke.

'*Tai.*' That was Phélan, enraged; I distantly heard footsteps; but before he could reach me, the bottom rushed out of my world and I fell into darkness.

I FELL, AND KEPT falling. Deep water received me, deep and dark; wide-eyed, panicking, I stared helplessly into thick, intense blackness. A whirl of boisterous currents tossed me in circles, pummelled me with a force that had nothing to do with nature.

I felt caught in the grip of some capricious game, spun like a top, tumbling like a doll made of rags—

Fionn's pearls, still clutched in one hand, glowed like stars in the deep, but that's all, they *shone*, what use was a light to me when I was *drowning*—

Not that I took it calmly when something tried to *take* them— the currents whirled me around until I was dizzy, and tore at my hands, trying to loosen my grip on them, but they're Fionn's, and if I had to die before I'd give up something important to her then *so be it*—

The water wouldn't end, and I couldn't *breathe*, couldn't see, couldn't *breathe*—

Something heavy barrelled into me, and I was borne upwards — I hoped it was upwards — my lungs were on fire—

My head broke the surface, encountered clear air. I choked, vomiting up water — and then dragged in an enormous lungful of sweet, sweet oxygen, surprised that I possessed the power to do so.

After a few panicked, heaving breaths, I calmed enough to look around me.

Lights bobbed on the near horizon. The vague shapes of darkened verdure loomed from the shadows, gently limned in wan moonlight. A park. I was in a river, winding through a park.

Swimming in slow circles around me was Fionn, seal-shaped and pissed off. I knew this from the choppy nature of her movements; ordinarily she's a being of effortless grace.

I took a few more breaths, marvelling at my capacity to do so without choking. Fi and her ways with water.

'Okay,' I said aloud. 'Maybe that wasn't the best idea.'

Fionn's only response to this handsome concession was to shove me with her nose, in the process alerting me to the existence of a humbling quantity of deep aches in my rather abused physique. I'd have bruises tomorrow.

'I'm sorry!' I said. 'Fuck's sake, should I have just watched you wander into danger alone?'

Fionn said something, but since it emerged garbled, and she kept slipping into a seal's chattering vocabulary, I didn't understand a word.

I could guess, though.

'It's not that I thought you couldn't handle it,' I said, spinning in a slow circle as I trod water. Nothing else of much note caught my eye. 'It's that nobody should be running off without backup. Didn't we *learn* that? Besides, how the fuck could you know that you could handle it?'

The seal vanished, leaving a wringing-wet Fionn in its place. She snatched her pearls from me and restored them to her wrist, after which she visibly calmed down. 'If you hadn't had those you'd be dead,' she informed me. 'You'd have drowned long before I got to you.'

'If I hadn't had them, maybe you'd be dead,' I retorted. 'Unless I miss my guess, we're in the Thames Barrier Park, a ways upstream from where Narasel's body was found. Whatever happened to her was supposed to be *your* fate, and it's got to have something to do with your unusual jewellery choices. Do all selkies have those pearls?'

'In a manner of speaking,' said Fionn shortly.

I waited, but she said nothing more. 'And?' I prompted. 'Now isn't the time to be secretive about this stuff, Fi.'

'You might thank me for saving your life.'

'You might thank me for saving yours.'

'You did no such thing. If the pearls are a danger, why aren't *you* dead?'

I sighed, beginning to shiver again. 'Other than your own tender ministrations — for which, indeed, I thank you — I'm not a selkie. Whatever power took us there had a strong interest in your pearls, Fi, but me? I felt ... flushed, like waste. Like something else was meant to happen between that pool and this river, and we skipped to the end. Because I didn't meet the criteria, and apparently, neither did you.'

'A delightful piece of wild speculation, for which we have no evidence.'

'True,' I agreed. 'But when Narasel showed up in these waters she was stone dead, and you palpably aren't. And sure, we don't know that she ever went near those weird-as-fuck pools, but we have quite the stack of coincidences piling up if she didn't.'

I heard her sigh. Then she had hold of me, and was towing me towards the distant bank with remarkable strength, considering her rail-thin physique. 'I can swim,' I informed her.

She ignored that. 'You're freezing to death,' she informed me calmly.

'Fair point.'

We reached the bank, and I was mercilessly shoved up and out onto the hard, cold ground. I got up at once and began pacing, as if that would somehow make me warmer. Honestly. '*One* day,' I said, somewhat indistinctly around my chattering teeth. 'We're back together for *one* day and already we're wandering the city in our underwear in the small hours of the morning, soaked to the skin, after a near brush with death. *Still* got it, Fi.' I punched the air with one fist.

'Good,' said Fionn. 'If you're capable of joking, you probably aren't about to drop dead.'

'I love you, too.'

'As for your speculations,' she said, ignoring that with aplomb. 'I wouldn't say that I think you're wrong. Something... tried to...' She paused. 'I felt... drained. Downed like a cup of water, and spat out again. I barely had the energy to take seal-form.'

'And the pearls?' I prompted. 'What the hell are they, Fi?'

In answer, Fionn appeared before me, and the moonlight somehow caught and lingered in her skin, her hair; she glimmered with pure magic, and every mote of light, every drop of water clinging to her pale skin was a pearl, or something like it.

'Oh,' I said.

'If someone stripped you of your voice,' said Fionn, letting the radiance fade once more. 'You could imagine how it feels to be stripped of my pearls.'

'I don't know. I only have the one voice, but you seem to be well supplied with pearls.'

Fionn trailed her fingers in the water, sending up a spray. Each droplet became a fresh, lambent pearl, and sank slowly into the deep. 'These, though,' she said, indicating her bracelet, 'are the oldest and rarest that I have. It would take me a century to replace them.'

'What do they have to do with your shapeshifting? Your seal-skin?'

'Nothing. Take my pearls and you weaken me. Take my skin and... you enslave me.'

I paced faster. 'I wonder if we're barking up the wrong tree here. Is this about selkie-skins, or is it about selkie's pearls?' I said. 'Or both? And while we're thinking about that, how about we go get warm or something? I haven't exactly tried, but I'm pretty sure I can't sing my way out of a bout of hypothermia.'

'Besides that, Daix and Phélan are still trapped.'

'Yep, we should absolutely do something decisive and heroic about that, too.'

I won't admit to having stripped a set of suitably warm garments off some hapless passer-by, because nobody would ever respect me again. Let's just say my lucky stars shone brightly that night, and leave it at that.

I might also assert that it was a warmish night in April and no one was in any danger of freezing to death if they hadn't taken an impromptu and ill-advised dip in the river first.

Anyway, somewhat better clad, Fionn and I made our way back to the Selkie's Pearls club in rather grim silence. I was *thinking*, and no doubt Fi was, too. Trying to puzzle the pieces together. What did this peculiar club have to do with Narasel, or Mearil, or Melly? I could well believe that Cellann might have been brought there by Brianne, if we hadn't intervened. Having got the idiot girl's attention with an expensive gift and admittance to an exclusive club, it wouldn't have taken much to coax her into leaving Eventide again in Brianne's company. Only drop a few hints about a joint *even more exclusive*, and the foolish child would go anywhere, with anyone.

No doubt, either, that those pools of water would have had much the same effect on Cellann that they'd had on Fionn. And with nobody to intervene, she would have wandered straight in. Pearls and all.

And gone... where? Because while Narasel had turned up dead in those same river-waters, Melly and Mearil had not.

At least, not yet.

So where were they?

I was becoming increasingly certain that the operation was more about selkies' powers than their skins. Not that a canny and ruthless operator wouldn't take full advantage of an opportunity to make a few quid on the side; I hadn't forgotten Tully's tip about a few scummy sluagh and a selkie-skin sale.

The question of what *we* had to do with it was a whole other problem. We weren't being targeted, precisely; if we were, Fionn would have been the first selkie taken. And it wouldn't have been all that hard to do it. Hit her quickly, take her by surprise; she was a fashion designer now, no longer the hard and wary *fatale* of yesteryear.

No, we weren't the target. Not exactly. But we were being baited.

I shook my head. 'I can't make it make sense.'

'Not yet,' Fionn agreed. 'But we do not lack for leads, now. There's much work to be done.'

'Right. Get Daix on it, for a start. Use her surveillance, her networks, for information. I'll get back on Tully at the Puca, see if I can track them from the sealskin end. And you—'

'I have a plan,' said Fionn.

'Super,' I said, rather warily, for there was a cold note in her voice I didn't like. I mean, Fi's always a bit chilly, but this was diamond-hard. 'Why don't we talk it over?'

'Later.'

'Now would be—'

She made a *cease and desist* gesture. 'Later. Look.'

I followed the direction of her pointing finger, and saw... a faint flicker on the horizon, a glimmer of light behind the looming shadows of darkened buildings.

Fire.

'Oh, for—' I snarled, and began to run. 'Fuck's sake. *Daix.*'

We made it back to Selkie's Pearls in two minutes flat, and there to greet us was a vision of actual nightmare. The club, such as it had been, was gone. At least, some of it was probably still there, but between us and it was a wall of green-tinged flame, roaring with all the infernal voices of hell. Black smoke poured gleefully into the sky, and from somewhere within I heard the protesting groans of a collapsing building.

I noted with distant approval that the fire was neatly contained. Not a lick of flame touched the buildings on either side of the club.

'So they're dead,' I gasped, pausing to recover my breath. The heat of those flames was beyond anything natural. I took several steps back.

'Oh, completely,' said Fionn, watching impassively. 'No doubt about it.'

'Nothing could survive such an inferno.' I turned away from the fire and scanned the shadows, eyes narrowed. 'Nothing left for us to do but mourn. Deeply. And for always.'

'Oh, *fine*,' growled Daix, and emerged from an alley. Greenish flames wove through her fingers, and lit up her eyes. 'Couldn't you have been a *bit* sad?'

'You wanted us to *pretend*?'

'Like you aren't a master of pretence, Tai.'

'Yes, but I only roll out the cold-blooded manipulation for special people.'

Daix scowled, and the flames around her fingers died out.

'I always liked that cool eye effect,' I added. 'Creepy as fuck.'

She grinned. 'Isn't it?'

'You *had* to burn the place down, I suppose?'

'How else was I supposed to get out?'

'Something something *less blatantly destructive*, but remembering I'm talking to Daix — no. There was no other conceivable way.'

'Nice of you two to ride to my rescue, though.' She blew us a kiss.

'Yes, also we're fine, thanks for asking.'

'Was on my way to the river to pull your lifeless corpses out of it. Now I can go straight home and put my favourite socks on, yay.'

'You have favourite socks.'

'There are people who don't have favourite socks?'

I abandoned the whole line of enquiry. 'You managed not to also burn Phélan alive and screaming, I assume?'

'Why would you assume that.'

Fionn intervened before I could beat Daix to death with her own boots. 'We did end up in the river,' she said, calmly. 'We'll compose a suitable report about it shortly.'

'Reports? Seriously? Fi, I thought we'd moved past this.'

'We need detail. Writing things down helps.'

Daix sighed.

'And yes, I expect you to produce a similar report of your findings for us.'

'Damnit.'

'Also, while I fully understand and support your burning of the club—'

'*See*, Tai? Fi gets it.'

'—if you were hoping to keep a low profile hereafter that's more or less busted it, hasn't it?'

'That place identified me by name, and locked the door after me. What would be the point?'

Fionn inclined her head. 'Perhaps that's fair. But—'

'Fi,' I said. 'She's right. It's too late for caution. It was too late from the first moment they took Narasel. We're supposed to be involved in this.'

'I just... I'm not used to working this way.'

I wrapped a comforting arm around her. 'I know. I miss the days of calculated lying, ruthless deceit, and stealthing around in fabulous disguises too. Maybe next time.' I squeezed her shoulders, and released her. 'What we are *now* is a crew of pissed-off Fatales, with awe-inspiring power to cause harm.'

'Right,' said Daix, and stomped one booted foot for emphasis. 'It's time to kick some ass.'

'You've been watching way too many action movies,' I told her.

'Define this "too many".'

'Can we return to the subject of Phélan just for a second?'

'What about him.'

'Still breathing, yes or no?'

'I don't see how that's any of my business.'

'It—'

'*Or* yours, either.'

'It's my business because I asked him here. Sort of. If he got burned to death by my pyromaniac maverick of a partner it's a little bit my problem, isn't it?'

'If you're going to insist on mooning around after moody sluagh types I don't see what's so wrong with Rudy. He's cute.'

'*Daix.*'

'Fine. He's alive, okay? But only because I love you.'

'And you stashed him where exactly?'

'*I* stashed him nowhere. Where he's stashed himself, who knows.'

If he was still lurking around somewhere and had any intention of showing himself, he'd have done so by now. I suppressed a traitorous feeling of disappointed hurt, and firmly dismissed the subject. He was fine. He could tend his own damned burns. 'Okay. It's time to retreat and regroup. Fi, I still think you weren't supposed to be making it out of here tonight, so you might want to be extra careful.'

'As in, how?'

'As in, don't go home. Or back to your studio.'

'But you'll be fine to go back to *your* home, considering your own damned roommate is among the missing?'

Oops. I'd touched a nerve. 'I *know* you can handle literally anything,' I said. 'But I also know you need sleep, and nobody does a great job of fighting off mortal peril while unconscious.'

'Fair,' said Fionn. 'Where then do you suggest I go?'

'*You*, nowhere. *We* are going to my bolt hole.'

'You have a bolt hole?' said Daix. 'Oh no, is it a *secret* bolt hole? A place no one could possibly know about but *you*?'

'Yes, I'm sure you know all about it,' I said. 'But no one else has had quite your incentive for tracking my every movement, now have they?'

'We're going,' said Fi, sounding weary.

'I have hot chocolate,' I offered. '*And* excellent socks.'

'Was that an invitation?' said Daix. 'I can't always tell around all the sarcasm.'

'Yes, and it expires in ten seconds.'
'*My* house hasn't been compromised.'
'Six seconds.'
'I could go there right now.'
'Three.'
'Get my *own, favourite* socks on.'
'And expired.'
'Damn you, Tai.'
'Three-person chocolate and sock party it is.'

11

— · —

FIONN

Tai's BOLT HOLE, AS she describes it, turned out to be a cellar. Entered via an unassuming door positioned halfway down a shabby alley of no notable features whatsoever, the place is discreet, to say the least. Considering how much gramarye Tai has shrouding the door, I'd be surprised if anybody ever discovered it unless they were looking for it. Which Daix probably was.

'People don't notice that you come into this alley and never come out again?' I asked, as Tai negotiated with the door.

'It isn't a dead end. It's a shortcut. Tube station just down the way.' She tilted her head in the direction of the opposite end of the alley. 'If I'm worried, I have an illusory me wander out the other end, and disappear into the Underground.'

'You've improved at glamours.'

By way of answer, Tai hummed a few notes in two-part harmony, and a vaguely Tai-shaped shadow flitted away down the narrow street, and faded out of sight. 'It isn't really a glamour,' she said, opening the door. 'It's more that I ordered your brain to perceive one. I used to do it a lot, back in the bad old days.'

'Not on *us*, though,' I said.

'Right. Not usually on you.'

'Stay out of my brain,' said Daix.

'Daix, nobody in their right mind wants to have anything to do with your brain.' She ushered the two of us ahead of her, and I stepped through the door. The space beyond was both dark and dank, judging from the smell, and led away into a blank void.

Daix held up one small fist wreathed in clear flame, and the void resolved into a stairwell leading down. 'Nice place,' she said, starting down it.

'It's not so bad below,' said Tai, giving me a gentle shove from behind.

I went down. The stairs wound around in a spiral, and ended at last in the aforementioned cellar. Its crumbling stonework and gothic-pointed arches suggested a medieval construction. While chilly, the place was more comfortable than I might have expected considering the approach: thick rugs covered much of the floor, and Tai had manoeuvred a shabby but comfortable old Chesterfield into position before a blackened fireplace. Matching chairs flanked the sofa. Once Tai had switched on a pair of standard lamps with charming Art Deco shades, and Daix had encouraged the hearth to develop a warming fire, the cellar grew cheerful. Tai compounded the effect by switching on a dusty gramophone; the strains of an old night club song filled the room.

'You're right,' said Daix, flopping onto the sofa. 'It's not so bad down here at all.'

'How did you get hold of this place?' I asked, reposing myself in one of the armchairs. Chesterfields can be unforgiving articles of furniture, but this one had been broken in long ago. I began, a little, to relax.

'Pheriko found it.' Tai disappeared into another, shadowed room; light flared where she passed. 'The building belongs to some connection of hers,' she called back. I heard sounds of a kettle boiling, mugs clinking. 'Wasn't using it, so we do. Sometimes.'

'What the hell does Pheriko want with a bolt hole,' said Daix.

'Photographers,' I murmured. 'Can be a nuisance.'

'Right. You'd know all about that.' Daix rolled her eyes.

'Not so much. My brand is famous, but I'm not personally so.' And I took care to keep it that way. Few people want to deal with that kind of attention, and the fae... very much not. Some say I ought never to have entered the world of fashion at all, that it isn't safe. Someday, my identity will be compromised and my true nature discovered by the non-fae world.

Perhaps. But a life spent crouching in the shadows, paralysed by fear, is no life at all. And I've spent enough of my life like that.

The same questions apply to Tai, of course, with still greater force. But Tai being Tai, I am pretty sure she doesn't care.

'What she said.' Tai returned bearing a chipped dinner plate, atop which were balanced three gigantic mugs smelling, gorgeously, of chocolate. 'Also, it's a quiet spot. We come down here to compose, sometimes.'

Daix snatched up a steaming mug, miraculously spilling none of it. Half the contents were gone in a blink.

'Oh,' said Tai, watching this performance with some bemusement. 'I forgot about that whole fire-proof thing.'

Daix chugged the rest in three gulps, and smiled sweetly. 'You just watched me fail to immolate myself *despite* my best efforts, which, I might add, were significant. You know I'm fire-proof. What you mean is you forgot the *heat-proof* thing.'

'I remain uncertain of its usefulness,' said Tai, taking the other chair, and settling with her own mug. 'You drank that too quickly to appreciate it. Fi and I, on the other hand, will go on appreciating ours for at least ten glorious minutes.'

'Meh,' said Daix. 'Life's too short.'

'You *literally* came over with the Conqueror and you're saying life's too short to savour hot chocolate.'

'Right.'

'That's your stance on the finer things in life.'

'No, just on hot chocolate.'

Tai met my gaze, and rolled her eyes. I grimaced in sympathy, but inside I was smiling. It's been such a long, long time.

'I've... missed you two,' I said.

Daix sat bolt upright. 'Fionn. Did you just admit to a *feeling*?'

'A mild one,' I said. 'Let's not get carried away.'

'She missed us a *little*,' said Tai, smirking at me. 'Every other Tuesday in March.'

'No, no,' I murmured. 'Much more than that.'

'Also Wednesdays in August.'

'Right.'

'I'm overcome,' said Daix. 'What a tribute.'

'Still waiting for yours,' said Tai.

'Good luck with that.'

I sipped chocolate. 'Daix's spent the past eighty years stalking our every move. She didn't so much miss us as *obsessively* miss us.'

'Untrue,' said Daix.

Tai looked at the ceiling. 'Tell me you aren't going to deny the whole twenty-four-hour surveillance thing.'

'Not at all,' said Daix. 'But for eighty *years*? You people aren't nearly interesting enough.'

'Okay, how long for?'

'That's classified.'

Tai smirked, and returned to her mug.

'So,' I said. 'If we are to work together again—'

'Who said anything about that?' interjected Daix.

'Agreed by tacit vote,' said Tai. 'Including yours, or why the hell are you here?'

Daix scowled. 'Fine.'

'If we're to work together again,' I resumed. 'We perhaps need to agree on a course of action.'

'Before we do that, we probably need to make sure we're all on the same page with what we've got so far,' Tai said.

I nodded. 'Fair. Tai, would you like to begin?'

Half an hour later, we'd covered all three of the missing selkies; the finding of Narasel's body in Faerd's waters; Tully's hints about a seal-skin sale at the Puca; the questions surrounding Eventide and Selkie's Pearls; my experiences in the strange pools at the new club, and Tai's; Brianne Lamarre; and the Quinn-Diamhor family.

'One thing that doesn't make sense,' Tai said. 'If Mea was taken at the airport, and signs do suggest she was: why? Does that mean she was never at Eventide?'

'It suggests she was never at Selkie's Pearls,' I said. 'Or at least, that she didn't walk in there voluntarily. But she may have been at Eventide.'

'Snatched before she could leave the country,' said Daix. 'They weren't finished with her, and didn't want her getting away.'

Tai frowned, plainly worried. 'I suppose that makes sense,' she sighed.

'We need to find out where that waterway was supposed to take me,' I said.

Tai looked at me. 'You don't think the river was the intended destination.'

'No. Why would it be? Nothing happened there. I think you may have been right when you spoke of being – *waste*. We were dumped there in the same way as Narasel's body. And I think perhaps you were also right when you said I would not have been, if I'd had my pearls.'

'Tell me you aren't thinking what I think you're thinking.'

'I am,' I admitted. 'But I can't go back and try it again. Daix's seen to that.' There would be nothing left of the club by now; Daix's fires burned fast, and *hot*. The pools were gone.

Daix gave Tai an imaginary hat-tip. 'You're welcome.'

Tai glared at me. 'Were you always this reckless?'

'Were you?' I countered.

'Yes.'

'There you go, then.'

'But that's me. That was sort of my *thing*. You're meant to be the sane one.'

'No. I was the fearful, cautious one. I'm less so, now.'

Tai gave me a long, wordless look, in which I read a mixture of understanding and annoyance. 'You weren't always that. I've seen you face incredible odds, and without a trace of fear.'

'I had the fear,' I said. 'Circumstances frequently compelled me to ignore it.'

One of Tai's eyebrows rose, slightly. 'Okay. And why are you different now?'

I subjected that question to a moment's thought. 'Perhaps it ceased to matter whether I got hurt.'

Tai's dark eyes darkened further, and narrowed. 'What—'

'Stop it,' Daix snapped. 'If you two want to soothe each other's boo-boos, save it for another time. We're working here.'

'Apologies,' I said. 'You're right.'

'Indeed,' said Tai. 'Since Fi's been denied the opportunity to perform a feat of awe-inspiring heroism at great personal cost, we'll have to do it the other way.'

'I tremble at the prospect of *the other way*,' I said. 'You've got that reckless look about you.'

'Oh, but it's all right when you do it?'

'Stop it,' Daix growled.

'I do have a plan,' said Tai. 'Neither of you will like it.'

'I'll probably *love* it,' said Daix.

Tai inclined her head. 'Fair. Fi, I need your permission to be certifiably insane for a bit.'

'Do you *need* my permission?'

'I'd... okay, I'd like your permission. Please.'

'You may have it, if you must. *With* the proviso that you don't get yourself killed.'

'Or you, either,' she said. 'Let's pretend we all still care about whether you live or die, hm?'

'All right. Nobody gets killed.'

She nodded.

'Are you going to share the details?'

'Later, maybe. For now, it's best if you two proceed as you were intending anyway. Daix, anything else you can dig up about the Quinn-Diamhors' doings might help. Also get in touch with your shadier contacts and find out about any illegal seal-skin sales or trades going on.'

'I love it when things get *shady*,' Daix grinned. 'Can I pose as a buyer?'

'Perfect. You're evil incarnate and you've always wanted a selkie slave of your very own.'

'Sounds like me.'

'Pearls, too,' I put in.

Daix frowned. 'All right, but why would I want to buy selkies' pearls?'

'For one thing,' I said, 'they're among the rarest, most beautiful pearls money can buy, and tend to fetch spectacular prices.'

'So there's plain old material value. Okay.'

'For another, they... may confer some limited gramarye upon the wearer.'

'May? That's awfully wishy-washy, Fionn.'

'No selkie *wants* to be separated from their pearls,' I said coldly. 'So it's not something that's been studied much, hm? But there are stories—'

'And you did say I'd probably have drowned if I hadn't had yours,' Tai put in.

'Right. I am not certain of that, and I have zero interest in running experiments to find out how quickly you drown without them.'

Tai's lips quirked in a sideways smile. 'Seconded. Though you know, it really felt like I was drowning. At the risk of sounding shockingly ungrateful, they could have worked a *bit* better.'

'Still, you didn't drown, so your experience offers some limited support for the idea. Which is partly why I begin to think the missing selkies may be more about selkie gramarye than about selkie slaves.'

'Why not both?' said Daix. 'By this account, you selkie-types are just dripping in value. Can't think why there hasn't been a selkie trafficking operation before.'

Her words chilled me, because they were true.

'Snatch a selkie from the airport,' said Tai, grimly. 'Or a club. Use her skin to enslave her. Force her to hand over her pearls, and all the gramarye therein.'

'Use the magic, traffick the bitch,' said Daix.

'Daix, some sensitivity please,' I said, icily. 'We're talking about Tai's room-mate here.'

'Sorry,' muttered Daix.

'Narasel died,' said Tai. 'Maybe – maybe she was an experiment gone wrong.'

'I didn't drown — because I still had my skin, and could shape-shift,' I agreed. 'You didn't because you had some of my gramarye. If they stripped Narasel of skin *and* pearls during that initial process—'

'When she went into the water, at the club,' Tai nodded.

'Then she suffered the same fate we did, only she hadn't the means left to survive it.'

Tai's lips tightened. 'Maybe they didn't expect that outcome. After all, she was valuable merchandise.'

I ignored the sick feeling Tai's vocabulary gave me. *Merchandise.* 'If this is all true, it ought to be encouraging,' I offered. 'Mearil, Melly and any others shouldn't be in imminent danger of their lives. They're worth too much for that.'

'I hope you're right,' said Tai. 'But the same questions remain. Where are they? If they're to be bound and sold into slavery – how? By whom, and *to* whom? And what's being done with their pearls and their gramarye?'

'In other words,' I said. 'Who wants a taste of selkie powers enough to set up such an operation as this?'

'And who has the clout to be so damned public about it?' said Daix. 'It's not exactly a subtle operation, is it?'

Tai nodded. 'Someone feels powerful enough to get away with it.'

'Someone who knows *us*,' I said. 'Let's not forget: we've been deliberately baited.'

I felt Tai's gaze on me again, and met her eyes. It isn't always easy to do that. She knows me too well.

'Fi,' said she.

'Yes.'

'Please tell me you aren't going to go out there and deliberately get yourself snatched.'

'How would I do that?'

'I don't know, by swanning around visibly unprotected until somebody hauls you off the street?'

'If they were going to snatch me, why haven't they already?'

'I mean, I agree, but they sort of *tried*, by sending us to that damned club. And you weren't meant to make it out of there.'

'So you're worried I'll be the next Mearil.'

'Having evaded the trap, more obvious tactics may be employed.'

I sighed. 'Are you sure it would be the wrong thing for me to do?'

'*Yes.* How the hell can you ask me that.'

'I'd find out what's going on.'

'Fi, you – you of *all people* can't risk being slave-taken again. How the hell long did it take you to get over it last time?'

I found I had nothing to say. *Had* I ever got over it, really?

'Exactly,' she said.

'And what's *your* plan, then?' I said.

'*I'm* going to get slave-taken.'

I went very still. 'What?'

'You saw what I did up on the street, right? I can make people look at me and see you. If you'll lend me those pearls one more time – I'll get them back for you, I *swear*—'

'Tai, you can't do that.'

'Why not? It won't affect me like it would affect you. I can't be genuinely enslaved, I can just act like I am. And since it's not a thing I've been traumatised by in the past, it won't hurt me like it would hurt you.'

'No. Absolutely not.'

'But—'

'I have a better idea,' said Daix.

Tai narrowed her eyes at me, then turned her attention to Daix. 'Which is?'

'If I'm posing as a buyer, Tai can pose as a seller.' Daix beamed at me. 'And she's selling *you*.'

'What?' I said, faintly.

'Story time!' Daix gave a gleeful little bounce, and adopted a smoky voice. 'The enigmatic fatales, braving the underworld night after night in the service of the oppressed—'

'Get on with it,' sighed Tai.

Daix shot her a poisonous look, and resumed her usual tones. 'Until the mission that ended us, and it all went wrong. Eighty years pass and we don't even talk to each other. So far, so true?'

'Okay,' said Tai, cautiously.

'Well. Despite signs of a tentative reconciliation in the past two days, resentments among us remain intense. Tai has got close to Fionn again, *not* because she's generously forgiven that detestable selkie for her part at Ravensbrück but because she's harbouring treachery in her ample bosom. Perhaps Tai isn't broken up about her room-mate's disappearance at all. Perhaps she even had something to do with it. Perhaps she'd like to do the same thing to Fionn.'

'So I'm evil and I'd like to sell out my old partner for cash,' said Tai.

'Maybe cash, maybe something better. We can talk about that.'

'Sounds like me.'

'I *know*!'

'And you're gleefully on board with this because you're Daix, and we all *know* you're evil.'

'Correct.' Daix shrugged. 'There always were plenty who saw us that way. Why not capitalise on it?'

'If you can't beat them...' said Tai, rolling her eyes.

Daix's grin was vicious. 'Join them.'

Both of them looked at me. Waiting.

'No,' I said. 'We're not doing the stupid motto, Daix. Not again.'

'Just this one time,' she pleaded. 'For me?'

'No!'

'Look, we'll even cue you in again. If you can't beat them—'

Tai's eyes twinkled. 'Join them. Come on, Fi. It's as true now as ever.'

I permitted myself a short sigh. '*Then break them.*'

Daix clapped. 'We're still so *cool.*'

'And evil,' said Tai. '*So* evil.'

Daix was right. Back in the day, we'd developed a certain moral flexibility, because it suited our purposes. It's hard to battle evil head-on, sometimes. It can be done, but it's the hard road.

Easier to do it from the inside. Easier to make yourself one of them – *then* take them apart. We'd played so many roles over the years, reinvented ourselves over and over again, employed disguise after disguise...

People had noticed eventually, of course. That's where the legend came from. The mysterious fatales, shadowy figures behind the ruin of many an underworld scheme.

That's one of the things that had gone so wrong. They'd figured out who we were.

But maybe we could use that, this time.

'All right,' I said. 'I'll agree, because it's far better than any scheme where Tai gets taken.'

'To be very clear on one point,' Tai said, eyeing Daix. 'At no point are we actually going to sell Fi.'

'Can't we?'

'Never, ever, and no.'

'Damnit. That complicates things.'

'Hey, if it comes to that, I can still masquerade as Fi.'

'No—' I began.

Daix brightened. 'Great. That's settled. Now we just have to figure out who we're going to trade Fi *to.*'

'I'm employing Phélan,' said Tai.

'Like you needed an excuse.'

'It's not an excuse. He probably knows something that we could use. Might have connections.'

'I'd love to mercilessly mock you some more,' said Daix, 'but unfortunately, you're right.'

'Fine. So I'll do that. Daix, you do your thing. Fi...'

I waited, stone cold.

'I know you're hating this, and I'm sorry.'

'Thanks.'

'It's going to be worth it.'

'Better be.'

Tai winced. 'Will you get on Jane's case, as planned? Back-stage gossip, word among the modelling agencies, that kind of thing—'

'It's done. I'll also be talking to Faerd. I have new questions for him.'

Tai nodded. 'And I'll pay a visit to the Booted Puca again. See if I can catch these mythical sluagh with the sealskin market.'

12

—·—

TAI

I'D CALLED PHÉLAN AGAIN before Fi, Daix and I ever got as far as my cellar hideaway. Honestly, the plan to use myself as Fionn-shaped bait had been circling in my mind for a while.

I still wasn't sure I was ready to relinquish it altogether. But Daix's plan had merit, too.

Either way, I needed to pick Phélan's brains.

The man had the sense not to shadow me, this time – or at least, not to let me *know* that he had. He did what I'd expected him to do. He went to my house.

I knew he was there from the moment I opened the front door. I've never been able to decide whether or not I'm imagining things, when it comes to Phélan. He has an impact on things people have no business messing with, like *atmosphere*, and shadows, and the precise quality of the silence.

Atmosphere: subtly tense.

Shadows: deeper than they ought to be, like holes in the world.

Silence: *profound.*

I closed and locked the door behind me, and dropped my keys on a nearby shelf. 'Hi, Phélan.'

'Tai.' The word emerged from the depths of the darkness. Phélan didn't.

I switched on the light.

He was standing – no, *lurking* – at the rear of my living room, leaning against the wall in a pose of deceptive casualness. He didn't move, but he did squint against the sudden light.

'Sorry,' I said, stepping out of my shoes. 'But I really don't need you being *dark* and *shadowy* all over my personal space.'

'Still finding that devastatingly attractive?'

'Still finding it incredibly annoying.'

'That's what I said.'

'You do know those things aren't meant to be the same, right?'

He shrugged. 'If it works.'

'It doesn't work. I mean, it's pretty much the textbook definition of an unhealthy relationship.'

'Since no part of this has ever been a relationship, I shall go right on being *dark and shadowy*.'

'I knew there was a reason I didn't talk to you for a decade. Or eight.'

Phélan's mouth tightened.

'That being so,' I continued, 'why exactly did you give me your number?'

I'd come home one day, several years ago, to find a note on my pillow. My fucking *pillow*. It had nothing on it save somebody's mobile phone number, hastily scrawled in black ink. I didn't need to recognise Phélan's writing to know it was his.

'And by the way,' I added, 'if you were actively *trying* to be as creepy as possible you couldn't have done a better job.'

'That's fair,' he said, surprisingly serious.

'So? What the hell were you doing.'

'I wanted you to know I was looking out for you.'

'By breaking into my room and leaving your contact details in my actual bed.'

'I... yes.'

'There's a term for that kind of thing.'

'Don't say stalker.'

'*That's* the one.'

'I haven't been stalking you.'

'Except for the pillow-note thing. Oh, and following me to the club tonight.'

'Looking out for you.'

'That's not how you do that.'

He shrugged. 'Okay, answer me this then: why did you save my number?'

'Because... I happen to be an idiot.'

He grinned, which was annoying, because my traitorous heart performed a somersault on the spot. 'Me too.'

'Okay. Good to clear that up.' I sank into an armchair, and sat with my arms folded. 'While I fully see the appeal of looming over me from an intimidating height, it's also fine to sit down.'

'Thank you,' he said politely, quite as though I'd been courteous as well, and sat down across from me.

We engaged in a little mutual staring.

'Right,' I said, sitting up a little straighter. 'Business. I called you because I do actually need your help.'

'I recall.'

That reminded me of the evening's events; my gaze strayed, guiltily, to the burns on his neck. 'I'm sorry about the... Daix, thing.'

'I know. I've always been pretty sorry about the Daix thing, too.'

'I don't think she's set fire to anyone in years. It's hard for her.'

'I sympathise.'

Knowing Phélan, he literally might.

'Are we getting around to why you called me?' he prompted.

'I called you because you're the worst person I know.'

A slight frown. 'Right.'

'If anyone of my acquaintance is likely to have their fingers deep in this pie, it's you.'

'I think that was an insult,' said Phélan. 'Not even a pretend insult, either.'

'It was.'

'Thank you.'

'It's fair.' Phélan had *so often* turned out to be involved in some scheme we were disrupting, if never very deeply. He was never the mastermind, never really committed himself to any scheme of infamy, but he was more than happy to make use of other people's if it benefited him somehow.

His face registered annoyance, briefly, then turned rueful. 'It is fair. Why don't you fill me in about this particular pie?'

'It's not just about that selkie they pulled out of the river. There are more.' I gave him a rapid precis of the developments thus far, and our suspicions as to the probable motives. Phélan listened in silence; I couldn't tell, from his face, what he was thinking.

'So when I heard that some mysterious sluagh's been trying to flog one or more selkie-skins on the quiet,' I concluded, 'naturally I thought of you.'

'Gratifying.'

'So? Anything for me?'

'I'm not a slaver.'

'I'm both pleased because I'd rather you weren't, and disappointed because that doesn't help me find Mearil.'

'I haven't heard anything about this. But I should've.'

'Can you—'

He cut me off with a gesture. 'Yes, I can make enquiries.'

'Great. Please do that. Actually though, I was going to ask if you'll back me up at Tully's while I investigate.'

'You're asking me to go to the Puca with you.'

'It's not a date.'

'I wasn't suggesting it was.'

I glared. 'If I'm going to sell Fionn, it stands to reason I need to know who to sell her to. And that I'd use your connections. You and I can approach these people, find out who's in the market for selkie-slaves—'

Phélan held up a hand. 'We're... selling Fionn.'

'Obviously.'

'I knew there was bad blood between the fatales these days, but not *that* bad.'

'Get over it. We're *ostensibly* selling Fionn, because I know where she hides her sealskin, therefore why wouldn't I.'

'Why indeed.'

'So we're agreed?'

'I don't see why you need my help charming these amateurs.'

'I've never needed any help with *that*.'

His lips twitched. 'So? What do you need me for?'

'I can't remember where I left my aura of badness, so I need to borrow yours.'

'Tai. You're still completely fatal.'

I beamed. 'Thanks.'

'But I'll help.'

'Great. I'll owe you.'

'Interesting.' He sat forward, fixing me with a dark, intent stare. 'What will you owe me?'

I held that gaze, because no way is the bastard going to intimidate me. 'Would you accept... one Tai-hug?'

'A pitiful offer. I'm going to need at least five.'

'It... it was pitiful, wasn't it? Clearly I've forgotten how to reward my flunkies, too.'

'Flunky.'

I nodded.

'Penalty awarded. The price is now ten Tai-hugs.'

'*Ten*? Ridiculous. Have you forgotten what these things are *worth*?'

'Not in the least. That's why I want ten.'

'I can go as high as four,' I countered.

'Six, and that's my final offer.'

'You drive a hard bargain.'

He shrugged. 'So go borrow someone else's aura of badness.'

'Five and a half and it's a deal.'

'Half?'

'Yes.'

'Half a hug.'

'It's within the bounds of possibility.'

'Fine. Five and a half Tai-hugs, but only because I'd love to watch you attempt to half-hug anybody.'

He had a point. I never do things by halves, and certainly not hugs. 'Challenge accepted.' I held out my hand; we shook to seal the deal.

'Right, meet me at the Puca tonight,' I said. 'Around six. We'll camp until these assholes show up.'

'What if they don't?'

'Then we'll go back the next night. Or we'll get a lead from Tully. I don't know, okay? We're winging it.'

He grinned. 'And that's the Tai I know and love.'

'A deranged screw-up?'

'A deranged and *affectionate* screw-up.'

'Yes, I guess I missed you too.'

I SNATCHED A FEW hours' sleep, because a semi-comatose Tai is all kinds of no fun. But somewhere around lunchtime, I was woken by the sound of the front door slamming shut, the jangle of keys dropped into the tray, and the *thud* of something solid hitting the floor.

Coronis, with luggage.

'Tai!' she yelled.

I wrenched my befuddled consciousness out of sleep-land and back into something like reality. It cost me an effort. By the time I'd hauled myself out of bed, donned a vaguely respectable garment, and shuffled as far as the door, Coronis was already barging through it.

'She's not here,' I said, noting the way Coronis's hazy grey eyes searched my room.

'You haven't found her.'

'Not yet.'

'Shit.' Coronis slumped onto the edge of my bed, her gauzy, silvered wings fluttering with agitation, and put her face into her hands.

'I know.' I sat beside her, and put an arm around her, drawing her into a hug. 'We're trying, believe me.'

'Looks more like you're sleeping.'

'Because I was up most of the night, looking for Mea.'

Coronis sighed, and sat up. 'Sorry. That was bitchy.'

I gave her an extra, reassuring squeeze before I released her. 'I'll tell you about it in a minute, but I actually have some questions I want to ask you.'

'Anything.' Coronis, a cloud nymph, is a storm in a tea-cup at the best of times. Now tension and worry had made her steely, brittle. The look she gave me cut me to the heart, for beneath a surface chill — like winter rainwater — she was hungry for a reason to hope. I had little to offer.

'We may have traced a connection between Mearil and a few other selkies,' I began. 'And those other selkies all have links to the Eventide club. Do you know it?'

'Shit,' said Coronis, again. 'Mea went there. About two weeks back.'

My heart leapt — and sank. 'Tell me.'

'She was so damned excited about it. Bought a new dress and everything.'

'You didn't go with her?'

Coronis shook her head. 'She went with a friend. Brianne. They invited me, but I — said no. I hate places like that. But I should've gone. Shit, Tai, I *never* should have let her go alone.'

My head spun; I barely heard the rest of Coronis's words. 'Brianne? Brianne Lamarre?'

Coronis came back from the guilt spiral she was busily falling down; her gaze sharpened. 'You know her.'

'*Mea* knows her? You told me she hadn't made any new friends recently.'

'Well, and she hasn't. She's been friends with Brianne for a month or two, must be. Met at some work-related thing.'

'I... would characterise that as *recent*, Cor.'

'I thought you meant, in the last week or two.'

'Anybody *else* she's taken up with in the last couple of months?'

'Not to my knowledge. Just Brianne.'

'So Brianne fucking Lamarre took Mea to Eventide two weeks ago. Or, ten days or so before she disappeared.'

That explained how Mea's movements had been known. If she'd seen Brianne as a friend, naturally she'd have told her about her upcoming trip away. But perhaps not much in advance. Had Brianne tried to lure her to Eventide again — or to the Pearls club — only to be declined on account of Mea's upcoming flight? They'd had to scramble to grab her before she left the country.

Brianne Lamarre.

'Okay, hold these thoughts,' I said, reaching for my phone. Fi and Daix needed to know about this. Brianne absolutely wasn't just bait, and her approach of that poor, naïve idiot of a selkie, Cellann, was neither innocent nor a coincidence. She was deeply involved in the scheme, and had been laying plans for weeks. Had she been cosying up to Narasel and Melly, too? Likely.

We should've eviscerated her back at Eventide, when we had the chance. Instead, we'd alerted her to our involvement, confirmed that we'd taken the damned bait, and then... let her go, because *then* we hadn't had sound enough reason to do otherwise.

I ought to have known. *We* ought to have known.

Where the hell she was now was anybody's guess, but I feared we wouldn't be seeing her again. Not until she was ready for us. We'd face her on her terms, not ours.

Damnit.

'Daix,' I said when she picked up the call. 'Tell me you've had your creepy surveillance thing going on Brianne Lamarre.'

'I thought my *creepy surveillance thing* was a totally unjustifiable invasion of privacy.'

'It is when you're running it on *me*.'

'Oh, sure. Hate it 'til you love it. See, Tai, you *need* me.'

'For once, Daix, I'm going to say: cut the jokes. This is important.'

'*You*? Cut the *jokes*? Now I *know* shit's got serious.'

'Daix. Do you know where Brianne Lamarre is?'

She hesitated.

Daix is the incorrigible smart mouth, with an answer for everything. I know, I know; coming from me, that's rich. But you really can't shut Daix up.

For her to be at a loss for an answer, however briefly, is never a good sign.

'You don't know,' I filled in.

'I *had* her, I swear. Then she — vanished.'

'Vanished.'

Daix paused again, a silence I'd term, in her case, deafening. 'Okay, she clocked me.'

'You? You were personally tailing her?'

'Not *me* as in physically me. What, you think I have nothing better to do than follow vaguely questionable people around all day in the hope they'll do something shady?'

'She's a lot more than vaguely questionable, Daix. She lured Mearil to Eventide; Coronis just confirmed it. There can be no doubt she's behind all this, so tell me again about how you lost her.'

'*I* lost her? You weren't even trying!'

'You're right. That was unjust. But could we just get *on* with it.'

Daix sighed. 'I put someone on her tail. Someone *good*. One of my best, but it's like she was expecting it. She spotted him in next to no time, and — I kid you not — blew him a goddamned *kiss* before she... vanished.'

'Vanished as in, how?'

'As in, no fucking clue, Tai. She was there and then she wasn't.'

'Wasn't visibly there or wasn't *there*?'

'Whatever the distinction might have been, my agent wasn't able to determine.'

'So she's gone.'

'Yep.'

My turn for a lengthy silence, turning over this unwelcome news. I broke it at last by saying, 'Daix, I don't think it's *like* she was expecting to be followed. I think she *was*. She approached Mearil weeks ago, made a friend of her — precisely in the furtherance of this godawful scheme. She was ready for you. Hell, she probably knows all the people you'd send to tail her.'

Daix's subsequent silence was more of the fuming variety. 'Fine, I was out-jockeyed,' she finally said. 'Happy?'

'It's not your fault,' I said, though I had to conquer a mild urge to tear her face off even as I said it. 'We've all screwed up. We got complacent. Lazy. Unwary. And for some reason, Brianne Lamarre is taking great pleasure in taking advantage of that.'

'Yes, what's got into her anyway?'

'We've talked about this. If there's someone from back in the day who's trying to settle scores, we didn't really consider Brianne. Sure, we saw her with that selkie at Eventide, but — what the hell did we ever do to her to deserve this kind of shit?'

'No clue,' said Daix. 'Did we fuck up some scheme of hers that I've forgotten about?'

'Not to my knowledge.'

'Then, what?

'I don't know. Let's find out where the hell she vanished to, shall we? Then we can ask her ourselves.'

Daix growled something. 'Fine, I'm on it. Call you when I've got something.'

She hung up.

I sent Fionn a text. *Fi. Brianne Lamarre's our culprit. Any chance you can go back to Eventide tonight? Doubt she'll show up, but you could maybe ask around.*

'Right,' I said to Coronis. 'The ladies are chasing up on Brianne. I've got other fish to fry.'

'Right. And what am I supposed to do?'

My phone buzzed: Fionn. 'Hang on,' I said absently, reading. *Can and will. Are you sure about Bri, though?*

'Right. You need to... wait,' I said to Coronis.

'Wait? That's it? I need to help, Tai. Give me something to do.'

'All right. What do you want to do?'

'I can go to Eventide—'

'How are you going to get in?'

She opened her mouth, paused, and closed it again. 'Well—'

'Forget it. I've got someone on that. What else?'

'I...'

'Hang on. There is a thing. Just a second.'

I typed back to Fionn. *Fairly, yes. I'd go with you but I'm committed to the Puca with P.*

'Brianne,' I said to Coronis. 'She and Mea were friends for several weeks?'

'I... yes, so she said. She didn't mention her name until, maybe, three or four weeks ago, but it seemed like she wasn't a brand new acquaintance then.'

'She have a phone number for Brianne? An address?'

'If she had a number for Brianne, it'll be on her phone, which presumably is on her.' Coronis brightened. 'Hey, maybe we could trace—'

'The phone. No. Brianne's no amateur. If Mea had a phone on her, they'd have tossed it long ago.'

'Oh.'

'I know. It's so annoying dealing with people who know what they're doing. So she wouldn't have a record of Brianne's details anywhere?'

Coronis shrugged. 'You searched her room. Did you find an address book or anything?'

'Anything so helpful, yet so old-fashioned literally nobody does that anymore? No. I did not.'

Message from Fionn. *Careful at the Puca.*

She didn't add, *careful with Phélan*, but I got that message anyway.

I wrote back. *Careful at Eventide.*

'Your job then, if you need me to tell you,' I said to Coronis, 'is to turn this place upside down and see if anything related to Brianne falls out. A number would be great. An address, better. But honestly, I'll take anything.'

Coronis nodded. 'What are you going to do?'

'I'm delving into the heart of mortal peril by gate-crashing a sluagh crime party.'

Coronis's eyes grew larger. 'You really are a fatale.'

'I thought you called that already.'

'It's one thing to realise it intellectually. Different to see it in practice. I've always known you as a slouch with a great voice.'

'Thanks. Wasn't always such a slouch. Anyway, the mortal peril's tonight. Right now, I badly need a sandwich.'

I returned to the Booted Puca an hour or so ahead of my agreed meeting with Phélan. I wanted time to get my bearings, settle in, talk to Tully... and watch the goings-on. You can learn so much without having to ask a single question, just by paying attention to what's going on around you.

Of course, it was too much to expect that Brianne Lamarre would be sitting at a corner table, nursing a drink and chatting about her evil plans at a penetrating volume. Or that the mysterious sluagh gang Tully had mentioned would be neatly arranged around a table, buying and selling selkie-skins — and therefore, slaves — just at the moment I wanted to be spying on them. Such glorious coincidences of timing aren't absolutely unheard of, but they're rare.

Still, there's always gossip. *Always* gossip.

'Hey, Tully,' I said, wandering up to the bar. I'd chosen to dress down this time, dark jeans and a tank top. I didn't want to be nearly so eye-catching as I was last night at Eventide. 'Get me one of whatever's popular today.'

'We're all over the pale ales today,' answered Tully. He grabbed a slim, hazily-blue bottle and presented it to me.

'Starlight Frostbite,' I read. 'Sold.'

He beamed. 'It's as good as it sounds,' he promised, pouring me a tall glass. And it was; one sip froze my lips blue, in a *good* way.

I paid, and took a moment to survey the pub. About half the tables were taken, several with lone drinkers, the rest with groups. None of them looked like the sluagh gang I was on the watch for. 'Tully,' I said, in a lower voice. 'Does Brianne Lamarre come in here?'

'Not... openly.'

'Oh?'

Tully tapped one green-gold eye.

'Let me see if I can parse that,' I said. 'Glamoured. Thinks she's concealed but you're wise to those tricks.'

'Pays to be, with this job.'

'Uh huh. She meet with anybody noteworthy when she's here?'

He twinkled at me. 'You got someone in mind?'

'A certain sluagh gang who may or may not be peddling particularly questionable contraband.'

'Not that I've seen.'

I nodded. Made sense enough. If Brianne was behind the scheme, she might be using these sluagh to fence the skins, but she wouldn't need to meet them in so public a place for that. Those arrangements would've been made elsewhere. No, the sluagh were here looking for buyers.

Leaning against the bar, I asked, casually, 'And Phélan Astrophel?'

Tully gave a nod. 'Seen him, a time or two.'

'He meeting with these sluagh at all?'

'Happen you should ask him yerself,' said Tully, and winked. With a tilt of his head, he indicated a corner behind me. I turned.

A tall figure sat there with his back to the wall. He wore a dark suit, very sharp, with a black homburg — like that would hide his face enough to conceal him from me.

I shouldn't have been surprised that Phélan had the same idea as me, and arrived early. What surprised me was that he'd managed to slip in without my noticing. I'm damned sure he hadn't been there when I walked in.

'Thanks, Tully,' I sighed. 'I'll do that.' I grabbed my glass of Starlight Frostbite and stalked over to Phélan's table.

'Look at you, cleaning up all nice,' I said as I sank into a seat.

He looked up, and, surprisingly, smiled. 'Tai. No sultry gown today?'

'How did you know I was up to my eyeballs in gowns yesterday?'

'Oh, I doubt very much you were up to your anything in gowns,' he returned. '*Down*, maybe. To about, here?' He made a vague gesture in the direction of my cleavage area.

'As you can see,' I said, folding my arms upon the table-top. 'I'm not breaking that out for you.'

'How do I get that deal again?'

'Start by answering my questions. Did you follow me to Eventide?'

'I'm tempted to let you keep thinking that, but no. Just a guess. The Tai of old had a taste for luxury.'

'I'm not the Tai of old.'

'That's becoming clear.' Phélan signalled Tully. A black glass bottle of something came duly floating over, followed by an empty glass.

'If you think you like that,' said Phélan, nodding at my Frost-bite. 'You should try this.'

'I'm good. Can't think clearly with too much alcoholic brain freeze.'

'Maybe I'm not too interested in your thinking clearly.'

'Phélan, this is business. Flirt some other time.'

He sighed, took off his hat, and tossed it on a vacant chair. 'All right. You spoke of questions, plural. What were the rest?'

'I was just asking Tully whether you've ever been seen rubbing elbows with these selkie-trafficking sluagh.'

'I told you. I'm no slaver.'

'So you did.'

'Doesn't seem like you were listening.'

I shrugged. 'I want to believe you. Considering everything, though, it's not unwise to ask questions.'

'And Tully said what?'

'Said to ask you myself. Which is interesting, because *I* never saw you come in, and I was expecting you.'

Phélan's gaze flicked to the bar, and the unassuming clurichaun presently polishing glasses. 'Tully's got all sorts of hidden depths.'

'Probably needs to. Can't be easy lording it over the only truly neutral ground in the city.'

'I wouldn't underestimate him.'

'It's okay. I'm fairly sure he likes me.'

'That being your weapon of choice.' Phélan gave me an unreadable look.

'Pure likeability?' I grinned. 'It's true. I'm everyone's favourite gal. Except when I'm *really* not.'

Phélan took a drink. I waited, but no rejoinder emerged.

'You missed your cue to tell me how unpopular I am with you,' I said.

'Is that something you need to hear?'

'Need, no. But it's *fun*.'

Phélan said nothing. I'd lost his attention; he was looking past me, at something unfolding out of my field of vision.

'That,' he said after a moment, 'is Nelo Lysander.'

I resisted the urge to turn and gawk, with an effort. 'And he is?'

'A… cousin, of sorts.' Phélan didn't look happy to see him.

Sluagh can be funny about family. By which I mean, family ties are supposed to be *everything*. They're more tribal than clannish, though the effect is much the same. If you could get Phélan and all his extended family connections into one place, under the right — or badly wrong — circumstances, they'd troop, and when they troop you get a Wild Hunt, and then… seriously, run for cover.

Phélan tends to steer clear of his family.

'This isn't a connection you're happy about,' I surmised.

Phélan didn't answer right away. He was watching Lysander's doings with an intent interest, and his face had gone hard and cold.

Abruptly, he looked away. Back at me. 'He's not so bad. But he is a damned fool.'

With which words, he rose and abandoned our table, heading for Nelo Lysander.

I followed.

Nelo looked nothing like Phélan, but then, the connection between them was likely remote. He had short-cropped brown hair, a style of dress that was casual to the point of slobbishness, a smiling mouth, and intensely pale eyes. Eerily pale. He looked like the kind of guy who could look up the ghost of your great-grandma, have a cosy chat, and then eat her for lunch.

Which is to say he was a strange blend of joviality and fucking scary. That's sluagh for you.

'Nelo,' said Phélan. A vacant seat beckoned, but he didn't take it, preferring, apparently, to loom over his distant cousin.

Nelo Lysander had a couple of friends with him, but they all went quiet when Phélan showed up. One was sluagh; the other looked like half sluagh, half troll. Interesting.

'Hey, if it isn't Phélan,' said Nelo, with an expansive, easy smile. 'Sit down, buddy. And your lady friend, too.' His pale eyes shifted to me, appraising. Appreciative, in ways I didn't appreciate. Assessing.

'Tai,' I said, and, remembering the role I was playing, I smiled into those creepy eyes, and held out my hand. '*Not* Phélan's lady friend.'

Nelo shook my hand, holding it slightly too long. 'I like her already,' he informed Phélan.

'She's everyone's favourite gal,' he agreed, and took the proffered seat. I accepted one from Nelo's half-troll friend, taking a moment to size him up as I did so. You don't see half-trolls very often. This one had the appearance of being uncomfortable with himself, rather self-effacing. Much more so than a man of his physical advantages ought to be; he was intimidating. I awarded him a smile, rather more genuine than the one I'd bestowed upon Nelo. He smiled back.

The third person at the table, the other sluagh, said nothing and did nothing. He watched. He had an air of stillness that suggested high alertness, and a busy mind. What was he reading into the situation? What did he make of me, or of Phélan's appearance? I couldn't read him.

'Here on business?' said Phélan, and repeated his send-me-drinks gesture to Tully.

Nelo looked from Phélan to me. 'Might be,' he said cautiously.

'Don't be shy of Tai,' said Phélan. 'She's in business, too.'

'Oh? And what business might that be?' Nelo directed this question at me, ignoring Phélan.

Tricky. You can't exactly come right out and *say* you're trying to sell your erstwhile best friend into slavery and you'd like to make use of your new acquaintance's contacts to do it.

'I've heard there's money in furs, lately,' I said.

Nelo nodded. 'Plenty. Lots of fine ladies like yourself, wanting a bit of luxury.'

Nelo didn't seem to be catching my drift. His friend, though... maybe. Something had changed with him, too subtle to put my finger on. But I had his attention.

'Nothing too common, though,' I continued, briefly catching the eye of Nelo's friend. 'I'm looking to deal in the rarer kind.'

'Might be I can put you in the way of an associate of mine,' offered Nelo. Half his attention was on Phélan as he said it; looking to win his cousin's approval, was he? I might be able to use that.

I smiled on Nelo. 'I could use some contacts.'

Nelo's friend abruptly spoke. 'Buyer?'

'Seller.'

Nelo watched this exchange, still smiling. 'Maybe you and Drevan should get acquainted, hm? Seems like maybe you could help each other out.'

Drevan, as seemed to be his wont, said nothing.

'Same trade, hm?' I suggested.

'New thing,' said Nelo. 'Could be—'

'Shut it, Nelo,' said Drevan. He looked long at me, jaw set. Nothing about his demeanour seemed welcoming, or conciliatory. But, he hadn't walked away either.

In appearance, he was thoroughly unassuming, in ways that I might call cultivated. Serviceable haircut, unremarkable brown. In build, neither heavy nor especially thin, and while he was in decent shape he didn't have the look of a man in fighting condition. Faded blue jeans, a dark t-shirt and a black jacket. Average.

A man dedicated to going unnoticed, in short. That tends to get my attention.

'Hey, I promise, I'm not here to trade on your patch,' I said, smiling. 'Just, I could use a few pointers, you know?'

'Help the good lady out, Drevan,' said Nelo. 'Any friend of Phélan's, right?'

I dislike playing the helpless female card, as a rule. It's demeaning. But, fuck me, it *works*. Few men can resist an opportunity to explain something to an attractive female, and this guy was no exception. Drevan didn't visibly soften, but a little of the tension went out of that clenched jaw, and he looked away. 'Sure.'

'Fantastic,' I said. 'I'm pretty sure of my *supply*. I just need to figure out where to take it.'

Drevan looked at me. Still unreadable, but I had his attention.

After that, I permitted the conversation to slide into other subjects. Wouldn't do to belabour the point; Drevan would either pursue it, or not.

I have to say, outside of the angle I was trying to work, Nelo and his friends were pretty good company. Especially his half-troll bodyguard – for such he must have been, let's be clear here. His name, I eventually learned, was Paulan, and he had a taciturn quality I found appealing. Perhaps because it registered with me as shy, rather than pugnacious, like Drevan. I had the feeling, throughout the next hour of drinking and talking, that he was sometimes studying me. Covertly, of course, so I didn't let on that I had noticed. What was he trying to figure out about me?

I wasn't surprised when, as Phélan and I rose to leave, Paulan soon found an excuse to follow us.

'Ma'am,' he called after me, bringing me to a halt a few steps beyond the Puca's front door.

'How courteous,' I said easily, turning. 'No one's called me "ma'am" since about nineteen forty.' Except Rudy, but only in jest, so I wasn't going to count it.

Paulan looked sideways at Phélan.

'You appear to be somewhat *de trop*,' I informed Phélan.

He didn't move.

I lowered my voice. 'If you imagine I can't handle myself around your friends, kindly reconsider.'

'This isn't a patronising show of gallantry,' Phélan retorted.

'Then what is it?'

He had no answer to that, seemingly, for he said nothing, and withdrew with a scowl.

'Sorry,' I said to Paulan. 'Phélan's...' Phélan's what? I couldn't think of any single word that could encapsulate all the odd and inscrutable attitudes that were his. I shrugged this off with a smile.

'Your *supply*,' said Paulan, without responding to this. 'You were speaking of — skins, weren't you?'

'I believe I said furs.'

'Drevan's into something... new,' said Paulan.

'Behind Nelo's back, hm?'

Paulan nodded. 'I'm not here to talk smack about Nelo, but Drevan's got ideas.'

I sighed inwardly. I didn't need to get tangled up with a leadership squabble among Nelo's gang, whatever the hell they were up to. That said, I had got the impression that Nelo wasn't quite the brightest star in the sky. I could see how that would frustrate a man like Drevan.

Perhaps this, too, was something I could use.

So what did Paulan want? I thought fast.

'You think he'll win?' I hazarded.

'He has support.'

Aha. 'But not Phélan's.'

'Phélan and Nelo are family.'

And among the sluagh, that meant everything. Phélan would never support the deposition of a cousin of his – unless he was suitably motivated, because after all, we're still talking about Phélan here.

Paulan wasn't talking like a man who felt a deep and abiding loyalty for either Nelo or Drevan. Probably he was just worried about where his ass was going to land when the dust settled.

'If Drevan prevails,' I said, 'I can try to get Phélan on side for you. Can't promise, but I'm not awful at this.'

He nodded. 'I've got information.'

'About Drevan's buyers.'

'I'm usually present.'

'Influence for information, then?'

He nodded.

'Consider it done.'

Paulan nodded. 'There's a building on West Hendon Broadway. Derelict. You got something to sell, show up tomorrow night. Auction starts at ten.'

'And Drevan?'

'He won't stop you.'

So he was acting with Drevan's knowledge and consent – or at least, he could presume far enough on Drevan's favour to feel certain of his support. I revised my ideas about Paulan's neutrality.

'I'll be there,' I told him, and tipped my hat. 'Appreciate it.'

He nodded, and returned inside.

I returned to Phélan.

'There's a power struggle going on,' I said, falling into step beside him.

'Drevan trying to unseat Nelo again?'

'It's happened before?'

'Nelo will deal with it.'

'I promised I'd use my influence with you.'

He looked down at me. It was dark, and since his eyes were shadowed beneath the brim of his homburg, I couldn't decipher his expression. 'Sounds like fun,' he said.

'*All* kinds of fun. But if you're determined on this policy of non-interference, there isn't a whole lot of point in my unleashing the feminine wiles tonight.'

'Who said anything about determined.'

I grinned. 'All right, hold that thought. In the meantime, we have a date for tomorrow night.'

'Let me guess. The kind of date that in no way resembles an actual date.'

'Unless gate-crashing a highly illegal selkie slave market in my company sounds likely to turn you on, in which case, suit up.'

He shook his head. 'Life's been so *quiet* without you.'

'I refuse to believe any part of that statement.'

'Would you accept quieter?'

'Allowable.'

We emerged from the Puca's lands onto Adelaide Road, which was... random. It's always random. I've never ended up on the same street twice.

Phélan paused in front of a tall block of flats, light from its many windows casting half-shadows onto his face.

'Problem?' I said.

'Are we done for tonight?'

'I've no other use to make of your connections just now, if that's what you mean.'

'I thought it was my aura of badness.'

'Or that either.'

He nodded. 'I was going to suggest going for a drink, but we've done that.'

I'd absorbed more than enough peculiar Puca beverages for one evening, that was for sure. Especially since I was very much on the job.

'Any other ideas?' he said, watching me.

'Are we talking about the kind of date that in every way resembles a date.'

'Let's say yes.'

'In that case, no.'

'I'd like to change my previous answer.'

I grinned. 'You know it's a bad idea.'

'I know nothing of the kind.'

'Track record of total disaster, etc, etc.'

'You worry too much.' He turned, and began to walk away from me.

'Tomorrow,' I called after him.

'Yes, yes.' He was briefly illuminated by the yellow glow of a nearby street lamp, then faded into the shadows beyond.

I lingered a moment, wondering if he would come back. When he didn't, I stepped around the side of the block of flats, and concealed myself in a dark spot, beyond the reach of the lamps.

Daix picked up on the third ring. 'Tai. Tell me shit.'

'I've got a lead.'

'*Yes.*'

I ran her through the evening's developments, glossing over some of Phélan's contributions. Daix tended to get incendiary on that subject. 'So, more names for you,' I concluded. 'This Drevan Somebody has links to tomorrow's auction. If he has any known associates besides Nelo—'

'I know, I know. I get the drill.'

'Sorry. Anyway, feel like showing up?'

'Me?'

'Why not?'

'Why not, because I'm always the bridesmaid.' I could hear the scowl in Daix's voice, even if she spoke lightly.

'Who's the bride in this scenario?'

'Fionn.'

'Ah. Don't worry, she's coming too.'

'Sweet. All the girls together again.'

Her tone dripped sarcasm, or perhaps it was venom.

'So, *are* you coming?' I persevered. 'If you're passing yourself off as a buyer in this charming scenario, you'd want to be at this auction.'

'You mean I get to show up and make it *rain*.'

'I'll take that over burning the place down, sure.'

She was grinning as she said, 'Party. I'll dress up.'

'Great. Now go away. I have to talk to Fi.'

'Okay, but I think you're rushing things. It's customary to wait until at least the fourth date before you propose marriage.'

'Speaking from experience, are you?'

'Yes.'

I blinked. 'No further questions.'

'Damnit. Should've hooked you with that one.'

'Too obvious.'

'Worth a try. Oh! I have a nugget of news for you, too.'

'Sounds promising,' I said.

'Guess who has links-by-marriage to the loaded and fashionable Quinn-Diamhor family.'

'Please say Brianne.'

'Got it in one.' Daix sounded incredibly pleased with herself, but I let it pass. She'd earned it. 'Brianne Lamarre's mother was a Quinn-Diamhor by birth. Married a bit beneath herself, by popular opinion, but our girl Bri's been cultivating those connections.'

'Good job.'

'That was a compliment, Tai. A real one.'

'Yes, yes it was. I'm guessing you haven't found Brianne herself yet?'

'That sounded more like an insult.'

'Only a bit. Anything else for me?'

'You expect such a lot from a girl.'

I grinned. 'Call me when you've got more. Bye.'

It took me a few minutes to work up the will to call Fi. This wasn't going to be the fun kind of conversation.

'Fi,' I said when she picked up. 'Hey. You busy?'

'I've a few minutes. Something afoot?'

'Rather.' I took a breath. 'Look. I know we lost touch for a while there, but we were always good friends before, and…'

'Mm?' she prompted.

'And I was wondering if it's too soon to drag you to a slave auction and sell you to the highest bidder.'

13

— · —

FIONN

'Wʜᴀᴛ?' I sᴀɪᴅ, ᴍᴏᴍᴇɴᴛᴀʀɪʟʏ breathless.

'May I mercilessly barter you for personal gain,' came Tai's voice down the phone.

I drew in air, with difficulty. 'Tai—' I began.

'Come on! It'll be fun!'

'It will be *anything but fun.*'

She sighed. 'I know. I do.'

'I don't think you do, or you wouldn't make a joke out of it.' Her words had hit me with the force of a brick, or perhaps a whole flurry of bricks. I felt bruised. A *slave auction*? For selkies?

'Right.' Tai paused; I could almost hear her swallowing the next jest she'd doubtless been planning to make. 'Fair. I'm sorry. I thought it might make it easier—'

'Shall we move ahead to the explanations?' I said, keeping my voice even with an effort.

'Sorry.' The story that followed grew a little confused; I gathered it had a lot to do with Phélan, inevitably. But the salient point was: a selkie slave-auction, tomorrow night. My stomach turned over. Would my fellow selkies be there in person, or would it only be their sealskins changing hands? Tai obviously concluded the former. Perhaps she was right.

In which case, perhaps Melly and Mearil would be there. There may be more, too – selkies whose absences we had not yet learned of.

Even if it was only their skins, this was our chance to find out who was conducting this abominable little business. Perhaps we could even stop them – tomorrow. Before they had chance to do anything... else. Anything *worse*.

'So you need me there to back up your claims,' I concluded when Tai had finished.

'Right. I need to prove to these people that I'm not trying to play games. I have to show that I've really got the goods.'

'And a sealskin wouldn't be sufficient by itself?'

'That's... up to you. I can walk in there with you openly, or you can skulk in the shadows and delve into unpleasant truths while I attempt to flog your sealskin to the highest bidder.'

'Can't figure out which one of those sounds less appealing.'

'We won't use your actual sealskin,' said Tai quickly.

'Damn right you won't.'

Tai didn't respond. I recognised the manoeuvre. She was giving me space to think, time to consider – confident that I'd come down on her side of the fence, once I had.

I did not have words to express my horror at being expected to *play-act* at being slave-taken again. I could absolutely do it, and very convincingly. I've had enough practice, Hags help me, and it isn't the sort of thing you forget. But to dive back into that kind of darkness is a lot to ask of a woman.

I couldn't say no, though. What else were we going to do? We had to be at that auction, and Tai was right: she couldn't show up empty-handed. A fake sealskin wasn't going to cut it.

'I'll be there,' I said. 'I'll get back to you on the details.'

'I love you,' said Tai.

'You always say that when I've agreed to do something for you.'

'No. I always say that when you've agreed to do something unspeakably brave and devastatingly unpleasant for me.'

'Remind me how that keeps happening.'

'I don't know, maybe consider a job change?'

'I *had* a job change. I'm a specialist in haute couture. I'm not supposed to be doing devastatingly unpleasant things anymore.'

'After tomorrow, we'll go to a theme park,' said Tai. 'A whole day. You and me.'

'A theme park.'

'You know what those are, right?'

'They're for kids.'

'They're for kids *and adults*, Fi.'

'Adults *with* kids. You know, parents.'

'If you want to borrow a child for the day, that's fine with me, but it'll be way more fun without.'

'I'll think about it.'

Tai went off to engage in obscure Tai-type things, and I returned to my own business. Thoughts of the next night's auction unsettled me; I put them forcibly out of my mind, and concentrated on the problems of today.

I had two tasks on my agenda. One, get in touch with Faerd. I wanted to talk to him about our recent discoveries, see if anything rang any new bells with him. And, who knew, perhaps he had uncovered some new information on his own.

And the other: Eventide. I had agreed to go back. Indeed, I was dressed for it already, in a moon-coloured satin gown and blue diamonds. I'd been on the point of leaving when Tai had called me; my taxi was waiting.

On the journey there, I composed myself as best I could, pushing away all the parts of Fionn that disturbed my peace. I was a lake of cool waters, placid and serene. I was a *fatale*, effortlessly capable, imperturbably confident. I could handle anything.

By the time my taxi drew up outside of the Eventide club, I almost believed it.

The club had attracted a photographer or two tonight, and the bouncers, for whatever reason, had not sent them off. I paused, and permitted a picture or two, before I went inside. No sense in hiding my attendance; Brianne knew we were involved, and I was there to track her down.

The idea that Brianne herself might be behind the repulsive selkie scheme had yet to make sense to me. Of course, it wasn't impossible. The lady had neither feelings nor standards to make such a business repellent to her, after all. But so direct an operation wasn't her style, either. She was always a more shadowy presence, attaching herself to the schemes of others as it suited her, but mostly independent. Like a female Phélan, really. I wondered if the comparison had ever entered Tai's mind.

Regardless, Brianne as mastermind did not sit right with me. A great deal of time had passed, certainly, and people could change in unanticipated ways; they did so all the time. Even so, I expected to find someone else at the heart of this mess. Someone upon whose right hand Brianne was contented to sit.

But I had no idea who that might be.

Eventide was packed, unexpectedly so. I paused upon entry, and surveyed the room. Scarcely space to manoeuvre, and the din was almost unbearable. Such a crush – and the photographers outside – usually meant a celebrity or two was in attendance, a cut or three above the usual level. I spotted the culprit after a time: a prominent actress who'd been in several films lately. She was leannan sith, of course – unbeknownst to most, though she made for a controversial figure among the fae. There were plenty who'd judge her for seeking or accepting such fame; under such constant scrutiny, could she keep her fae nature a secret?

I had never made it my business to care. I avoided her, taking my time as I wandered through the room. If Brianne was here, she would be well concealed in this crowd. I kept an eye out for flashes of green hair, or perhaps that distinctive laugh of hers, but I encountered neither.

Someone touched my elbow, lightly. 'Fionn, wasn't it?'

I turned to find Tai's friend, Rudy, hovering nearby. He wore the standard metalhead's outfit of all-black, adorned with an occasional silver-based accent; nothing to interest me. But his demeanour was friendly.

'We met the other night,' I said, remembering to smile. 'Rudy, yes?'

He nodded. 'Tai with you?'

'Not tonight. Were you hoping to see her?'

Rudy took a moment to work out a response. 'It was nice to run into her, that's all. Have you two been friends long?'

'About a thousand years.'

'Oh. Then you know her well.'

'Used to. Tell me something, Rudy. Have you seen Brianne Lamarre here tonight?'

'Not so far. She was in last night, though.'

So she might still turn up. I resolved to wait. 'Thanks. How about Cellann? You know, the young model she was with.'

'She was in last night, too.'

Same time as Brianne. Good, on the one hand; she was still well, or at least, she had been as of yesterday. But she and Brianne were at Eventide together — less good.

Rudy drifted a little nearer, and lowered his voice. 'Those questions you were asking. Last time.'

'Yes?'

'I've been keeping an eye out.'

I nodded, and waited.

'I can't always tell who's selkie and who isn't, understand. Not if they don't make it obvious. But it seems to me we've had more selkies than usual coming in here lately.'

'Are they all seen with Brianne?'

'Not necessarily, but I can't be here all the time.'

That matched up with our conclusions thus far: Eventide was being used as some kind of honey trap, led by Brianne. But that only helped us so far. What I wanted was an opportunity either to wring some truths out of Brianne, or to follow her out of here and see where she went.

'Then again,' said Rudy, with an odd smile. '*You're* a selkie, aren't you? And I don't remember seeing you here before this week.'

I studied Rudy, unsure of his point. 'It's the presence of the others that's drawn me,' I said. 'Or rather, their absence from where they're supposed to be.'

He smiled wider. 'You ladies are a bit confused, aren't you?'

'I beg your pardon.'

'Consider Tai,' he said. 'She's a sweetheart, isn't she? Barely knows me, but trusts me anyway. Delightful quality. You'd think a history like hers would have made her more paranoid.'

'Did she tell you about her history?'

Rudy went on without answering me. 'And then we come to you. Waltzing in here the other day, Tai in tow, openly asking questions about things you really should have left alone. I'd expected better.'

I took a step away from Rudy. 'What could you possibly have expected?'

'That the pair of you would've had more sense than to advertise your intentions *quite* so openly. Or that you'd have better sense than to saunter back in here alone. Tai couldn't be here to back you up? Or did you think you'd be safe among so many people?'

Rudy's behaviour had changed. Gone was the congenial manner, the slight, amiable foolishness. Gone was the flirtatiousness of the other night. There was something cold about him now, and hard; unsympathetic.

'You're involved in this,' I said quietly.

'What, you thought that Tai has any clue who to trust?'

'She deserves better from you.'

He shrugged. 'Bitch has been avoiding me for years. Thinks she's too good for me. And you — you're worse, aren't you? Stuck up prima donna. And tragically over-confident.'

My knives were in my hands before he'd got halfway through this speech. I didn't want to openly pull them in such company — besides, given the quantity of people around me I had barely any room to move. But I got them between me and Rudy before I spoke. 'You're exactly Brianne's type, hm? Entitled attitude. Fragile ego. Tragically easy to butter up.'

His gaze flicked to the short, bright-silver blades pointed towards him. 'Nice move,' he said. 'Wrong target.'

Brianne's voice purred in my ear, 'Hello, darling. Did I tell you how much I've missed you?'

I had no time to react, no time to turn. The barest pinprick of sensation alerted me to her attack: a dart perhaps, or more likely a needle, jabbed into my bare left arm.

'Brianne,' I snarled, already unsteady on my feet. 'Can't say I've missed you *at all*.'

'I wonder if sweet Tai would say the same?'

The clamour in the club seemed to grow louder and louder, buzzing in my ears. My vision clouded. Brianne caught me as I fell, in a surprisingly gentle grip.

'There, there,' she murmured. 'Feeling a bit faint, hm? It's all these *people*, darling. We'll get you somewhere nice and quiet, and you'll feel better.'

I wanted to call her every name under the sun. I wanted to make sashimi of her with my beautiful knives. But before I'd had time to decide where on her exquisite person I'd begin, I dropped into darkness.

I woke slowly, and painfully, my abused head objecting to consciousness with every breath. Opening my eyes, I experienced a moment's blind panic, for I saw nothing but blank darkness. *Was I blind?*

No. Likely not, only left somewhere without lights. I forced myself to breathe, slowly and deeply, until the sensations of panic faded.

Well. Rudland Mathis, of Tormented Wraith. Tai was going to smash his teeth in with those fabulous gauntlets of hers, and I hoped I'd get to watch.

We had a major problem on our hands. For the moment, though, escape loomed rather larger as a priority.

Where the hell was I.

I was freezing cold, for one thing. I still wore my flimsy satin evening gown, and nothing much else. My shoes had fallen off my feet during transit; either that or they'd been intentionally taken from me. The knives I'd been holding were, of course, gone, as was the third blade I kept in a thigh-sheath.

I wasn't bound, which was curious, but convenient.

I could smell water. Neither fresh nor salt: stagnant, dead water. And something else: mild decay, not that of biological matter but of old, rotting wood and earth.

A derelict building, in all likelihood. Had I been dumped at the old car factory, the one Tai had said was hosting the auction? That would make sense. Perhaps Brianne and Rudy intended to make me part of the wares.

My bracelet... the nakedness of my left wrist told me my pearls were gone.

Of course they were.

So was my phone.

Well, then. I drew myself to my feet, carefully. My head throbbed with nauseating intensity, and I almost toppled over again. Several minutes of breathing passed before I felt steady enough to venture away from the spot in which I'd been lying.

I'd chosen a high-necked gown for the evening. Not my usual style, but there had been a purpose to it. It cost me a few moments' awkward fumbling to retrieve my pearls — the real ones — from their hiding-place; I'd hung them around my neck upon a long length of near-invisibly translucent silk, trusting to the gown's folds of satin and my undergarments to hide them. Those, and Brianne's obliging combination of cockiness and lack of imagination. She thought she had caught me unawares, too rusty to anticipate her plans. And I *was* rusty, no doubt about it — but nowhere near fool enough to go looking for *her* without taking precautions.

The other precaution was called Daix, and she'd been watching Eventide's rear entrance since before I arrived. Brianne might be wise to such a trick, certainly; we never used to show up anywhere alone, given the choice. But few people got the drop on Daix. She'd be along soon.

In the meantime. I separated one precious pearl from the string, and placed it upon my tongue. It felt cool there, tasted of salt.

I swallowed it. Immediately, the vestiges of my fatigue, confusion and dizziness faded away. My limbs strengthened, my head cleared, and I stood taller.

It hurt a little to seek those dead pools of water, but it wouldn't be the first time I'd dealt with stagnancy. It left a lingering bad taste, and I'd have another headache, but no matter. I forced myself to focus on the water, and in doing so, the stench of it threatened to turn my stomach. The taste of it flooded my mouth; I gritted my teeth on a surge of nausea.

Worth it, though, for this borrowed kinship allowed me to sense where it lay. Little of it was in the room with me; here there was only the dampness of leaking ceilings and mildew. But the water was not far away. I called it to me, and it came, seeping under the door and running across the concrete floor to reach me.

'Would kill for a light,' I muttered, and stepped carefully in the direction the water had come from. There lay the door, and egress. I sloshed through puddles of foul-smelling water, my bare skin shrinking from the contact. I moved slowly, wary of a collision with obstacles I couldn't see, but nothing impeded me. Soon, my outstretched arms encountered a wall, soft with rotten wallpaper and mould; my shrinking fingers groped their way from there to the hard panels of a closed door.

Excellent.

I concentrated, and the water flowed up to engulf the door. Decades of slow decay took place in the space of a minute or two; the water rotted the wood through, and, softened to the point of collapse, it sagged and fell.

I stepped through. I'd hoped a light of some sort might greet me on the other side, even if at some distance, but the environs were as pitch-dark as the room I'd left. This wouldn't do. I'd have to risk the exposure of my pearls, even if it meant alerting Brianne to my continued possession of them. I retrieved them, restored them to my wrist, and a moment's thought produced a dulcet white glow.

Better. The soft light was everything, compared to the blank nothingness of before. It illuminated the long, narrow and decrepit corridor in which I stood, a bleak, featureless passage etched with the marks of long neglect. No clues met my eyes as to where I was, or where I should go to escape the building, so I picked a direction at random and set off.

The uneven floor hurt my feet, and I regretted the loss of my shoes. I was shivering, too, beyond the possibility of controlling myself. I made a mental note of all these discomforts and indignities, and resolved to take the price of them out of Brianne's hide at some near-future date.

I reached the end of the corridor, followed it around to the right — and paused, for a new scent reached me. Smoke.

I broke into a trot, following the aroma of smoke through another couple of passageways and across a large hall piled with assorted rubbish. Down a flight of stairs. I kept my senses alert as I ran, still attuned with what little water remained in the building; if there'd been sign or scent of another person somewhere

— or, more specifically, another selkie — I'd have caught it. But there was nothing. For the moment, at least, I was the only prisoner on this site.

At last, I discovered the main doors — large enough to drive a car through, and hanging open. A figure stood between me and escape.

A small, compact figure wreathed in green-tinged flame.

'Finally,' said the walking torch. 'Take your damned time, Fi. Not like we're in a hurry or anything.'

'Are we though?' I said, slowing to a stop.

'I've got people tailing Brianne but they're bound to lose her soon. We have to get on that.'

'Did she see you?'

'Showed no sign of it, but that doesn't necessarily mean much. If you're done with your little holiday, shall we go?'

'I'm finished here.'

'Yes? You get everything set up?'

I nodded. 'The waters will watch for me. Everything that goes on in here for the next twenty-four hours, I'll know.'

'Great, well. Better be worth this little adventure.' Daix turned and walked out.

I followed, at a safe distance. She had a point: getting myself snatched by Brianne had been a risky strategy, and one I'd had to conceal from Tai. She'd never have gone for it, and with reason enough; it could have turned out a lot worse. But we needed an edge in this putrid game, and I'd willingly taken the gamble. 'Was it absolutely necessary to set yourself on fire?' I said to Daix as we walked out of the big front doors.

'High visibility. Figured I'd make it easy on you.'

'Good of you. Oh, and by the way, I was betrayed.'

'Oh?' said Daix, letting her flames die back a bit. 'By whom?'

'One Rudy Mathis. Acquaintance of Tai's. Some kind of metalhead with a nice guy complex and a crush on Brianne. And, I think, on Tai.'

'And?'

'And, it took me a little too long to figure him out. If you've got your phone, better warn Tai. He might go after her.'

Daix rolled her eyes, extracted a phone from her pocket, and punched a message into it with unnecessary force. 'Amateurs,' she muttered, shoving it back into her pocket.

'I am justly chastised.'

'I meant Rudy Mathis. What, some kind of idiot with a grudge? Is that what we're dealing with now? I remember when criminals used to be professionals.'

'I remember when *we* used to be professionals.'

She was kind, if condescending enough to pat me on the shoulder. 'Never mind Fi, you've still got me.'

'And Tai, if she'll forgive me for this stunt.'

'Do we have to tell her?'

'Of course we do.'

'I'm just saying. Maybe we don't have to tell her. I don't remember signing any full disclosure agreements.'

'Of course we have to tell her. It wouldn't be right not to.'

'It wasn't right not to tell her *before* we pulled this "stunt." What's wrong with not telling her afterwards, either?'

To my chagrin, her logic held up at least as well as mine did.

I'm not even sure why I was so worried about telling Tai, either before *or* after. Daix I'd enlisted to my cause without a moment's doubt — because I knew she'd be up for it, and I also knew she wouldn't care about the risks, either to herself or to me.

Tai would care. About the latter, if not the former. She'd been showing some mother hen tendencies, which I hoped would wear off given a little time, and (hopefully) a lack of Ravensbrück-level disasters. I could hardly tell her I was capable of looking after myself; hadn't we all proved how spectacularly untrue that could sometimes be?

Plus, I was a hypocrite. I was more worried about Tai out there alone than I'd ever used to be, back... before.

We'd lost confidence in ourselves, *and* in each other. Hopefully, both of those things would improve with time.

'So where are we?' I said, when we reached the street. The darkness and general dereliction were no help to me in pinpointing our location, though the source of the unpleasant smells became clear: this was a fly-tipper's paradise.

'Old car factory,' said Daix. 'West Hendon Broadway.'

The same place the auction was to take place on the morrow. That's what I'd been hoping for, though the confirmation cost me a moment's unease as well. Dumping me in *there* proved my fears about the ultimate goal: I was to be sold off at auction. I, or my pearls, or more likely both. I wondered how long it would take Brianne to realise she had stripped me of a fake set.

I knew what to expect when I returned home. Before I'd left my flat, I'd hidden or removed anything I didn't want a burglar to discover, though this didn't include the seal-skin they'd undoubtedly be looking for. I didn't keep that at home. Or at the studio.

'You were lucky, you know that?' said Daix suddenly. 'Hiding your real pearls on a string around your neck? Wouldn't have taken a lot of searching to find them, hm?'

'She thought me caught unawares,' I said. 'We've been retired so long, we're civilians now, at least in her eyes. I was in no danger.'

'Pride comes before a fall, as we've proved,' said Daix, with unwonted seriousness. 'What were you going to do if you were wrong about her?'

'You mean Escape Plan B?'

'*Tell* me you had an Escape Plan B. Please.'

'Course I did.' I smiled. 'I didn't hide all the pearls around my neck.'

Daix stopped walking, and eyed me with deep suspicion. 'Where else could you possibly have... oh.'

'Right.'

'*Oh*. Fi, that's not right.'

I shrugged. 'I was pretty sure even Brianne wouldn't search me *that* thoroughly.'

Daix shook her head, and resumed walking. 'I wouldn't put it past her.'

'That's why I had Escape Plan C.'

'And that was?'

'You.'

'Ha. And I thought I wasn't allowed to burn the place down.'

'Not today. Maybe tomorrow.'

'I look forward to tomorrow.'

'So these people you have on Brianne's tail? Were we doing something with that?'

'Oh. Right.' Daix called somebody. I waited in silence.

'Yep,' she said, hanging up the phone again. 'They lost her.'

'You need better people.'

Daix shrugged. 'Would've been nice if you could've got some kind of tracking device onto her. You know they have things like that now?'

'Handy, and I'd love it if you'd get hold of some. But I hadn't the opportunity this time. Befuddled kidnapping victim, re-member?'

'Oh, did she drug you?'

'Heavily.'

'Bitch.'

'I know.'

'Fi, that does mean she's not completely underestimating you. You realise that, right?'

'Got it.'

'Just making sure.'

I smiled. 'If we don't have anything else on the agenda for tonight, here's where I leave you.'

'Deserter.'

'Stuff to do.'

'Like, straighten up your flat.'

'Yes. Later.'

I resisted further questions from Daix, wandering away from her. She didn't follow; she had her own stuff to do.

I was heading for the river. We were close enough that I could smell the water: clean, sharp, with the faint, underlying foulness of pollution. You don't get clear, pure water anywhere near a city, let alone running through it.

I didn't pause when I reached the shore, but dived straight in, shifting mid-air. When I hit the water I was seal-shaped and fur-clad. I swam hard and fast, heading for Faerd's waters. In nocturnal terms, it was early yet. He'd be awake somewhere. I had a plan to put in motion, for which I'd be needing his help, and it had to be in place by the morning.

14

— • —

TAI

HEADS-UP, RAN DAIX'S MESSAGE. *Rudy's full of shit. Keep clear.*

That was it.

I'd arrived home alone. Daix's fabulously vague communication had arrived shortly afterwards.

What? I texted back. Full of shit how? Keep clear why? I resolved to enrol Daix in a communications seminar at my earliest opportunity.

Being Daix, she did not deign to respond.

Coronis had been busy in my absence. The house was…dishevelled, to say the least. The mishmash of paraphernalia that Mea and I owned between the two of us — an eclectic mix of books and DVDs (mostly mine), video games, knickknacks and odd kitchen gadgets (mostly Mea's), and assorted unclassifiables — were largely transferred from their regular haunts to every other conceivable surface in the building.

Coronis stood in the midst of this chaos, engaged in a frenzy of activity. She barely looked round when I came in. 'I can't find *anything*,' she growled. 'All this *crap* and not one thing of use.'

'Nothing about Brianne, hm?' I said, stepping around a stack of shabby paperbacks to hang up my coat.

'I started in her room. Nothing. Nothing *anywhere*.'

Having ransacked every space in the house, including the bathroom and the kitchen, Coronis had clearly done a thorough job. She was agitated; she barely stood still for more than two seconds together, and her wings were a silvery blur of motion.

'It's okay,' I said. 'Coronis. It's okay to stop.'

'But I haven't *found* anything,' she said, the last word breaking in a sob. 'I haven't helped.'

I moved her way with vague thoughts of offering comfort, though I wasn't sure what; was a hug going to help? But she rounded on me. 'You *must* have come up with something, right? What did you pick up at the Puca? Do you know where she is?'

'I'm... fairly sure I know where she'll be tomorrow,' I said. 'Or at least, her skin.' I gave her a rapid precis of the evening's developments, acutely aware that she was in no way pleased or reassured. Her expression grew darker as I talked.

'An *auction*?' she exploded. 'They're selling her at a hags-cursed *auction*?'

'Well, no,' I said, gently grasping her shoulders, and inviting her to sit down. 'They're going to try to sell her at an auction, and I'm going to prevent them. Take a breath. Did you eat today?'

'Stop fussing,' she said irritably, but she did sit, and she did breathe. 'Okay. What's your plan, and how can I help?'

'I'll be there tomorrow night. So will Fi, and Daix. We've got a plan. Roles, disguises, schemes, everything. It's very like old times.' My misty smile soon faded again when I registered Coronis's expression. 'Er, right. The *plan*, is to establish whether our missing selkies are there or not, and if so, retrieve them. Plus their skins, pearls, or anything else that's been taken.'

'Just... retrieve them. Right.' Coronis nodded. 'Great plan.'

'Details to be filled in tomorrow.' I shrugged. 'Or... not. I mean, we used to wing things quite a lot.'

'That worked out well for you, on the whole?'

'More often than it didn't.' I stubbornly refused to think about our last mission together. That had been the exception to a long-established rule. 'Anyway, it's not that we won't be preparing at all. I'm going to the old car factory first thing in the morning to check it out. *Carefully*,' I added hastily, encountering Coronis's gimlet eye. 'I'll sneak. I'm good at sneaking. Once we get an idea of the space, that'll help a lot tomorrow night. And if there's anybody there already, all the better. I'll spy.' I was smiling. I couldn't help it. When was the last time I'd got chance to commit a bit of solid espionage?

Coronis rubbed at her eyes. 'You're meant to be professionals, but I have to tell you, Tai, this isn't sounding like it.'

'Harsh but fair. No, wait. Not fair. This sort of job was child's play, back in the day.'

'And that was a long time ago.'

'Truth.' I went into the kitchen, grabbed a couple of bags of crisps, and returned to the living room. 'Here,' I said, handing one to Coronis. 'Eat, then sleep. And sleep soundly, knowing that I hear you and you're right and I will work on the details of this non-plan before the auction begins.'

Coronis, mollified, accepted the packet. We crunched crisps in silence for a couple of minutes, both of us weary. I wished I could catch a bit of sleep myself, but I didn't feel there was time. Coronis was right: tomorrow wasn't far away, and I had a lot of work to do if we weren't going to screw up at the auction.

This train of thought came to an abrupt halt when the door-bell rang.

I was instantly alert. 'What the hell time is it.'

'After three. Who the hell rings doorbells at 3am?'

'In my experience? No one with the best intentions.' I dropped my crisps, and drifted towards the door. There's a motion-triggered light on the porch, and a spyhole in the door itself; some of my old, paranoid habits never did leave me. I moved silently on the carpet in stocking feet, and peered through the door.

Rudy stood waiting.

My thoughts flew back to Daix's near-incomprehensible message. *Rudy's full of shit. Keep clear.* I still didn't have much of an idea what that meant, but his turning up on my doorstep at this hour clearly wasn't a good development.

I padded silently back through to the living room. 'Cor,' I said softly. 'Go into your room and shut the door. Wedge it with something heavy. Don't come out until I say.'

Coronis didn't argue. She was gone in a moment, the door closing behind her.

I went back to the front door, walking normally this time, and yanked it open. 'Rudy!' I beamed, slurring the name slightly. 'Hey!'

'Tai.' He gave an easy smile. 'You took your time.'

'Just got in. Had to pee.'

'Oh? Drinking party?'

I nodded enthusiastically. 'Was at the Puca. Downed... *a few* drinks.' I giggled.

Rudy shook his head, still smiling. 'Drinking on duty, hm? Not too professional.'

'Duty?'

'The other Fatales here?' He leaned slightly to one side, trying to see around me into the house.

'Pheriko and Orandine? No. They don't live here, Rudy.' I made an expansive gesture. 'Said it wouldn't work for us to live *and* work together.'

'I'm not talking about your bandmates,' said Rudy. 'I'm talking about your old partners.'

So. Rudy had heard stories after all. I let the drunk demeanour fade a little. 'And why are you looking for them?'

'I'm not. I'm just making sure.'

'I never gave you my home address, did I?'

'Nope.'

Rudy moved fast. He blocked my attempt to shut the door on him, barged inside, and grabbed me by the hair, pulling it and twisting it. I felt a sharp pressure in the small of my back: probably a knife.

'Ow,' I snarled. 'Rudy, what the *fuck*.'

He shoved the front door closed, and pushed me ahead of him into the living room. 'You keep in touch with them all this time?' he said, speaking rapidly. 'Stayed friends?'

'Not even a little bit.' I kept a wary eye on him as best I could, letting him walk me into the centre of the room. He stood looking around, visibly frustrated.

'Right, sure. So Fionn wouldn't, say, give you anything important to keep for her? Like when the two of you showed up at Eventide together?'

'Not to my knowledge—*ow*.' Rudy had yanked my head back, a gesture of frustration.

'So all this mess. That wasn't you having the same idea?'

'What? Rudy, I've no idea what you—*ow!*'

'Did you find it, Tai? You'd better hand it over.'

'I've no idea what you're on about, but you're pissing me off.'

'Poor baby. I'm talking about Fionn's sealskin. Are you keeping it for her?'

'That's what you're after, hm?'

'You give me that sealskin and maybe I won't torch your place.'

'Tsk. Rudy, you were always the *nice* one.'

'Much good it did me. You never looked twice at me, did you?'

'Is that what this is about? I wouldn't fuck you?'

'Stuck-up bitches think you're—'

He got no further with this charming sentiment, for I'd turned in his grip, grabbed the hand that held the knife, and yanked it away from me. In the same movement, my free hand landed him a smashing blow to the jaw. He stumbled back, clutching his face.

'Now, if you thought these were some sort of cute affectation,' I said, holding up my gauntleted fists, 'you've learned differently.'

His face twisted with rage. His arm whipped up; he hurled the knife at my head.

I dodged with embarrassing ease. 'Appalling throw,' I chided. 'Face it, Rudy. You aren't cut out for this shit. You're a drummer, not a thug.'

He began grabbing random articles from the heaps of stuff around him, chucking each one at me. He had *some* aim, and strength enough to throw with force. I winced as something heavy struck my arm, and bounced off.

'Did Brianne put you up to this?' I persevered. 'Met her at Eventide, did you? I bet you were flattered by the attention. Egotistical enough to imagine she meant it. What has she had you doing for her, hm?'

'That sealskin,' he growled. 'I'll find it, with or without your help.'

'So that's your big assignment? Smash and grab? Take back the trophy, win your prize?' I was growing angry. The next object he threw — a book — I caught mid-air and hurled back at him. It hit him in the face.

Rudy didn't answer. Hags knew what bullshit he'd spun to justify his actions to himself, but I could see I wasn't going to reach him with words.

'Her sealskin isn't here,' I spat. 'Nor is it with Daix, so forget that idea. Now get the hell out of my house.'

'Like you'd tell me the truth—'

Unwise. Rudy received the benefit of another polite introduction to my gauntlets, and retreated from the encounter with a bleeding face and a possible fractured jaw. He backed up, howling — and ran.

I gave him thirty seconds' head start — just long enough for him to imagine himself unpursued, and for me to acquire a coat, and shoes — and then I took off after him.

If I was lucky, Rudy would flee straight back to Brianne — and I'd be only a minute behind him.

Whether Rudy was trying to reach Brianne or not, I soon realised where he was headed.

He ran straight for the Selkies' Pearls club.

Obviously the news of its abrupt demise hadn't reached him.

'The *fuck*,' he snarled, and stopped, panting for breath and cursing, before the burned-out wreck of the once luxurious nightclub.

I hung back in the shadows, unwilling, just yet, to let him see me. He hadn't seemed to imagine that pursuit might be a possibility — further proof of his utter amateurishness. I wondered what the hell Brianne was thinking, employing a dilettante like him. Was it just because she realised he and I knew each other? Did she imagine he'd have some kind of leverage over me? I could imagine Rudy boasting of the connection.

When he'd finished swearing, and got his breath back, Rudy pulled out a phone. I'd had to stop in the shadows of a building across the street; too far away to hear what he was saying, but that it pertained to the state of the club was certain, for he gestured repeatedly at the burned husk, and once I heard him shout, '*It's fucking wrecked.*'

At long, *long* last he seemed to grow wise to the likelihood of pursuit — or whoever he was talking to had alerted him to the idea — for he began turning in circles, looking around for… well, me, probably.

I let him imagine himself safe.

He said something else into the phone, shaking his head. Something emphatic. *I wasn't followed, okay? Stop worrying. I know what I'm doing.* Something like that, most like. The sort of thing characteristic of the kind of shithead Rudy had turned out to be. Overconfidence teamed with a degree of ignorance so profound, it'd almost be cute, if he wasn't such a dick.

I waited until he'd hung up the phone before I considered my move. He didn't seem to know what to do next, right away. He stood staring at the club, radiating indecision.

Then he turned, and began to head back my way.

I stepped silently out of my hiding spot and waited for him to notice me.

Took him a little while; he wasn't paying attention.

'*Shit,*' he swore, when at last it occurred to him that those weren't just fetchingly-proportioned shadows ahead of him. 'Tai. Fuck.'

'Yes, it is I,' I agreed, stepping forward. 'Though why this should come as such a huge surprise I've no idea. You should've listened to your buddy. I mean, of *course* I was going to follow you.'

I was close enough to see the expression of acute rage that crossed his face. Jeez, how had I missed all these charming personality traits in Rudy? The nice guy routine should never have worked so well on me.

Fuck, I'd lost my edge.

'So,' I persevered, when he didn't speak. 'What were you expecting to find out here, hm? Meeting up with the lovely Brianne, perhaps? Or someone else?'

'Like I'd tell you.'

'You should. Honestly, Rudy. Just because I showed up at Eventide with Fionn, doesn't make us bosom buddies.'

His eyes narrowed. 'What are you saying?'

'I'm saying we didn't talk for the past eighty years and with good reason. We're far from friends now. If you'd just *told* me you were in the market for a certain sealskin, maybe we could've helped each other out.'

Rudy watched me, wary. Good; maybe he'd learned a thing or two. 'Why didn't you tell me this earlier?'

'You mean when you were trying to remove a kidney by main force? You're right. Perfect conditions for a cosy chat.'

'I was told the two of you were thick as thieves. That you'd always back her up.'

'Brianne's information is eighty years out of date. She hasn't exactly shown up to talk to me, either.'

'So you're... what, playing her?'

'Something like that.'

'Why?'

'Scores to settle.'

'Scores? Like what?'

'If you've heard the tales, Rudy, you might recall there used to be four of us.'

He nodded. 'Happen I've heard mention of that, yeah.'

'Yeah. Well. Fi bailed on us at Ravensbrück and we ended up losing Silise. She deserves to know how that feels.'

I crossed my fingers behind my back, hoping it would assuage the faint pang of guilt I felt. It was a lie, if only a small one. Fi hadn't bailed. She *had* fucked up, but then, we all had. We were all responsible for Sil's death. But I needed to make Rudy — and by extension, Brianne — believe that I blamed Fi.

I waited while all this sank into whatever Rudy considered his brain. 'You said you don't have her sealskin,' he said.

'I don't. No way she'd trust me with it now. But I've been working on her. I've got access to her studio, maybe even her flat. If anybody could get it, it'd be me.'

Rudy said nothing, so I tried a smile on him. Sweet, coaxing, flirtatious. 'Work with me on this, Rudy. Better than fighting, right?'

'If this is some kind of play—' he warned, trying to sound tough.

My smile widened. Hooked. 'I know, I know. I'll let you extract a kidney. Hell, I'll serve it on a silver platter for you. Toasted.'

'Okay, so. What are you suggesting? You'll get the skin?'

'Yes.'

'Then what? Flog it to Brianne and disappear with the cash?'

'I could — if Brianne didn't hate me. She won't even talk to me. I'll need your help to get to her.'

'So we split the proceeds.'

'Fifty fifty.'

He wasn't sold. He was suspicious. Good. I'd hate to think so poorly of his sense as all that. 'You don't need the cash,' he said.

'Neither do you.'

He shrugged. 'There are other perks.' Like, Brianne's *favour*, whatever he thought that was going to consist of.

'Right,' I said. 'Other perks. Like *revenge*. You ever hate someone that much, Rudy? So much you'd do *anything* to make them pay?'

'Never knew you had it in you,' he said. Hags curse him, he sounded impressed.

I stepped a little nearer. 'Yes, well. Turns out you underestimated me, hm?'

He smiled. 'That's more like it,' he said, and *touched my hair*. Just ran his fingers through it, as though he had every damned right to feel up any part of me he chose.

I resisted the impulse to slug him, but it cost me. 'You get my number along with my address?' I said, matching him smile for smile.

'You bet.'

'Great. Call me, and I've got your number. I'll call *you* when I've got the goods.'

Following a few further pleasantries unworthy of recounting, I was able to retreat. I did so at a saunter — a *sashay*, even — though I badly wanted to just cut and run. Sleazebag. People like that can be so easy to fool, because shit like this looks perfectly reasonable to them. If Rudy had no problem enslaving Fi for the sake of getting in with Brianne, why would he suspect *my* motives when I proposed to do much the same?

If I ever got a chance to extract a kidney or two from Rudy, he'd be a goner inside of a week.

Better yet, I'd let Fi do it. She has those knives. I doubt she's had an opportunity to use them in a while.

I waited until I was well clear of Rudy before I dropped the act. When Rudy's call came in, I immediately passed his number to Daix (*'Made a "deal" with Rudy, no thanks to your spectacularly unhelpful message. Contact details as follows'*).

Then I called Fi.

'You know that Rudy wants to sell your ass?' I said when she picked up.

'So I discovered. Didn't Daix tell you?'

'After a fashion.'

'She said she'd warned you. Are you all right?'

'I'm *fine*. I mean, of course I'm fine. Rudy's a piece of cake. Do you happen to have your sealskin handy?'

Her voice grew guarded. 'Why?'

'I'm going to have to wave *something* compelling in front of his face or I'll never get him to take me to Brianne.'

'I see.'

'I mean, I could try just taking my bra off but I doubt that'd be enough at this point.'

'Tai.'

'Yes.'

'You are not taking my sealskin anywhere near these people.'

'Okay, but then do you happen to know a way to fake a selkie skin? And it'd have to be a damn good fake, Fi.'

'No.'

'Besides, there's the whole auction thing going on tomorrow and I'm still down to attend as a seller but high and dry on the *saleable goods* part.'

'Still no. You can't fake a selkie skin. Any idiot could tell the difference, and Brianne isn't an idiot. Neither is whoever's hosting the auction, I imagine.'

'This is a problem.'

'It's all right. I have a solution.'

'Oh?'

'I'll tell you about it later.'

'...Do you happen to have two solutions? 'Cause I've sort of double-booked myself here and I can't give the same sealskin to Rudy *and* sell it at auction.'

'Can't help you with that. Pick one.'

'Damnit.'

'Thinking on the fly is all well and good—'

'Until someone loses an eye. Got it.'

'Or a partner.'

'Ouch.'

We were silent for a moment after that. Even I didn't have the heart to joke the memory of Sil away.

The problem wasn't a problem, I decided. I'd go to the auction tomorrow, and if nothing came of *that*, I could use Rudy later. Always nice to have options on top of options, and maybe an extra option just in case.

'Anyway,' I said after a minute. 'I'd, um, better go home and let Coronis out.'

'You... what? Out of where?'

'I *might* have left her barricaded into her bedroom. In my defence, I got excited about hightailing it after Rudy and forgot about her.'

'Tai.'

'I'm not used to having civilians in the field, Fi.'

'Go liberate Coronis. Then come see me.'

'Ma'am.'

I hung up.

15

— · —

FIONN

TWO HOURS BEFORE TAI'S call, I was back in the water and heading upriver.

I'd gone out there expecting an hour's search for Faerd, if not more. But I was met before I'd been longer than twenty minutes afloat.

'*Fionn of Cuath-Tor*,' came a voice out of the shadows. 'Faerd summons you.'

I dislike being *summoned,* for it assumes a degree of authority over me that I don't choose to acknowledge. But since I'd wanted to find Faerd anyway, and I assuredly needed his help, I kept my dislike of this terminology to myself. 'Then I'll follow,' I told the wispy asrai messenger, and I did, though not without difficulty; she was fast, and agitated. Even, perhaps, annoyed.

'Something troubles you?' I said, after a few minutes' silent forging upriver. The intense blackness of the waters were no impediment for her, for the asrai are nocturnal, with a sensitivity of vision to exceed even my seal's keen eyes. I followed more by sound than by sight, listening for every *swish* of the currents that washed around her undulating form.

'We have been seeking you this *long* while,' she snapped, without so much as a slight turn of her head; I barely heard the words.

'I am sorry,' I said coolly. 'I did not know myself sought for. Faerd, I believe, knows where to find me.'

My irritable messenger made no reply. I focused on following her pale, darting shape through the shadows, and soon enough she began to slow, leading me into the deeper depths of the water. I heard fresh sounds: someone else had joined us.

'Fionn,' said Faerd, and came swimming slowly into view. As pale as the waters were dark, he looked the very water-ghost the asrai are sometimes called. 'I'd begun to despair.'

Growing tired of these chastisements, I retorted, 'Could you not have sent someone to find me, if it were so urgent?'

'No one wants to step out of the waters. Not now.'

That silenced me, for a moment. The asrai are not comfortable out of water, but this was something else. This was outright fear. 'Have *your* people been harmed?'

Faerd did not answer, at least not immediately. He murmured something to his messenger in a tongue I could not follow, and she left us. Then he said: 'The drowned selkie.'

'Yes. Narasel. You've heard something?'

'Gained something.' He floated a slow circle around me, and a heaviness settled over me. I felt an odd pull of kinship, laced with a sharp repulsion.

A sealskin. Another selkie's skin.

'Her skin was not found, I think you said.'

'It remains unaccounted for,' I said cautiously. 'Where did you acquire this?'

'It was brought to me by one of my own. Tossed upon the morning tide, they said, and adrift.'

'Someone threw it in the river.'

'So it appears.'

Thrown away, like useless rubbish. A surge of rage left me shaking, and sick. Narasel's killer had kept it a while, perhaps thinking to turn it to use. May have tried to sell it, even, but they'd failed, for the skin of a dead selkie has no magic left in it; is only a hide.

A thing not everyone knew.

'I thank you,' I said to Faerd. 'I will see that it is well treated.'

I wasn't immediately sure how I would achieve that. Most likely it ought to be returned to Narasel's people, if I could find out which clan she'd belonged to. That would have to wait a little while.

I engaged in a moment's gratitude that it had been returned to the water, and not hurled into the garbage.

And paused. Why *had* it ended up in the Thames? Was that happenstance?

I folded the thought away for later reflection, for Faerd was speaking. 'There has been no harm to my people.'

'Good.'

'Yet. But there is fear that we will not escape the persecution our wave-cousins have suffered.'

'To my knowledge,' I said cautiously, 'it is selkies only that are of interest to these people.'

'Why?'

'Skins. And pearls.'

'Theft, then.'

'Yes. Yes, exactly. Narasel's death may not have been intended. A... process of theirs went awry.'

Faerd was silent. I could imagine his thoughts. An asrai may be taken captive, as may any being, but there exists no such tool like the selkie-skin, to compel their obedience. Not lastingly. If Tai and I were right, and theft, not murder, was the purpose of the scheme, then the asrai should be safe from it.

'Thank you,' said Faerd. 'I am in your debt.'

Either for the reassurance, or the service I intended to perform for Narasel's sealskin, I wasn't sure which. But I needed his help, so I accepted the debt. 'I have a boon to ask of you.'

'Name it.'

'There are others like Narasel still without liberty.'

'So it is said.'

'Tomorrow night, it is my intention to attempt their rescue. If they can make it to the waters, will you give shelter?'

'We will.'

'There may be pursuit.'

'If so, it will be dealt with.'

I considered the problem of Cellann of Indra-Tath. Perhaps I ought to send her to Faerd's waters right away. She would be safer there than she would be wandering London alone.

But to do so would be to draw further attention to ourselves and our interference, in ways which would conflict with the role we were attempting to play. Mine was the role of prey, to Tai's and Daix's predator; to shepherd those like me to safety in no way fit with our story.

And Cellann may not consent to go. The girl had not seemed to me to possess much in the way of sense, and we had little with which to persuade her. Only the death of Narasel, which could be called accident, and a wild tale of missing persons impossible to prove.

'Have you further word for me?' I asked of Faerd. 'Did aught of Narasel's fate reach you, besides her skin?'

'I have heard nothing of use.'

Disappointing, but perhaps this was no longer a useful line of enquiry. Not wishing to linger too long in the asrai's waters, I thanked Faerd and withdrew. The pearls I'd made from the stagnant pools at the old car factory were with me still, but submersion confused them, muddied their link to the waters from which they were fashioned. If I wanted them to work for me, I'd have to get back to dry land.

TAI'S PHONE CALL, SOON afterwards, recalled Narasel's sealskin to my mind immediately. An irreverent use to put it to, of course, and I suffered a pang of remorse upon proposing the idea. But Narasel was not here to receive offence, and besides, we were on the trail of her killer.

Were it me, I'd want to help, even if direct assistance had been put forever out of my power.

So I swallowed my conscience, and set aside the sealskin to put into Tai's possession. What would she choose to do with it? I had to smile at her airy admission of having double-booked herself; very Tai, to get herself into a tangled series of messes, and work out an extrication plan somewhat later. To her credit, she probably would. I didn't need to worry for her.

In the meantime, I had more preparations to make for the auction, namely regarding Cellann. Was there something I needed to do for her?

Was there some way I could use her? Especially without making any open approach.

I thought back to the only occasion I'd encountered her in person: at Eventide. She had been wearing one of my gowns.

Gifts. The girl liked gifts, especially the expensive kind.

My poor pearls. Once all this was over, I'd have to devote some serious time to replenishing them.

I hadn't more than formed the thought before my attention was arrested, and all ideas of Cellann flew out of my mind.

My pearls awoke.

Not my ancients, my lustres, but my new ones; the pearls I'd formed out of the waters at the car factory. Stained and muddied, these, no shine to their surfaces at all. I hated to look at them, hated more to touch or wear them. But they'd served their purpose.

Someone wandered the derelict halls in which I had, briefly, been held captive.

I sank into the nearest chair, thankful that my flat was quiet tonight. No noise, no company to distract me. Closing my eyes, I let every idea empty out of my mind, save one: those stagnant pools and the link I'd forged with them. Sensations washed over me.

Someone's feet stepped softly through the puddles, spilling droplets beyond the borders of the pools. The foul water sank into the fabric of their shoes, their socks — stockings in fact, flimsy and delicate, barely absorbent — a lady? Brianne. Surely, it must be.

I waited, sought for further signs. The cadence of those steps: slow and deliberate. No hurry there, no flurry of activity ahead of the proposed auction. What was this lady's purpose, then, in entering the building?

I thought of Tai, or Daix, but discarded the idea. Nothing about this person matched either: the movements were wrong, the proportions... the scent. A hint of a deep, floral fragrance caught at me, distracting. I didn't recognise it.

The waters knew her. She'd been there before. When I was brought in, perhaps? Was this my captor?

Was it Brianne?

It had to be; it was the only explanation that made any sense. But I couldn't be certain. Too many nagging dissimilarities, too many subtle signs...

Besides that, a *familiarity*. I could not shake the sense that I, too, had seen her before, that I knew her as the waters did...

At last it dawned on me. What the evidence of my pearls was telling me, what the waters saw: I did know her.

I'd known her very well, long ago, and she was dead.

She was dead; she'd been dead for eighty years.

I couldn't breathe. The pearls fell from my fingers and spilled across the floor, unheeded; I fought for air, frozen with horror. And beneath that, *hope.*

It couldn't be. It *couldn't* be.

Could the waters be wrong?

How long I sat frozen in this state, I could not have said. I was woken abruptly from the trance by the sound of a pounding upon the door, and Tai's voice, yelling for me. 'Fi?'

'Moment,' I called, or tried to; the word came out as a cracked whisper, and Tai didn't hear it.

'*Fi!* Open the damned door!'

I shot out of the chair, made it to the door in three great strides, and hauled it open.

Tai stood staring at me, eyes wide and petrified. She let out a breath when she saw me, relief quickly giving way to annoyance.

'I only thought you were *dead,*' she growled, stalking past me into the hall.

'Sorry,' I mumbled. 'Sorry, I was...' I couldn't finish the sentence. I closed the door, and it was a moment before I could turn and meet her gaze again.

Tai's eyebrows went up. 'What?'

I tried to speak, but the words didn't come.

'Fi.' Tai gripped my arms and gave me a tiny shake. 'Pull it together. What's happened now?'

'I saw...' I paused, cleared my throat. 'At the car factory. You know I wrought pearls from the waters there? When they took me?'

'No, but good. And?'

'They... someone's there now.'

Tai nodded. She was not unfamiliar with the method; I'd used it in the past. 'Tell me it's Brianne? I'll be down there in a jiffy to remove a couple of important articles of her anatomy.'

'It wasn't Brianne.'

'Damnit.'

'I... I'm fairly sure it wasn't Brianne.'

Tai took a long look at my face, then steered me to a chair. 'All right, deep breath. You're a big girl, you can do this.'

'Silise,' I blurted.

'What?'

'I saw Silise.'

'No fucking way.'

'It was her.'

'Fionn of Cuath-Tor, Silise is *dead*. It couldn't have been her.'

'Nonetheless.' I breathed deep, and managed to stop shaking. 'I'm certain of it.'

'Can't be. Someone's screwing with you. How clear a vision do you actually get with this trick, anyway?'

'Not... not that clear. It's more impressions, senses—'

'So you didn't see her.'

'Not exactly—'

Tai sat back. 'As I said. Someone's screwing with you. With *us*. Again.'

That could be true. I thought back, tried to imagine how it might be possible to fake all the impressions I'd received. It seemed... improbable. 'But, Tai, how could anybody be that familiar with Silise except Silise herself? Every movement of hers, her gestures, her demeanour — that stuff is far harder to fake than a face. You know that.'

'Well.' Tai stood up. 'One way to find out,' she said cheerfully. 'Let's go down there right now.'

'If you're right, then this is another trap.'

'And if you're right, our long-lost best friend is down there waiting for us.'

Tai's words triggered what was left of my critical thinking. Shock and... other emotions had temporarily disordered my wits, but my head was clearing. 'No. You're right. If she was alive somehow, why would she be at *this* building, of all places? And why wouldn't she have *told* us?'

Tai nodded. 'This is some game of Brianne's. It's clever, I grant you.'

I frowned, still disquieted. 'But how could Brianne know Silise so well? And, Tai, she'd have to have realised I would work pearls from those waters, she'd have to have known what that meant, what I could do—'

'Perhaps she does know all that. She's been watching us a long time, planning this little game for a while. That much is clear.'

'She? Or someone else?'

'Like who?'

I just looked at her.

'Silise is dead,' said Tai firmly. 'I don't know how Brianne is doing this either, but it's just a game. It has to be.' She headed for the door. 'You coming?'

'Where? The old car factory?'

'Where else? Let's go find out what Bri's up to now.'

'You remember the part where this is a trap?'

'Yep.' Tai beamed at me.

'And maybe we could stay ahead of this game by not walking straight into this trap, the way we did at the club?' I knew myself a hypocrite as I spoke; I'd let Brianne trap me, let her cart me to the old car factory. I'd done it with sound reason, and with good results. But I couldn't just let *Tai* throw herself to the wolves.

'At least it was an informative process,' said Tai.

'A process that would have killed you, if you hadn't happened to thieve my pearls beforehand.'

'You were the one that walked face-first into the water.'

'I wasn't in any danger.'

'And how did you figure that, exactly? *You're* the selkie, Fi, and those are turning up dead lately. Hell, you've been kidnapped since then and you can still say you weren't in any danger?'

I was silent. I had no answer to make, unless I wanted to confess my little scheme to her. I couldn't.

'Perhaps you mean you were in no danger you didn't find acceptable,' Tai continued.

Too true for argument. Still I said nothing.

'Okay well, if you've got some kind of death wish going on, this is a great way to further that goal.' Tai beamed at me again, but there was an edge to it this time, something cold behind her eyes. 'And if that's Silise down there, she obviously doesn't love us anymore, so let's go give her a chance to kill you.'

'*Us*, Tai.'

'Oh, you're not worried about you but you are about me? That's sweet.'

'We lost Silise because we didn't look after each other. I won't make that mistake again.'

Her brows went up, her expression one of withering scepticism.

'I didn't expect you to follow me into that pool,' I said. 'I mean, *why* would you?'

'If you'd like to think back to everything you said about ten seconds ago, I believe you'll find it applicable.'

'What?'

'Didn't want to let you go alone.'

'Which turned out to be pretty stupid, didn't it.'

Tai shook her head, chose not to answer that. 'Are we going to the car factory or not?'

'Not. We're sticking to the plan. We can't afford any more screw-ups before tomorrow's auction.'

Tai accepted this without a blink. What she might privately have thought of it, I couldn't have guessed. 'Fine. About that solution you said you had?'

Wordlessly, I retrieved Narasel's sealskin from where I had laid it, reverently, over the back of my sofa.

Tai hadn't registered its presence before. She received it in silence, and nodded once to me. 'Narasel's?'

'Yes.'

'I'll bring it back to you.'

Tai said it with emphasis, meaning she'd bring it back to me even if she had to leave a limb behind in the process. 'Her family will want it,' I said.

'They shall have it.' She stroked the fur softly. 'I'd better get some sleep,' she said. 'I'll see you for the auction?'

Ah yes, the part where I got to pretend my best friend hated me enough to sell me for cash. Perhaps it was the abrupt way the question of Silise had been raised tonight, but the prospect made me nauseous.

Still. Needs must. 'Come here first,' I told Tai. 'If you like, we can even stage a betrayal scene.'

Her mischievous smile gleamed. 'Great. I'll bring the big guns to take you down.'

And then we'd walk out of here, Tai wielding Narasel's seal-skin like it was mine, me acting the part of a woman whose will has been torn away and used against her.

Good times.

'Sleep well,' I said. 'You'll need it.'

16

— · —

TAI

WE DID THE BETRAYAL scene.

Maybe it was absurd. In fact, *definitely* it was absurd. But you never know who might be watching, right? And it helped get us in role.

The sort of thing we used to do, back in the day.

'Hello, Fionn,' I said, coldly, when she opened the door to her flat.

She looked me over, cool as a mountain stream. 'A gun? Really? That was never your style.'

Damnit, I knew I shouldn't have gone for the gun. It might have been only a prop, but it felt good! Powerful! 'It gets the point across,' I said, sounding only slightly defensive. I tightened my grip on the weapon, shaking my head. Keep it together. I was evil Tai today.

'So what is this, a double cross?' said Fi softly. 'Tai. Has it come to this?'

Just the right note of tragedy in her tone, and her chin held high. 'Don't make me laugh,' I hissed.

Her eyes twinkled, briefly. 'You're here to kill me,' she said.

'No. I'm here to claim you.'

An eyebrow went up, and she grinned. 'Sounds interesting.'

'I have your sealskin! You never thought I'd find it, did you?'

'No! Not my sealskin!' Fionn gasped. 'This is the literal end.'

'I know. I'm never getting invited to your birthday party again, am I?'

'Never!'

'Well, fuck it.' I lowered the gun. 'We're going to have to do better than this when we get to the car factory.'

'Yes, yes. Tell me, are you a benevolent betrayer? Do I get to wear shoes?'

'Sure.'

'Maybe even a coat.'

'Wimp. No. Like any kidnapper worth their salt would let you grab outerwear.'

'You're right. No coat. Did you want to drag me by the hair?'

'Yes. Did you grow it out especially?'

'Just for you.'

I took hold of some of the hair in question, and gave it a tug. 'Right, come on. Bring the skin.'

'I'm supposed to carry it? How does that make sense?'

'I'll take it later.'

'Better take it now. Brianne's got people watching my front door.'

'Has she? I didn't see them when I came in.'

'Then you've got sloppy.'

'Or they were very well hidden.'

Fionn grinned. 'Okay, Daix told me.'

'Oh yes, Daix. Where the hell is she, anyway?'

Fionn shrugged. 'Off doing her Daix thing. We'll see her at the factory, I expect.'

'Impossible. We *might* see someone of Daix's approximate height and proportions playing shamelessly to the crowd, however.'

'She gets bored,' said Fi.

'Somebody ought to get some fun out of this shit show,' I agreed. I took a steadying breath. Evil Tai. From here on, I had to be more convincing. Curtain up. 'Walk,' I told Fionn, in a cooler voice. Detached. 'We're going outside. Stop when you reach the street, and wait for me.'

Ehh. Fionn got into role in the blink of an eye, and she chilled me right down to my bones. Not that there was an obvious shift, nothing theatrical. Nothing you'd even notice, if you didn't know Fionn. The changes were subtle, and profound: a degree of passivity about her, an air of biddable docility. Something of liveliness slipped out of her face, and the steel went out of her eyes: she was as composed as ever, but more in the way of a *thing*, a doll, a creature built without independent will in the first place.

She nodded without meeting my eye, stepped past me, and set off down the hallway. Her gait was smooth and even, to the point of eeriness, like a graceful automaton.

I shuddered, and followed.

Down on the street, Fionn paused as instructed, stopped dead a few steps beyond the doors and waited. She barely moved.

A shadow rippled, and Phélan emerged. I didn't need to warn him about Brianne's spies: he knew his role, and however maddening the man could be, he was a professional. He tipped his hat to me, ignoring Fionn, except for casting a quick, appraising eye over her. Like a man evaluating a horse he, or someone else, might consider buying.

'All went well?' he enquired.

My only answer to this was to heft the sealskin, letting Phélan see it. 'Let's go.'

Phélan had a car waiting, dark and innocuous. We barely spoke on the drive across town. Fionn did as she was told, and sat in silence. I tried not to think too hard about where she was getting all her excellent method acting from. This was what she'd been like, when some long-ago psycho had stolen her sealskin for real. Even in all our years together, she'd never talked in detail about who that man had been, or why he'd done it. I only knew it had been someone very close to her.

Unthinkable.

I sat thinking about it without interruption until the car drew up on West Hendon Broadway. Phélan got out, and held the door for me, then for Fionn. We'd been dropped a short distance from the old car factory: we wanted a moment to orient ourselves, and maybe to check the place out, before we went in.

It was 9:45. Nearly showtime.

I leaned close to Fionn, made some pretence of adjusting her attire. I wanted her to look her best when I trotted her in front of the buyers, right?

'Anything?' I breathed, barely an audible whisper.

'Show's started,' she whispered back. Right. Fi's pearls from the factory would be a blaze of activity, feeding her a flood of sensations about the myriad people descending upon the building. Probably they were of little use, from here on: too much going on, too little detail. But Fi had brought them anyway, just in case.

They'd brought her no significant information yet, I surmised, for she said nothing more.

When I turned away from her, Phélan offered me his arm. 'Milady.'

I smiled brightly, and took it. 'Shall we?'

We sauntered up the wide street like we owned it, Fionn walking, as instructed, a pace or two ahead of us. As evil-Tai, I didn't want to take my eyes off my highly saleable prize; as real-Tai, I didn't want to let Fi out of my sight in case someone snatched her again. I didn't feel in control of this game. We were out of our depth in these waters, and I knew it. Fi knew it. There were too many questions still outstanding, too many mysteries, too many variables in play. Whoever was playing games with us was winning, at least for the moment. We needed to turn the tables — tonight. That meant keeping my wits about me.

And it meant sticking together. I couldn't let myself be separated from Fi, unless she had Daix at her back.

The car factory was a different place that night. It loomed still in decrepit shadow, a sad mess of empty windows and vanished potential; but now lights blazed in some of the echoing rooms within, and its air of melancholy desertion had given way to a buzz of activity.

There were guards on the door. Sluagh.

'Drevan's men,' said Phélan in a low voice.

Interesting. I hadn't expected that, and apparently, neither had Phélan. What did it mean? Was Drevan the organiser of this auction? I hadn't pegged him as possessing so much power, or initiative. I'd thought him focused on his leadership struggle with Nelo.

Perhaps this was part of it.

'Thetai Sarra Antha,' I announced as we reached the doors. 'With my escort, Phélan Astrophel.' Phélan tipped his hat.

'And the lady?' said one of the guards. Sluagh, the both of them, dark-clad and imposing.

'Introduce yourself,' I said briefly, coldly, to Fionn.

'Fionn of Cuath-Tor,' she said obediently. 'Slave.'

A moment's silence, while the two guards looked Fionn over. She'd dressed in one of her more fabulous gowns, a fluid, rippling confection of moon-white satin. Her hair was decked in pearls. She'd make a gorgeous auction piece.

We were waved through.

The hall beyond was empty, except for one person: short and lithe, a boggan perhaps, wearing an usher's uniform. This innocuous appearance was belied by a posture, an air, of authority; he quickly intercepted us. 'Madam,' he said to me, with a brief nod. 'Sir. I trust you've registered your lot in advance?' He was looking at Fionn, still and silent.

'Lot number seven,' I said. 'Fionn of Cuath-Tor. Sealskin and pearls included and intact.'

He nodded. His scrutiny was subtle, but intense: I didn't know what he was reading in me or Phélan, but that we were being tested was apparent enough.

Nothing I could do about that. Shouldn't be a problem: I was here as my real self, hiding nothing, except for the fact that Fionn was only pretending to be enslaved. But he'd have no reason to suspect that, and it was me and Phélan he was testing, not Fi.

'This way, please?' he said after a moment, and Phélan and I were led through a short succession of corridors, wanly lit with wisp-lights. The room designated for use for the auction was situated nearly in the heart of the building, a large open space now cleared of the machinery it must once have held. Thick with people already, all of them fae; a low hum of conversation greeted us as we were ushered in.

'Your lot will go under the hammer at 10:25,' our usher informed us. 'Make sure she's ready, please, and has all her accessories.'

I thanked the nice boggan, taking a moment to commit his face to memory. Someday I'd kill this one.

My smile gave none of this away, however, except perhaps to Phélan, who knew me far too well. His own smile went a little crooked when it landed on me.

I know, I know, I signalled with my eyes. *Work first, play later.*

We were attracting some attention — or rather, Fionn was. She walked slowly into the fray, head held high, eyes blank, and I walked behind her with my arms full of Narasel's sealskin and a bracelet of pearls on my arm that would pass for Fionn's anywhere. Heads turned to get a good look at her. One or two people recognised her; I heard her name repeated a few times, in shocked tones.

Someone put out a hand to stop me.

Paulan.

'That's your "supply"?' he asked, nodding at Fi.

'Quite a prize, no?' I smiled.

He nodded. 'She'll fetch a bit.' His manner was civil, even friendly. I couldn't tell what he thought of my showing up here with a slave to sell; whether he approved or not.

Then again, he was supporting Drevan's leadership claims, and Drevan seemed to be running this little show. I reminded myself not to like Paulan too much.

'We expect to do *fabulously* well,' I told Paulan with a wink. I watched him clock that word, "we", and look at Phélan. Reminding him of my influence, of who had the power here. He got the hint, touched his hat, received a nod from Phélan in return.

'Anything I should know?' I asked of Paulan, leaning nearer, and speaking low. Paulan had a table to himself, thus far; wherever Drevan was, or the rest of his men, I couldn't guess, but Paulan was probably parked here to observe, and keep the peace.

'You got your time slot?' he replied.

'Just now.'

'Keep to it. Tight schedule tonight.'

I raised an eyebrow, looked a question, but Paulan didn't go for it. 'Bold move,' he said instead, nodding towards Fionn. She stood a few feet away, still and silent, while a couple of auction-goers touched her hair, her gown, and inspected every part of her. Nothing showed on her face at all. Nothing.

'Rest of the goods are locked up,' Paulan elaborated. 'And the girls don't show until it's time.'

Meaning, Phélan and I were openly parading around with both "girl" and accessories, showing them off, while everyone else had taken the precaution of keeping the sealskins and pearls under guard somewhere, and their former owners, too. We'd more or less known that. Fionn's factory-pearls had remained quiet for the past twenty-four hours, so we knew the other selkies weren't being kept on the premises ahead of the auction.

'No harm in drumming up a little interest in advance, right?' I answered, and nodded towards Fionn. 'I'd say it's working like a charm.'

Paulan gave me an assessing look, and Phélan. It *was* a bold move on our part: we were as much as saying that we feared nothing and no one in this place, that we expected no interference with our merchandise that might put it — or us — at risk.

This is partly why I'd needed Phélan. If I'd shown up alone with Fi in tow, I'd be seen as a dilettante, a role I'd already adopted for Drevan's benefit. With Phélan at my back, we made a decent show of strength. Thetai Sarra Antha might be new to the selkie-trade, but she wasn't weak and she wasn't unconnected.

I saw most of this register in Paulan's eyes, though with a shade of something else I couldn't place. I hoped we hadn't made a misstep.

'Better put her somewhere out of sight for now,' Paulan recommended. 'Show's about to start.'

'Wouldn't be polite to upstage the competition,' I grinned. I took hold of Fionn's arm and towed her away, over to a more or less empty corner.

'If you could do that cool shadow trick,' I asked Phélan. 'That'd be handy.'

'Can't. Too much light in here.'

'You can't make a bit more shadow?'

He looked vaguely annoyed. 'Not how that works.'

'All you can do is, what, pull it about a bit.'

'Something like that. Why don't you sit still for a bit and don't talk, Tai, that ought to be enough.'

'You're doing enough *not talking* for the both of us,' I retorted, but he wasn't wrong. I parked Fionn against the wall, giving her arm a brief, supportive squeeze before I released it. I couldn't know what this charade was costing her, but I knew the answer was somewhere in the region of *way too fucking much*. I'd have to make it up to her somehow. Someday.

'Is that annoying you?' Phélan said, standing with his back to the wall, arms folded. 'Good.'

'Not really *annoying*,' I said, taking up a station on Fi's other side, and turning to watch the room. 'It's just unlike you.'

'Missing my silver tongue?'

'Awfully.'

Phélan smiled, faintly, and turned away his head.

'It's true,' I said. 'I actually am.'

This went unanswered, for the auction was palpably about to begin. They'd done a decent job of this space, whoever had been in charge of setting it up. Wisps clustered thickly under the high ceiling, their pallid glow casting the shadows out. The great stone blocks of the walls were festooned with grime and cobwebs, but the effect was not unpleasing under that flickering light; a certain gothic chic, one might say. Someone had hauled in a lot of tables and chairs, cheap plastic numbers no doubt, but covered in brocade cloth and with a wisp-light apiece, they contrived to be charming.

The front of the room was given over to a staging area, with a podium. A woman stood at the latter, dressed in a glittering black gown, her mane of dark hair lit with jewels. My heart stopped for a moment, expecting either Brianne or — impossibly — Silise, but this woman was neither. I didn't know her face.

'Ladies and gentlemen, welcome to tonight's auction,' she was saying in a low, resonant voice. I stiffened a bit, recognising some quality of the tone.

'What?' Phélan murmured to me. 'Someone you know.'

'No. Siren, though.'

'Ah.' He nodded. 'Great for crowd control.'

I had to smirk. He was right; if this crowd of criminals got too rowdy, it wouldn't hurt to have a siren as mistress of ceremonies. Smart move.

I let the rest of her words wash over me, not paying too much attention. The usual pleasantries: introductions; thanks for attendance; explanation as to the functioning of the auction, for those inexperienced. I was watching for the appearance of the first selkie. In fact, questions had been blossoming in my mind for the past ten minutes, thick and fast, and I cursed my inability to consult with Fionn. If the show was starting, where was the merchandise? Had they entered the building yet? If they had, Fionn might know; her pearls might differentiate fellow selkies from among the mess of other people arriving. But I couldn't know, and I couldn't ask Fi either. She certainly hadn't given anything away.

The mistress of ceremonies made a show of checking an elegant pocket-watch, worn around her neck on a silver chain. As she did so, the haunting notes of a great bell began to chime the hour: ten strikes. Ten o'clock. Auction open.

'Let's begin!' she called. 'Presented for your admiration and your bids, ladies and gentlemen: lot number one.'

I waited, scarcely breathing. Lot number one had not appeared. Nobody had entered the room, nobody was walking up to the staging area. The great room, with all its assembled guests, was breathlessly silent: nothing moved.

Beside me, Fionn twitched.

She had something to tell me, but she couldn't. Shit. I resisted the impulse to turn to her, talk to her, and kept my eyes on the stage.

After a moment, something changed.

I heard the faint sounds of running water.

The pool formed rapidly. Where previously there had been a bare stone floor, freshly swept, there now came a watery glimmer: aqua-blue, lit with its own ethereal glow. Those waters were never still; they flowed in a smooth spiral, slow, mesmerising.

Then, there came a face at the centre of that pool; a tousled mane of fair hair, untouched by the waters; a slim figure, clad in a simple white gown, rising smoothly from the deep. She wore pearls at her throat, her wrists, and woven in her hair, and her eyes were closed.

Mearil.

I didn't move a muscle, didn't make a sound, but Fi knew what I felt anyway. She leaned, fractionally, nearer to me.

Interestingly, so did Phélan.

The crowd applauded, and well they might: what a show! And how *deeply* fucking unhelpful, because if we'd expected to be able to move in and get these selkies out, we were nicely stymied. These were the same waters we'd seen at the Selkie's Pearls night club, the same portal device. Somehow, Fi had known nothing about it in advance, despite the pearls she'd made from the waters here. How had they kept it from her? How were they doing this?

Where the hell had they sent Mearil in from?

I wanted, desperately, to charge up there, grab Mea, deck the mistress of ceremonies (and anyone else who got in my way), and get the hell out. But I couldn't. Siren-song or no, I couldn't take on so many people, even with Phélan and Fionn to assist me. And while rescuing Mea was an objective of primary importance with me, to do so *now* would do nothing to help Melly, and any other selkies who were still being held. We had no idea where they were, and until we did I'd have to be cold and hard. Like Fi.

I controlled myself with an effort, gritting my teeth so hard my jaw began to hurt. Mercifully perhaps, Mea didn't open her eyes. Was she aware of the applause, or the laughter? Could she hear the mistress of ceremonies' description of her saleable points, or the numbers soon afterwards called out across the auction hall, climbing higher and higher? She appeared to be in some kind of a trance. A mixed blessing.

As Mea had appeared out of the waters, others had filtered into the staging area: guards. Now that the merchandise was beginning to appear on the premises, security was stepping up its efforts. Anybody hoping to get a free taste of the goods was to be strongly discouraged, and these were a tough lot, stone cold and bristling with menace. I didn't much fancy tangling with them myself.

Before my racing mind had time to come up with a course of action, Mea had gone. Sold. I looked sideways at the person who thought he had bought her: urisk, by the looks of him, none too tall, with a hard, unhandsome face and a goat's legs. He stood a little apart from the rest of the crowd, alone, and bristling with loneliness. If he imagined purchasing company was like to fix that, I'd have news for him later.

He had not won Mea uncontested. Competition for her had come from all over the room, but the urisk had two competitors in particular: a tall, cloaked figure, features indeterminate, and a ravishing golden-skinned woman whose air and features were, to me, suggestive of the naga.

The next selkie to appear was one I did not recognise, nor did she fit Melly's description. The same three fought among themselves for her, quickly outpacing the other bidders; the numbers grew shockingly high. The naga was the winner, this time; the urisk again, for the third; then the mysterious cloaked figure, who remained an enigma. I wondered, briefly, if this could be Daix, but dismissed the thought. The only thing I could be reasonably sure of was that the build was masculine, and he was certainly too tall. And too rich. He won a frag-ile-looking, blonde little flower of a selkie with a sum that would have purchased a house in Knightsbridge.

Fionn's turn approached. I took her arm again, and drifted towards the podium, Fi in tow and Phélan at my back. As the unfortunate blonde sank back into the glittering azure pool, I issued instructions to Fionn, and took up a station nearby.

Fionn walked out into the centre of the stage, avoiding the pool. She stood there in her satin and her pearls, head held high, as the mistress of ceremonies went smoothly through the long list of her assets and accomplishments. Ancients are among the more powerful of the fae, and Fionn was unquestionably the most powerful of the selkies on offer. Extraordinary beauty, said the MC, even for a selkie. Remarkable talent as a designer. Control of her company, Serenity. The list went on, more and more nauseating with every word.

Fionn bore it all without a flicker.

I kept my eyes on the urisk. He listened with close attention to every one of Fionn's proffered features, his eyes never wavering from her face. When the bidding opened, I was unsurprised to find him among the most aggressive.

Bids quickly went sky-high. Fionn was the jewel of this re-volting auction, and everybody there knew it. Sickened, I tuned out the bidding after a while, and turned my thoughts to my plan of action.

I didn't really have one. *We* didn't have one; our objective had been to discover the whereabouts of the selkies set to be auctioned, and we hadn't. I had no idea of the range of the enchantments operating those pools. Were the selkies nearby? They could be in another country for all we knew. Unlikely, but not impossible. Most likely they were somewhere in the city, but as to *where*—

Fionn was moving. I looked hard at her, trying to catch her eye, because she couldn't possibly be so reckless as to repeat her manoeuvre at the Pearls club, surely? *Surely*?

She could. She was showing herself off, on the face of it: turning slowly, displaying her figure, her gown, in a horrid mockery of her catwalk style. But every step took her nearer to the pool. When the bidding on her closed, she wouldn't walk offstage again and return to my side. She'd disappear into that damned pool.

I felt a grip on my elbow: Phélan. 'You're planning something crazy,' he hissed in my ear.

'*I'm* not,' I growled. '*She* is.'

'And you're going to follow, aren't you? Dive right in there after her, for all the world as though you aren't liable to drown in water.'

'I can't let her go alone.'

'She's at least as tough as you are.'

'Even so—'

'Look, *one* of you is a magical creature of the waters, and it isn't you. So tell me again how you expect to be able to help in there?'

My hands formed fists, nails digging into my skin hard enough to hurt. Damn him, he wasn't wrong. I didn't have Fionn's pearls this time; I'd drown in minutes. But what was I to do, then? Just stand there and watch Fi disappear, and hope she made it out again alive?

The auction seemed to be drawing to a close; Fionn was the last lot on the schedule. Perhaps that was why the urisk was heading my way. Had he won the bidding on Fionn? I hadn't caught the denouement. I waited, half my attention on Fionn and half on the urisk as he approached.

He gave me a curt nod. 'Nice score,' he said in a rich, gravelly tone, indicating Fionn. 'How'd you get ahold of her?'

'We go way back,' I said, coolly.

'Selling out your friends, is it?' He nodded again. 'If they're fool enough to give you the opportunity, fair play.'

Unsure where he was going with this line of enquiry, I merely lifted a brow, and waited.

He grinned, showing a mouthful of crooked teeth. 'Got any more where she came from? Something a bit shorter, by preference. Clever. And I like them... fiery.'

A suspicion darted into my mind, and I looked harder at the urisk. 'Do I know you?'

The grin widened.

'I—' I began, but got no further.

Several things happened at once.

The room erupted into applause, the bidding, and apparently the auction, finished.

Fionn raised her arms, took a step, and sank gracefully into the swirling pool, meeting my eyes only briefly as she vanished. I read a note of apology there, and determination.

And the urisk leaned into me, bumping me with his shoulders. Something cool fell into my hands, cool and smooth; a string of pearls.

'Go,' hissed the urisk, in a different voice entirely.

'*Daix*? What the—'

'What, you want to do questions? Now? Are you letting her go alone or what?'

I cast a last, frantic look at the roomful of fae, every one of them rotten to the core. Several of them had bought the selkies *we* were meant to protect; even now they were moving, preparing to collect their purchases, take them away, trap them forever. Something had to be *done* about that.

'I've got this,' hissed Daix. 'Fuck's sake, if you miss your chance *I will kill you.*'

'Right.' I grabbed the pearls in a tight fist and bolted for the pool.

The pool was closing, fading, its waters retracting. I closed the remaining distance in a leap, landed up to my ankles in chill waters; gasped as the cold spread to my legs and hips, drawing me down.

Only belatedly did I realise Phélan was a scant step behind me. His hands closed on me, drawing me close; where I went, he went.

We both went down, down into the dark, and as the waters closed over my head I heard Phélan beginning to choke.

17

— · —

FIONN

THE WATERS COULDN'T TOUCH me, this time. Not with my sealskin at my back, and my pearls intact.

But, they didn't try to.

Last time I'd travelled by these deceptively beautiful waters, there had been a... *greedy* quality to the procedure. I'd felt engulfed, torn at; near drained, by the time I'd emerged into the Thames. As though I'd been half absorbed.

This was different. Nothing tried to *take* anything from me. Instead of greed, these waters were exulting.

I felt *welcomed*.

As the waters closed over my head and dragged me down into darkness, I tried to tell myself this was a good thing. That there wasn't a *gloating* element to that welcome; that I hadn't done exactly what I'd told Tai I wouldn't, and walked straight into a trap set just for me.

Fool of a selkie. Of course I had.

Standing there on that stage, on display, while my desirability as a purchase was presented, delightedly, to the bidders, I'd been beset by a nagging feeling. That the previous unfortunates, popular as they'd proved, were only an opening act. *I* was the unwilling star of this show, the jewel in the crown. Why?

Ego told one story, fear another.

I was the oldest, the most powerful, the most beautiful: so said the MC. It could have been true.

But fear said: *this was a trap set for you*, and as I breathed in those azure waters in the cold and the dark, that fear grew louder.

We'd known since the Pearls club that some part of this mess was, somehow, directed at us. Had we failed to understand how much?

Had *everything* been a feint, a ploy, designed to bring me to this very moment?

What had I got myself into?

Tai, I'm sorry, I thought, uselessly, even as I knew I'd had no other choice. This pool, these waters, were the route straight through to the answers we hadn't found. This was the road to the resolution we needed. Whatever lay in wait for me on the other side, I'd have to face it.

Alone.

I breathed water and waited, making myself cool and cold, making myself ice. My racing heart slowed. By the time I opened my eyes, by the time the suffocating darkness ebbed, I was collected again, and ready.

I saw little, at first. Not due to a lack of light, but to an excess: the darkness had fled all at once, blasted out of existence by a dazzling, blinding radiance emanating from several sources at once. I blinked, water leaking from my tormented eyes. It melded seamlessly into the waters around me, saltwater added to saltwater.

For I remained submerged, and my senses told me I was deep under. My eyes grew slowly accustomed, and some of the blinding lights faded; I received a blanketing impression of deep blue, azure and turquoise, the colour of tropical ocean waters. *Shallow* ocean waters, but I was down in the deeps; how did that make sense?

'But is it the right one, this time?' came a voice, from somewhere: a woman's voice, deep and rich. 'Is this *she*?'

Movement: a ripple in the waters, a changing of the pressure. Someone approached. I saw a dim figure at first, indistinct. Then, mercifully, the dazzling light dimmed, and I could see.

Brianne?

'Ah! It is! Oh, well *done*, darlings.' Brianne beamed at me, a cruel twist to the smile. 'Welcome, the lady Fionn! I hope the accommodations are salubrious enough for you.'

She looked...different. Oh, as unruffled as ever, as at home under the sea as she had been at a table at the Eventide club, quaffing cocktails. Her hair, malachite-green, drifted with the currents; she was clad in silver weed, and sea-foam. Here was a woman whose confidence was in no way forced; a woman in her element. She belonged to the waters as much as I did.

'Is this your little scheme?' I demanded, sizing her up with a withering look. 'Short of palace attendants, were you? Needed some new blood?'

'Considering you just attended a certain auction, that surmise is unworthy of you.' Brianne spirited up a string of jewels with a whirl of her slim fingers, turning seawater to sun-coloured topaz. These she draped over my neck, and drifted back to observe the effects of her handiwork. 'Better,' she decided. 'You were rather under-dressed, darling.'

The jewels were pretty, but lifeless, nothing like my pearls. I stripped them off anyway. 'Fair,' I said, in answer to her challenge. 'But why spirit away all those selkies, just to sell them off? There are far easier ways to make money.'

Brianne just shook her head, and gave a tiny, disappointed sigh. 'Come on, darling. Think it through.'

I thought back over the past few days. We'd considered before that it wasn't the selkies that were wanted, or even their skins: it was the pearls. The clue was in the damned name of that club, set there to entrap us. In the fate of Narasel, dead in the water, her sealskin thrown after her — but her pearls had never reappeared. In the way those waters at the Pearls club had tried to wrest something from me — something I hadn't, at the time, possessed, and which Tai hadn't qualified, or consented, to surrender.

'What could you possibly *want* with the pearls?' I said, no nearer to comprehension. We were missing so much information; even now, I couldn't read Brianne, couldn't guess at her scheme. And where she had brought me remained a mystery.

'It isn't the pearls,' said she. 'Pretty as they are.' In illustration of this point, another whirl of her fingers produced a flurry of them, shell-pink and moon-white. She tossed these at me, and they settled over my shoulders, my hair. Empty and lifeless, like the topaz, however much they shone. 'But then, they aren't pearls, are they?' continued Brianne, studying me. 'Not as such. That is but a semblance. Symbolic. What they are, selkie, is *power*. And they represent an opportunity even I don't possess.'

'I don't believe there's much I can do that you cannot,' I said, and with truth. She was an ocean creature, like me; the waters loved her, could never harm her. In that, she was superior to a selkie: no sealskin to betray her, no way to wrest her powers from her. Only death could do that, and as I well knew, she was damned hard to kill.

'Perfectly true,' Brianne mused. 'Save for the seal shape, and to be honest with you, I don't fancy it. Elegant as you are in *this* form, you're a trifle less alluring in the other, hm?' She decorated me in a few more pearls, and a diamond or two; entertaining herself. Toying with me. 'All that *fur*. I appreciate a good mink as much as the next woman, but there is such a thing as too much, Fionn.'

'While I hate to interrupt the victory lap,' I said drily, 'could we perhaps skip to the end.'

Brianne's smile faded. 'Of all you *fatales*,' she said, coldly, 'you were always the least fun.'

This was too true for denial. Tai was all laughter and affection, and Daix would try anything once. Literally. Anything.

'Considering this is the third time I've been forcibly abducted this week,' I said, unimpressed, 'I don't think I owe you any *fun*.'

'Untrue. You walked into those waters of your own, free will, didn't you? Both times.' She waved a hand. 'Yes, yes, the charade. Frighteningly clever, I'm sure. But nobody who knew you could possibly believe it, darling.'

So much for Tai's scheme. 'What,' I said icily, 'do you want with the hags-cursed pearls, Bri.'

'Oh! Yes, that. Well.' She looked long at me, admiring — like I was a piece of meat. 'The one, thorny little problem with *my* various talents, love, is: they're a lot less transferrable.'

'I don't have the first idea what that means—' I began, but something disturbed the prismatic waters. Some frenzied thing, out of control, pulling the currents out of order.

'See, now. That's exactly what I mean,' said Brianne, no longer looking at me.

I drifted left, unwilling to turn my back on Brianne. We weren't alone in this dazzling little piece of undersea paradise: a couple of others had joined us. Land-folk, by the way they were thrashing about.

A flash of dark hair, and a face I knew, enlightened me.

Tai.

And Phélan?

I'd covered half the distance before I knew I was moving. 'Idiot,' I hissed as I reached her. 'Now who's got some kind of a death wish?'

Tai didn't — couldn't — answer. Her eyes, meeting mine, were wide and petrified, because her mouth and throat were full of water and she was drowning before my eyes—

Something pale glinted in her fingers: pearls.

'Right, *stop*,' I told her, ignoring Phélan. 'Give.' I stripped the pearls out of her hands — had it not occurred to her that merely holding the things wasn't enough this time? I yanked one out of the string, shoved it between Tai's lips, and held my hand over her mouth until she swallowed.

She took a breath.

I repeated this procedure, ungently, with Phélan. I didn't return the pearls to Tai. They were not mine: too new, too fresh, the layers of time and magic barely formed. I didn't waste time asking where they had come from.

'Lovely,' came Brianne's voice from behind me. In my panic over Tai, I had, for a moment, forgotten about the morgan. She came drifting up, and surveyed Tai and Phélan with great interest. '*Lovely*,' she repeated, with a wide smile. 'I hadn't *quite* courage enough to test the procedure this far below, I'll admit, but don't they work a treat? You are all being thoroughly helpful.'

I ignored this for the moment, still focused on Tai. She'd stopped thrashing as her panic ebbed, but she was still swimming like a brick. 'Don't fight with the water,' I told her. 'Try to go with the flow.'

She snorted, her eyes never leaving Brianne's face. 'Fi, please. I fight with *everything*.'

'And how's that working out for you,' said Phélan. He'd stripped off his coat, lost his hat somewhere. He was doing a better job than Tai, moving just enough to counteract the tugging pressure of the current. His words emerged indistinctly at first, but grew clearer as his body accustomed itself to the Undersea.

'I don't know, let's try an experiment,' said Tai, smiling at Brianne. 'For *science*.'

I wondered, then, if her ineptitude had been a show for Brianne's benefit, for she lunged at the morgan with all the sleek, confident power of a sea-creature herself. Her knee connected with Brianne's midriff, her fist with the morgan's face, and then her hands were around the throat in a throttling grip. '*What* have you done to Mearil?' she said, cold and hard. 'What the hell has all this been *for*?'

I learned, then, that we had never been alone, for several morrough — merfolk — flashed into view, their powerful fish-tails slicing through the waters. I was seized and held immobile; Tai was hauled off Brianne by two morrough guards and restrained, a shimmering blade held to her throat and a large hand held tight over her mouth. I couldn't see Phélan.

'Transferrable,' I said calmly, motionless in my captor's grip. It doesn't help to struggle. They'll only tighten their hold, trap you the more thoroughly for it. They'll only *hurt*.

Brianne was taking gasping breaths, rage twisting her perfect face. The anger soon faded, thrust away in favour of her usual, unruffled demeanour. I had the odd thought that I was looking at my mirror-twin; there, but for the Hags' grace, went I, one of these days.

'That is the problem with the sealskins, is it not?' I continued, while she composed herself. 'They work only for their owner, which I imagine you've verified for yourself by now. Why else would you discard Narasel's?'

Brianne's only reaction was a look of acute annoyance. She looked from me to Tai, as if to ascertain that we were still immobilised.

'But the pearls,' I said. 'That's a different matter. What have you done with them all, Bri? Narasel's, and Mearil's, and all the others? Several sets of them, albeit none quite as powerful as mine. That's why you needed to get hold of *me*, isn't it?'

'How long do you think they'll breathe water before they drown?' Brianne said, drifting nearer to me, her attention on Tai and Phélan. 'A day? A month?'

Did she imagine I'd pushed my own, dearly treasured pearls down their drowning throats? I might have, I supposed, if it were a choice between that or letting them perish.

Tai I would certainly have saved, even at such a cost.

Phélan, maybe.

I didn't correct Brianne. 'I've never had occasion to test the effect,' I said. 'But then, I don't choose to take up my residence in a tasteless undersea palace dripping in jewels.'

'A long time, I'd wager,' she said, ignoring my jab at her residence. 'That's the thing with morgans. They're highly territorial, with a taste for luxury. Tai once called them undersea magpies, and she's right. Brianne was a powerful morgan. She'd have a fiefdom somewhere, complete with a palace fit for a princess.

We were probably in it

'I expect so,' I agreed, and waited.

Brianne looked at me, and this time she didn't bother to smile. There was ice behind her eyes; I doubt she saw a person, merely a means to an end. 'I'll be needing the rest of those,' she said. 'All of them, please.'

It didn't do to give up the torn string of pearls too easily. I didn't want her to guess that they were not mine. I fought, and received a few stinging blows for my trouble. The pearls were pried from my fist by a hard-faced morrough, and delivered to Brianne.

She turned them over in her hands, staring at them with an odd kind of hunger. 'How long?' she said abruptly, looking at me. 'How long will these last?'

'You mean how long could a land-creature breathe water, with those at their disposal?'

Brianne nodded once.

'I told you, I have no idea. I've never given any away before.'

'Nobody you loved enough? Sad story.' Brianne's gaze flicked to Tai. 'Except, apparently, for her.'

'Except for Tai,' I agreed. 'Who are you planning to give them to?'

'That would be none of your business,' she said crisply. 'I'm afraid I'll be needing a lot more, however.'

'I don't have any more.'

'So make some. Make plenty. Nobody's leaving here until you do.'

'That isn't how this works. Those pearls are the product of centuries, I can't just spirit up some more.'

'That's a pity, isn't it? When you've been so obliging as to provide me with so much leverage. Bring them,' she said to her morrough. 'Take the lady Fionn into the crystal waters. The others... you know what to do with.'

'What?' I said sharply. 'What are you doing with Tai?'

'Hopefully, nothing,' said Brianne pleasantly. 'But that depends on you, doesn't it?'

'This is futile. I cannot work miracles for your convenience.' I fought against the grip that tightened upon me, to no avail; a morrough guard looped a bright-silver string around my neck, tightened it, began to pull. I was borne along, half-choked.

'Find a way,' said Brianne coldly. 'Or the whole damned lot of you will be face-down in the Thames by morning.'

THE CRYSTAL WATERS TURNED out to be a charming grotto, walled with coral and silver weed. Clear, jewel-toned waters flowed in a ceaseless whirl, intensely pure, and deeply attractive to me, under any other circumstances. I was thrust into the midst of it, and while I could not find the end of the silvery cord around my neck, it was fastened somewhere, fastened tight; when I tried to swim away, I was brought up short.

Not only that but the cord tightened, merciless, painfully compressing my throat.

I stayed where I was as the morrough swam away, grateful for small mercies. I was captive in truth, no longer just in seeming, and I had no obvious means of escape. But at least I had free use of my own will. My sealskin was safe, and I remained *me*, even under restraint.

I could work with it.

Stillness assisted me. The more I fought to escape, the more the silvery cord tightened, choking me, bruising my throat. When I stopped and held myself in peace and silence, it gradually loosened.

Breaking free by force was no option, then.

I turned my senses on those pure, perfect waters, and made a discovery. I knew this water. I'd immersed myself in it before, twice over: once at the Pearls club, and once at the auction. This was the source of the grasping pools, those waters that seemed half alive.

They were Brianne's work, then. That made sense. Hers was the power that animated the waters; hers the intimate knowledge of our history, our methods, that permitted her to lay traps for us with such success. Hers might be the resentment, too, that made such a scheme desirable. We hadn't always been enemies, but it was a long, long time since we'd been friends.

Details nagged at me still. I hadn't pegged Brianne as the mastermind of such a show, and neither had Tai, or Daix. We had been basing our ideas on the old Brianne, the one we'd known nearly a century before. Had she changed so much? Or were we right to think this wasn't her style?

I still believed she'd had help. Whose?

Above all: who was the intended recipient of so many pearls? She hadn't been exaggerating when she said she'd need a lot. If the pearls were all she'd wanted, she could have stolen them without half so much hassle. I didn't doubt that this was where she'd been keeping Mearil, and Melly, and the others. She probably had them performing the same task I had been set: manufacturing pearls for her, pearls with the latent powers she sought. She'd exhausted Narasel with the endeavour, pushed the girl until she'd drained herself dry in the attempt — and died. She had taken more care with the rest, pushed them only so far — and then sold them off for profit, ensnaring me in the process.

All for the sake of selkies' pearls.

Pearls she could give to... who? Who needed the gifts only a selkie could bestow?

Who mattered enough to Brianne to be worth all *this*?

Useless speculation. I didn't yet know, and no amount of thinking would produce the information I lacked. Thoughts of Tai, and Daix, drifted uneasily through my mind. Where had Tai been taken? What had become of Daix, left behind on the surface alone?

I remembered, briefly, the impressions of yesterday, brought to me by the stagnant pools of the car factory. Silise. A particularly cruel torment, those visions, and I mentally tipped my hat to Brianne for the manoeuvre.

I would have given such a lot to have Silise at my back. As a quartet, we'd been nigh unstoppable.

'You don't appear to be working very hard,' said Brianne, and I looked up sharply. She'd drifted in, so silently as to escape my notice. She maintained a station some way above me, forcing me to look up at her.

I didn't appreciate the humility of the posture.

'I told you,' I said evenly. 'I cannot miracle up centuries-old pearls for your convenience.'

'So you aren't even going to try? What a pity for poor Tai.'

'It isn't much good, is it? This notion of leverage. Once you've killed Phélan and Tai, what do you propose to do next?'

'A bluff! Charming. But I might think, after a century or so, you'd come up with something *new*.'

'Old habits die hard.'

'But old sirens die very easily, darling.'

'So, go kill her.' I shrugged. 'What's stopping you?'

For the first time, her face registered a flicker of uncertainty. 'You can't be serious.'

I looked her in the eye, hard as steel. 'You appear to have changed, Brianne. So have I. Eighty years is a long time.'

'True,' she said softly. 'But then, it wouldn't be the first time you've thrown a partner under the bus, now would it?'

'What?'

'Once there were four,' she said, drifting down, and nearer. 'Then there were three. Shall I make you a duo? Shall I really, darling?'

'A good tactic,' I said, as steadily as I could. 'Tormenting us over Silise. It did throw us for a moment or two, I will admit that much.'

'She was worth twenty of you.'

That gave me pause. 'I did not know you were at all acquainted with the matter.'

'The matter of Silise? No, of course you wouldn't. You were too... distracted, weren't you? You and Tai, wrapped up in each other. Best friends *forever*, and the others could go to hell for all you cared.'

I watched her through narrowed eyes, silent. Never would I admit that her words hurt, that she had found, with remarkable instinct, a sore point.

'I rather wonder that Daix bothers with either of you,' she went on. 'What could possess her to go on playing sidekick to your leading lady duo?'

'Where exactly are we going with this?'

'Silise would have left you,' said Brianne. 'Eventually.'

'She did,' I said, icily. 'She died.'

Brianne didn't answer immediately. She looked down at me with something like contempt, and when she spoke at last, it was no longer on the subject of Silise. 'Those pearls. Now.'

'No amount of threats will render the impossible achievable, Brianne.'

Brianne shook her head, sending her malachite-green locks floating in a flurry around her face. 'Pity, really. For all your faults, I do have *some* standards, darling. I was really hoping not to have to do this to you.' She lifted her voice, called over her shoulder, 'Bring that here, please. Thank you.'

A pair of morrough appeared behind her, carrying something between them. I knew instantly what it was; I didn't need to watch as they spread it out for me to see, showed me the length and breadth of it, the sleek, brown-furred contours of it, shot through with silver. I knew it the way I know the shape of my own face.

My sealskin.

The two morrough carried it to Brianne, who was looking at me with something like genuine pity in her face. 'I am sorry,' she said, and she sounded sincere. 'I don't think you altogether deserve this, but what choice have you given me? Hm? I need those pearls. If you won't do it even to save Tai — and really, all things considered, I shouldn't be surprised — well then, darling, I'll have to resort to desperate measures.'

She took up my sealskin, then, and she did it with all the malicious, self-serving intent I'd always known she possessed.

The moment she grasped it in her hands, clutched it tight, I felt *trapped,* caught, like an invisible net had been thrown over me. I breathed, and I could move, if I wanted to. But I couldn't remember why I might want to. I would do nothing until I received instructions from the one who held my sealskin.

Brianne drifted down and down, until her face was level with mine. 'Interesting,' she said, studying my expression. 'I thought I would feel more... triumph. Power. Something. But really, all I'm feeling is regret.'

I said nothing.

'Now then, those pearls. Make all you can, though you're to preserve your own existence, please, darling. I don't need another dead selkie on my hands.'

Something, deep inside, flinched. Narasel.

'And when we're finished here, who knows? Perhaps I'll let you have this back.' She hefted my sealskin, stroked it with tender fingers. 'After all,' she said, thoughtfully. 'Nobody makes gowns quite like you, do they?'

18

—·—

Tai

An undersea cell isn't that much different from the above-ground variety, as it turns out.

Superficially there are differences, sure. This one was prettier: all turquoise water and coral, and pearlescent fish that look like they were painted to match the décor (for all I know, they might have been). But bars of water-smoothed stone are still bars, and a locked door is still impassable without a key.

Brianne's guards had installed Phélan and I in the same cell, and while it's been some time since he and I have had to escape a confined situation together, I'm going to go ahead and call this a mistake on her part.

'I'm fastened to the wall,' I observed to Phélan, once the morrough had gone. I had a manacle, of sorts, attaching my left wrist to the craggy rock face around me: silvery and slender, it looked like it wouldn't hold a child, but when I tested it, the thing tightened around my skin and *bit*. I stopped trying to pull free.

Phélan was on the other side of the cell, glaring at me.

'Fine,' I said. 'You were right. I shouldn't have followed Fi down here. But you didn't have to come with me, did you?'

'I wasn't trying to come with you,' Phélan growled. 'I was trying to *stop* you.'

'Oh...'

'I, too, am fastened to the wall.'

'Sorry about that.'

'Any idea how long before we drown?'

I shrugged. 'Not a clue, but that sounds like a problem for future me.'

'Right.'

'*Current* me is more interested in getting out of this unusually pretty prison.'

Phélan visibly swallowed whatever of his irritation remained unvoiced, and set to work. I watched him test his own silvery bindings as I had, with the same result.

'You hang onto any of your knives?' I asked.

'Course not. What, you think we're dealing with a bunch of amateurs?'

I gave that due thought. 'Probably not,' I conceded. 'Though I don't know that Brianne was expecting this part.'

'She certainly wasn't expecting me.'

I opened my mouth, and let loose with a cacophony of shattering notes. The sounds sliced through the silence; behind me, rock splintered. The clear waters grew cloudy with rock-dust, but when they cleared, the silvery manacle remained unaffected.

'And that would be why I'm not gagged,' I observed. Damned Brianne. Whether she had expected me personally to end up down here or not, she'd proofed her arrangements against siren-song pretty well.

Phélan favoured me with a string of curses, and a couple of unflattering reflections upon my personal character and capabilities.

'All true,' I agreed. 'But I had to try it, didn't I?'

'Can't hear you,' he replied. 'Some idiot has shattered my eardrums.'

'Yes, yes.'

It occurred to me that he was looking rather pale. I watched with fascinated interest as he grew visibly paler by degrees, his dark eyes and hair turning ink-black against paper-white skin.

'Cool,' I breathed. 'I haven't seen this in *ages*.'

Phélan ignored that. The waters around him darkened and began to churn, storm-tossed. I glimpsed vague shapes in the choppy currents, pale wraith-figures, moon-bright and, by the looks of it, pissed off.

Par for the course. You set up a direct line to the departed in somebody's prison cell, you're going to get a few enraged ghosts on your hands.

Phélan wasn't having an easy time of it. The storm grew rapidly out of hand, trapping him at the centre, buffeting his suddenly frail figure about like a leaf in a hurricane.

Tsk. He *hated* it when they did that.

'*ENOUGH!*' he roared, followed by a string of echoing words in a language I didn't know. The dark syllables rang out, clear as a bell, compelling.

'We'll make a siren of you yet,' I complimented him.

The storm, though, did not much abate. '*Tai,*' I heard him gasp. 'A little — fucking — help?'

'Right! Sorry.' I began to sing, wordless stuff; it isn't the lyrics that matter, it's the melody. I strung three voices together in a soothing harmony, added a fourth with penetrating, commanding notes. I wanted to calm, and compel, and it worked: the wraiths trying to tear Phélan to pieces began to slow, the waters gradually settling back into their former tranquillity. As the tumult faded, I discerned, more distinctly, the wraiths: half-invisible in the clearwater, restless, drifting.

Phélan drifted with them, near motionless, breathing hard. And, let me tell you, breathing water when you aren't used to it is not easy. It *feels* wrong, even if it functions; you fight yourself for every breath, overcoming the panic reflex — *this is water, this is death* — only by force of will. I'm prepared to believe that would fade in time, but I wasn't doing a great job of it yet, and neither was Phélan.

Finally, he drew breath enough to speak. For me he spared only a withering flick of those black eyes; I made apology gestures.

To the wraiths, he said: 'Any idea how to get out of this mess?'

There followed a lot of bargaining, by the looks of it. When the wraiths answered, they spoke in the same jagged, rippling language he'd used before, and Phélan answered in kind. I didn't understand a word, but I knew a negotiation when I saw one. The wraiths remonstrated with Phélan, and Phélan did a lot of head-shaking in denial, followed by some kind of counter offer.

My attention wandered. Not that it isn't hellishly cool to watch Phélan bargaining with the souls of the restless dead, but I've seen it a time or two before. He'd be devilishly hungry later, and angry; it always soured his temper. I could see why.

A soft sound distracted me, not coming from Phélan and his wraiths. A sound like a sob, half-stifled. It came from somewhere behind me. I drifted that way, found to my interest that the silvery manacle lengthened itself as I moved. It didn't like me trying to take it off, then, but it had no objection to my travelling away from the wall.

Interesting.

'Hello?' I called, once I'd gone as far as I could go. The smooth stone bars blocked my progress any further; beyond them I could see only turquoise water. 'Anyone there?'

The sobbing sound stopped.

'I'm a friend,' I offered. 'Here, I'll prove it: Brianne Lamarre can go die in a fire.'

Silence followed. I began to think I'd imagined the sounds, or scared the maker of them away.

Then came an answer.

'You sound like someone I know, but that's unlikely, so! I'm going mad. Good choice. At least I'm hallucinating *nice* things.'

I knew the speaker before she'd uttered more than three words. 'Mea!' I shouted. 'At fucking last! Where are you?'

'See, that's exactly what Tai would say,' Mea agreed. 'Purposeless expletives and all.'

'It's been a bad week, okay? I'll swear all I want.' I reconsidered. 'Actually, no. You've had a far worse week, and I've *missed* you, so if you don't want me to swear I'll try to control myself.'

'That... isn't something I'd picture Tai saying.' Mea's voice, when she spoke again, seemed a little nearer. '*Am* I mad?'

'Possibly! But it is really me. I'm stuck at the moment, but we'll be getting you out soon.'

'We?' The voice sharpened. 'Coronis isn't with you?'

'Coronis is safe at home. I've got someone else with me, though, and he'll have us out in a trice.'

Phélan spoke, immediately behind me. I jumped. 'I don't know how you've survived all these years without me.'

I turned. He looked exhausted, like he hadn't slept or eaten in a week. 'I figured something else out,' I told him. 'Like always. You look like you could use some help.'

'Manacle's off,' he said, and he was right, it was. It had melted away so seamlessly I hadn't noticed it was gone. 'Your turn,' he added.

'What do you — oh. Right.' Phélan had got us unfastened from the wall, but the bars were still between us and open water. And Mea.

I sang. Phélan had the sense to clap his hands over his ears this time, not that I imagine it helped all that much. I sang in discordant, destroying four-part harmony and the walls shuddered and cracked around me. When I'd finished, the pretty, sea-smoothed bars lay shattered in a hundred pieces, and the water was thick with debris.

'Hey, we're not dead,' I enthused, delighted by the lack of Tai-crushing rubble.

Phélan must have been tired, for he let this perfect opportunity for an acid comment pass. He merely fell in beside me as I swam out past the confines of our cell, somewhat graceless, wishing futilely for fins. Even in her woman shape, Fionn's a creature of perfect grace in water. Phélan and I did the best we could.

My song had shattered the bars of Mea's prison as well, but she hadn't come out. I found her lurking at the back, hands over her head to protect herself from falling debris.

She was still shackled to the rock wall.

I looked at Phélan, but he shook his head, exhausted and mute.

Okay. The deal he'd struck with the wraiths only covered our bindings, not everyone's. I noticed, for the first time, that the souls had not all disappeared again; one stuck to Phélan like an incorporeal burr, wound vine-like about him. Couldn't be healthy, that, but I knew better than to question it.

I wasn't about to ask him to bargain with the dead again. By the looks of him, it would probably kill him.

Still, that left me with a dearth of options.

'Mea,' I said. 'It's okay, I've stopped.'

She came out from under her uplifted hands, and looked at me with tired eyes. I scarcely recognised her in her current state: she wore some kind of simple shift-dress, nothing like her usual garb, and her hair had, somehow, grown. A lot. More than that, there was something ethereal about her, something *other*; she looked selkie through-and-through, and I never usually got to see that.

'I can't go with you anyway,' she said. 'My sealskin's no longer my own.'

I didn't know what to say to that. I have little real idea what it means, to lose your sealskin; Fionn's never really talked about it, and I've never chosen to push the subject.

'No, I can't just *try*,' said Mea, reading some of this in my face. 'The thing is, I don't even remember how to want to. My place is here.'

Her place was here, because whoever owned her had decreed as much.

To get her out, we'd not only have to break her shackles. We'd also have to find, and retrieve, her scalskin.

'Are the others down here, too?' I asked.

'Somewhere about,' said Mea. There was a lifelessness to her demeanour that I despised; it wasn't even hopelessness, it went beyond that. The too-passive acceptance of a person who had... forgotten what it was like to be anything but what she now was. A slave.

I mentally added this situation to the list of reasons to eviscerate Brianne. 'Okay,' I said. 'We're going to fix this.'

Mea just looked at me in silence.

'Right?' I said to Phélan. 'We can make this better.'

He, too, looked at me in silence, a hollow-eyed stare that told me, clearer than words, that he was already tapped out. Phélan isn't the most powerful among the sluagh. He can do some fantastically freaky shit, don't get me wrong, but it takes a lot out of him.

I was still floundering around in my own, useless head for a way forward when the currents shifted around me, and grew cold. Colder.

'Again?' sighed Mea, turning her eyes upwards.

I looked up, too. A column of vivid, azure water descended, and swept Mea up in its swirling currents, turning her around and around, her pale hair flying.

'That's the — that's the portal,' I said. 'No. Mea—' I grabbed at her, trying to get hold of her somehow, but I couldn't maintain my grip; the current was ferociously strong. In seconds she was gone, spirited away. I tried to follow, ignoring Phélan's attempts to hold me back, but the waters slipped away from me and vanished.

Nothing but cool, clear, inanimate water was left.

'Shit,' I said, numbly. Where the hell had she been taken this time? Back into that wretched auction room, or somewhere else? Somewhere I'd never find her again?

Phélan, for once, didn't hassle me about it. He took my arm in a more or less gentle grip, and said nothing.

I chose to interpret the gesture as supportive.

'Right,' I said after a moment, pulling myself together. 'Mission Objective A: Rescue the Selkies, really isn't going well, but there's always Mission Objective B.'

'Which is?' said Phélan.

'Find Fionn. Then descend upon Brianne in righteous, tripartite fury and tear her to pieces.'

Easier said than done. A pithy little piece of triteness, that, and if I'm honest it could sum up pretty much every area of my life.

Phélan and I performed a laborious tour of those undersea cells and found every one of them empty. If there had been selkies held there besides Mea, they were gone now.

We didn't find Fionn.

'Brianne's keeping her someplace else,' I said in frustration, treading water.

'Stands to reason,' said Phélan. 'The rest of these people were just detritus.'

I shot him a glare. 'Mea isn't detritus.'

'To Brianne, she is,' said Phélan brutally. 'Toughen up, Tai.'

He was right. I could be as upset as I wanted — later. Right now, I had to be cold. As cold as Brianne.

And Fionn.

'Okay,' I said. 'So if Fionn was the real target all along: what does that mean? What does Brianne *want* with her?'

'No idea. But something about this is personal, and that means she'll be keeping Fionn close.'

That thought nauseated me. Mea's hopelessness and helplessness, so fresh in my mind, blended themselves with a vision of Fionn as I'd last seen her. Front and centre at the auction, acting the part of a soulless captive far too well.

I should never have taken Fionn there, but that, too, was a thought for another time.

'Wasn't up to you to decide that,' said Phélan unexpectedly.

I looked sideways at him. 'What?'

He pointed a finger at my face. 'I recognise that look. If you're going down a guilt spiral because we took Fionn to the auction, forget it. She would've gone anyway, and it wasn't up to you to tell her she couldn't.'

Phélan's always so bracing. I nodded. 'At least her skin's safe. However Brianne's holding Fionn, it'll be with manacles and bars, not—'

Not the subjugation of her entire soul by way of her sealskin. I couldn't say it.

'You're sure about that, are you?' said Phélan.

'No, but Fionn was. Utterly certain.'

'Her sealskin's that well-hidden, is it?' The look all over his still-gaunt face was sceptical. 'Could you work out where it is?'

'... Probably,' I allowed. 'But I know her better than anybody in the world. Brianne... I can't see how Brianne could *possibly...*'

'Better hope you're right,' said Phélan, giving voice to the unease unfurling within me.

'Shit,' I sighed. 'Okay. We find Brianne. And luckily, I do have an idea about that.'

'Oh?' Phélan fell in beside me as I kicked myself into motion again, swimming up this time. Out.

'It might be a long time since I considered her a friend,' I said. 'But some things don't change. We're somewhere in Brianne's territory right now, and Brianne Lamarre loves one thing above all others: luxury. There'll be a palace. There'll be an inner sanctum in said palace. It'll be dripping in pearls and gold and I'm pretty sure that's where she'll be.'

'With Fionn.'

'With Fionn.' Something about that juxtaposition of ideas nudged a faint thought, somewhere in my mind. We knew Brianne had some kind of an obsession with the glittering pearls a selkie like Fionn could make: it was the properties they possessed that interested her, more than the shining outer shell they came in. But she was a sea-creature, too: she didn't need those things. Was she selling them? She wouldn't be the first person to try that. An occasional selkie, fallen on hard times, would sell a pearl or two of their own; they were highly prized.

But all Brianne would gain by that was money. More gold, more jewels, and she was already drowning in both.

I still couldn't make sense of it, and for the present, I gave up the struggle. When we found Brianne, I could beat the answers out of her myself.

Until then, I had a palace to infiltrate.

19

FIONN

IT IS A PROCESS I used to enjoy — spinning up pearls out of nothing. A swirl of clearwater and salt, of air and deep magic, and something beautiful emerges. Something powerful. No dense, glossy nuggets of disharmony, these, resentfully expelled by beleaguered oysters; these glitter with promise, shine with all the layers of ancient magic I have in me.

If there is one capacity humankind and fae share alike, it's this: to take a brightness and darken it. To turn a joy into agony.

Brianne's morrough bodyguards — or whatever they were — had dumped me in what I supposed were the crystal waters she'd spoken of. The name was apt enough, the place enchanting. The waters never ceased moving around me, a fluid whirling, soft and restful; clear as new ice, tinted with colour, they were crystal indeed, were such a thing transformed into dulcet ocean.

They were also, effectually, a cage. Clear as the waters may be, I could not see beyond them, and while the gentle kaleidoscope of hues had beauty enough to delight the soul, the relentless motion had the latent power to turn a person sick, in time. Eventually.

I did my best not to repine, as I drifted alone in the midst of this mesmerising whirlpool. I had been given no instructions at all by my new mistress, save for the fashioning of pearls — or more rightly, powers, mine to conjure up, hers to take and use. And fashion I did, the only power left to me that of deliberate slowness. I could justify it, easily. She had told me not to exhaust myself. To keep myself alive.

Still, it exhausted me. Each new pearl siphoned off another drop of my soul, turned it to bejewelled enchantment for Brianne. Draining me.

Every time, I fought. The compulsion was not so strong, this time, I told myself. She who had taken my sealskin was nothing to me, not even a friend. An enemy, now. I need not suffer under lingering ties of love and loyalty; I had no obligation to please, no confusion of feeling.

Even so. It is a curious power, the selkie skin. Why the mere transferral of an object should bind my actions so, I could not say, but nor could I conquer it. Until my skin was once more my own, I'd do what Brianne said.

I'd hate it, but I would do it. My body moved on its own, no longer obeying my commands but receptive to another's.

And so the string of pearls grew longer, each new jewel a shade dimmer than the last, but radiant enough.

I wondered, dimly, when I would stop. At what point would Brianne's parting command — *preserve your own existence, please, darling* — take effect? How bone-deep would this weariness have to go before, at last, I could rest?

The answer was far too long in coming. I fashioned pearls of mist and magic until I wept with fatigue, and still I went on. I spun jewels of coldwater and gramarye until I'd have severed my own fingers rather than make another, and still I did not stop.

Only when I'd lost the strength to move, to think, to do more than wearily exist, did my wretched factory of pearls come to an end. My thoughts, sluggish as a silted river, barely formed words; the only word I could remember clearly was not even my own name, but another's.

Tai.

I drifted in slow circles, too weak even to hold myself steady against the currents. Perhaps I slept.

Time passed.

'Is this *all*?'

The words snapped me out of my daze, brought me back into my miserably bound flesh with a jolt.

Brianne.

She held my hard-won pearls in her thin hands, turning them over greedily, dissatisfied. 'Twelve,' she said. 'Only twelve, and look at you.' She did look at me then, a hard, cold stare, taking in my state of exhaustion. 'Perhaps, with rest—'

'No.' I said the word with a freezing coldness to match hers, but the word emerged too faintly. I'd barely strength enough left to speak.

'I was under the impression,' said Brianne, 'that I had eradicated defiance.'

So she had. I couldn't defy any command she chose to issue me, for where my own will used to be, now there was only hers. 'But not truth,' I managed.

Rest wouldn't restore the magic she'd forced me to drain for her benefit. Not in the way she meant: a good night's sleep or two, and back to work. It would be months — perhaps years — before I'd have it in me to fashion even a single jewel.

'I don't accept that,' said Brianne crisply. 'How often I've seen you *decked* in the things.' She made a sweeping gesture, indicating the flowing, water-drowned length of her hair. True. I sometimes appeared so, in my true state; mist-wreathed, rain-infused, with a hundred pearls woven into the black mass of my hair. But they were baubles, nothing more. A glamour only, a seeming.

'Not *those*,' I said, meaning the fruits of my exhausting labours, the precious dozen she now held so cheap.

Brianne gave a short, irritated sigh, her fingers closing tightly around my handiwork. She'd had me moved, somewhere in my slumber. The crystal waters remained, but they were lessened, here; a fleeting flurry of colour out of the corner of my eye, a gentle *tug* of movement and magic, scarcely felt.

I was in a chamber of spectacular grandeur. The walls shone with the pearlescence of mother-of-pearl; the distant ceiling gleamed shell-white. There were no windows, no glass here below; instead, arches through which the saltwater flowed freely, tangled in kelp and moss-green weed. Gold-and-silver gilding limned statuary in gentle fire, sun-and-moonglow. The floors were tiled mosaic.

I was on a dais, raised up like a queen, save that I remained bound by that silvery thread. A purposeless feature now, I thought with distant puzzlement, for I wouldn't run away. I no longer had that power.

Perhaps she just enjoyed the visual reminder of my servitude.

'Well, then,' said Brianne, regarding me with her elegant head tilted, her green-malachite hair tossed softly by the currents. 'What next to do with her, hm?'

The question not being directed at me, I was not obliged to answer. I remained silent, waiting.

Wondering. Whom was she addressing with the words? For I saw no one about save for the two of us; the water was heavy with silence.

Nonetheless, after a time, an answer came. 'I care not.'

The words were coolly spoken, in a voice feminine, if rather low. Something about the cadence of it tugged at my memory, but the feeling of familiarity faded. I hadn't the energy to pursue it.

'No?' said Brianne, her gaze shifting from me, a frown creasing her brow. 'But I got her for *you*.'

'No. You got her for what she could *do* for me, and she's done it.'

My head came up, for the feeling of recognition returned, strengthened. I knew that ringing, confident voice, knew the arrogance of it. I'd once drawn courage from the unflinching certainty of those tones, but not for years, not for *eighty years*, because she'd been gone.

I couldn't see her. I turned in the water, but she was hidden from me.

Brianne was watching me again. Watching with a cruel, amused glitter in her hard eyes. 'Something bothering you?' she smiled.

'Silise.' I half choked on the word, near overwhelmed with the wealth of memory, of pain, of confusion; of sheer *feeling* the brace of syllables provoked.

'No, darling, no,' said Brianne, all soothing softness, though the cruel smile widened. 'How could that be? She being so very *dead*.'

'She is dead,' I breathed. 'I know she's dead. *How are you doing this*?'

How was this possible? She'd already summoned a vision of Silise to torment me, back at the old car factory. A conjuration of movements, of scents, of nameless cues, *all* so perfectly reminiscent of Silise.

Now her voice. *Her* voice. Not just the contralto smoothness of it but her inflections, the lingering hint of Irish brogue, the *personality* of it.

'How?' I said again, a mere whisper, exhausted anew by my efforts to find what couldn't possibly be there.

'Dead, hm?' said Brianne, drifting nearer to me. 'Are you sure of that, Fionn? Entirely sure?'

'Yes.'

'No possibility of mistake?'

'I... *yes*.' I was. I had to be.

'Did you see her body?' Brianne pursued. 'Did you see it with your own eyes, snapped like a twig? Did you see those grey eyes emptied of life? All the stone-dead, inert *meat* of her corpse?'

I had to answer; my mistress desired it. 'Yes. I...think.'

'You *think*.' Brianne wasn't smiling now. Some intense emotion I couldn't read churned behind her eyes; her mouth was a hard line. 'Then you don't *know*, Fionn?'

'This is... mind games,' I said, with as much energy as I could muster. 'Spare me that, at least.'

'I don't see why I should.'

'Nor do I,' came Silise's voice again. 'I am thoroughly enjoying the spectacle, I confess.'

She was right behind me, or so it seemed, her voice very near. I began to turn, but Brianne's order stopped me cold, fired from between clenched teeth like a bullet: *'Don't move.'*

Silise spoke again, so close I could feel the disordered currents of the waters, the soft displacement she made with her words.

'You left me.'

'No,' I said, instantly. 'No. We came for you.'

'You came too late. You left too soon. Am I to thank you for the gesture?'

I was silent, bewildered.

Silise had disappeared, late in the second world war. We'd been in Austria, attempting to extract a pair of alven who'd got themselves into hot water. But the two alven had vanished before we'd managed to get them out, and so had Silise.

They'd ended up in Ravensbrück. A German concentration camp, just for women.

Silise was more than equal to the challenge, at least at first. When Tai, Daix and I got ourselves in, we found Silise had already got herself out — after a fashion.

But she never got the two alven out. She got caught, and executed.

So we'd thought.

We'd heard her death-song, her terrible ban-sith wail, and we'd *known*, somehow. This song was for *her*.

We'd seen... no. I'd seen nothing. But Tai had, and Daix. That eerie song, cut abruptly short, and a bleeding body that looked like hers...

Nothing had been the same after that. Recrimination, guilt and regret had torn the surviving fatales apart. We'd failed Silise, and none of us had ever forgiven ourselves — or each other.

And yet.

Could we have been wrong?

I said nothing; I couldn't have formed words under threat of my life. I waited, bowed with a nameless sense of dread, as Brianne stared coldly down upon me and *something* spoke behind me.

'I relied on you,' Silise went on, or the thing that spoke with Silise's voice. 'My fellow *fatales*, the unstoppable trio who'd always have my back. Isn't that right? But it wasn't you who came for me, in the end.'

Then I saw her. Silise in truth, in the flesh: ragged red hair, eyes as grey as a cold morning. Thinner, even, than she used to be, gaunt and pale: ban sith, a spectre made of flesh and blood.

She'd used to be vivid and bright, for all that. Warm and energetic, cocky and brittle. Always laughing.

Now she looked like death itself.

'Who do you think came to my rescue, in the end?' said Silise, unsmiling. 'Who was it who loved me enough to brave hell itself? It wasn't you.'

'It was me,' said Brianne.

I understood, then. How Silise was here, *here,* under the water, where she'd no business but to drown. Why Brianne had wanted every pearl of magic I could muster, why she'd grabbed every selkie in London. How she'd known what we would do, the three of us: me and Tai and Daix, why the scheme had seemed designed to bait us, torment us.

How Brianne had known where to find my selkie-skin.

Silise.

'I'm sorry,' I gasped. I had no other words in me, nothing else I could *say* around the fresh wave of horror, of guilt.

She'd been alive. Silise hadn't died at all, but we'd *left* her there, left her in Ravensbrück. If it hadn't been for Brianne, she probably *would* have been killed.

She was right to hate us.

'Sorry,' Silise repeated. She looked down upon me, chill as winter, hard as stone. 'Is that all? *Sorry*?'

I bowed my head. She was right: the mere word could never express the extent of my regret, nor hope to make up for the extent of our neglect. *Sorry* had no power here. Nothing could.

Silise gave a sigh, curiously tinged with annoyance. 'The thing is,' she said, not to me: to Brianne. 'If we keep her, we'll have to *do* something with her. Feed her. Find a use for her. *Look at her.*'

'A good point,' Brianne agreed. 'Let's get rid of her.'

The idea had a finality to it. I thought, with despair, of Tai and Daix. Would they ever know what had become of me? Would my body wash up in the river tomorrow morning, my selkie-skin thrown after? Would they know why I'd died?

Would they know Silise *lived*?

I hadn't the energy to argue, to persuade, even if I'd had the power. I had no options left, and I deserved none.

Some part of me, deep down, doubted, even then. Would Brianne kill me? *Could* Silise? However angry she was — however *justly* angry — we'd been the best of friends, once. Closer than sisters.

Looking at those wintry faces, those hard eyes, I couldn't be sure.

But I wasn't destined to find out.

Whatever Silise might have said in reply was lost in a raucous *wall* of sound, a wail as sharp and discordant as Silise's dread death-song. It shattered the smooth currents, turned the gentle flow to juddering waves.

A shock of crushing agony tore through me, slicing through my focus. I lost consciousness, perhaps, for a scant few seconds; when I revived, it was to a different scene altogether.

Brianne and Silise remained, but their tyranny was over. They were thralls, now, held spellbound by a new mistress altogether: Tai.

If I thought to see shock, or even surprise, when Tai came face-to-face with Silise, I was mistaken. I saw only a livid anger. She drifted upon the wave-tossed currents like an avenging fury, and if I'd thought Silise intimidating, well, she had nothing on Tai.

'Well! You've pissed me off pretty thoroughly, haven't you?' Tai said. 'Should've cut out my damned tongue while you had the chance, bitch.'

20

— · —

Tai

'Tai,' sighed Phélan. He was lurking somewhere behind me, for some reason. If he thought he was out of range of my songs there, he was an idiot.

'Yes?' I snapped.

'Don't gloat. An efficient hunter dispatches the prey quickly.'

I stared at Silise. Did I want to dispatch her?

I did. I really did. This hideous excuse for a friend hadn't bothered to tell us she'd survived Ravensbrück, instead choosing to spend *eighty years* nursing a pathetic grudge followed by some fucked up revenge mission? She thought this poisonous scheme was deserved, did she?

She and Brianne had hurt Mea. They'd caused the death of Narasel. And, most unforgivably, they'd enslaved Fionn.

And they'd got to her. I knew that look on Fionn's face. They'd broken her damned spirit, first by taking her sealskin and second by taking her peace of mind.

I paused to take a slightly petty pleasure in the vision of the two of them, enthralled by my siren-song. Puppets. I could make them do anything.

Considering they'd done the same thing to Fionn, I'd call it fair.

'First,' I said. 'I'll be needing Fionn's sealskin. *Bring it to me.*' I used three voices as I issued the command, blended together into a choral bludgeon. Overdoing it, really, but so what? They'd earned it.

It was Silise who obeyed, albeit with an expression of murderous rage in her eyes. I could make people do what I told them to do; I couldn't make them like it.

Fine by me.

I looked long at her as she put the heavy sealskin into my hands. What kind of a viper had we harboured in our midst for all those years? She'd been all warmth and bonhomie, once upon a time. I'd never thought she'd possessed this capacity for blank hatred.

I gave the sealskin to Fionn, first. I didn't watch as she regained possession of herself; a woman like Fi, hyper-controlled, intensely reserved... she'd want some privacy.

Instead, I advanced on Silise.

'Tell me there's more to this than Ravensbrück,' I said. '-*Eighty* years, Sil. An eight-decade grudge because of a mistake? *Really?*'

'A mistake?' she spat. 'You three took your sweet time showing up, didn't you? Do you have any idea what I had to *bear*?'

'Nope, because apparently communication is beyond you.'

'Pray you never find out, Tai.'

'Okay, thanks for the melodramatics, but let's skip to the relevant part.'

'Those alven,' she said. 'Gutted like goats, both of them. One after another, right in front of me. And I bet you don't even remember their names.'

'It's been eighty fucking years, of course I don't remember their damned names. But so what? I'm sorry we couldn't save them, but since when has a little violence rattled *you* so badly? You're a ban sith. Death is your *business*.'

'Yes,' she said, hollow-eyed and cold. 'Yes, it is. I sang them both into death, Tai, and many others, too. *So many others.*'

I began to get an inkling of what she was talking about. She was ban sith, a *banshee*, and she'd wound up stuck in a concentration camp for... well, not all that long, I'd thought. It'd taken us only a few weeks to figure out where she was, and get there.

A few weeks.

To Silise, those few weeks must have seemed longer. Much longer. She'd seen, *felt*, every approaching death; wailed out her heart for every last one.

And in those days, towards the end of the war, we were talking a lot of deaths. Fifty a day. Sixty, eighty... I didn't even know, but a *lot*.

'Shit,' I said. 'Sil... I'm sorry. I am.'

For some reason, that only enraged her more. If it weren't for my thrall still holding her fast, she'd have attacked me. I saw it in her face.

'Okay, you hate us, I get it,' I said quickly. 'But what did you expect? We did everything we could to find you. We *did* find you. But you'd vanished into the mist like a puff of fucking smoke and it took time, all right? We couldn't work miracles. We were just a group of tired, worried women doing our damned best. Sorry it wasn't enough for you.'

'It's too late,' said Silise. 'No amount of words will ever change what happened to me, and *nothing* will ever change how I feel about you.'

'Cool.' I shrugged.

She stared.

'What do you want me to do, commit seppuku? From where I'm sitting, my ex-best friend is a malevolent bitch with an entitled fucking attitude. What, you abandon us for a century, follow *that* up with a charming supervillain routine, and you expect to walk off with the moral high ground? That's a hard no.'

Brianne stirred. My thrall seemed to have hit her harder, for some reason, but why was I surprised? Silise always was hard to handle.

'Yes?' I said to Brianne. 'Go ahead and speak.'

'It was me,' she said, slowly, with some kind of difficulty. 'Me who found her, me who got her out. If I could do it, why couldn't you?'

'Something to do with the fact we thought she was dead, I expect. If you had better information, good for you.'

'I almost died,' grated Silise. 'I *felt my own death*, Tai. I almost bled out, *me*, conquered by a fucking SS nobody.'

'That would hurt my pride a bit, too,' I nodded.

'Let me go,' panted Brianne. 'You can't hold us like this forever.'

'Why the *fuck* would I want to? Fuck's sake.' I risked a look at Fionn; she'd gathered herself, to a point, though there was an empty look in her eyes I didn't like.

We'd work on that later.

'Let's ask the group, shall we?' I proposed. 'Phélan, what's your vote?'

'Kill them both.'

'Perfect. It's neat, it's tidy, it eliminates all possibility for future trouble. I like it. Fi?'

Fionn looked at the pair of them in silence, for a while. When she spoke, it wasn't to cast a vote; it was to ask a question. 'The pearls,' she said. 'Mine, and the others'. You wanted them for Silise? So she could breathe down here?'

Brianne nodded her head, once.

'You love her.'

'More than anything.'

I rolled my eyes. '*Right*, because she's so fucking cuddly.'

'Tai,' said Fi, on a slight sigh. 'If you love *me*, shut up.'

I drew a finger across my lips, indicating total silence going forward. Probably.

'I'd rather not kill you,' she said, looking with admirable calm at Brianne, and Silise. 'You probably deserve death more than Narasel did, but I won't be the one to make that call. Neither will Tai.'

'Hey,' I said. 'That's not—'

'*Tai.*'

'Don't make me thrall you.'

'Like you'd even think about it.'

She had me there.

I shut up. Again.

'However,' she said, more coldly. 'If you're discovered to be involved in any more such schemes, I'll change my mind. And if you dare enslave another selkie ever, ever again, I'll slit your throats myself.' Her face hardened. 'Slowly.'

I shivered, a little. Fi in *this* mood is scary beyond all reason; I'm glad she's never turned that kind of icy anger upon me.

Silise wasn't buying it. 'So we just slink meekly away like good little girls, and that's that?' she snarled. 'No. My morrough—'

'Won't be coming to your rescue, sorry,' I put in. There had only been a few of them, after all, and they hadn't been expecting Phélan. Or me. Or the spectre Phélan had picked up in the cells, *who*, as it turned out, had a bit of a grudge going on of their own.

That took the wind out of Silise — a little. 'Forget it,' she said. 'I'm not backing down. You all deserve to *pay*.'

'I'd say we have,' said Fionn. 'You've led us a merry dance this past week. You've hurt several of those we love. You've hurt *us*. And besides all that, our best friend is dead. The Silise we knew is gone forever; all that's left of her is *you*.'

Fi said this with such revulsion, such contempt, I wasn't surprised it shut Silise up.

I also wasn't surprised to see a renewed depth of hatred in our erstwhile buddy's eyes. She was proud, like Fi; she wouldn't like being so graciously spared. She'd rather die.

Fionn absolutely knew that.

'It's no good,' I said to Fi. 'They aren't going to just walk away.'

'I know,' Fionn answered, with the ghost of a smile. 'Someone's going to have to do something about that, wouldn't you say?'

'You mean someone's going to have to punch their lights out?' I flexed my hands, curled my fingers into fists in sheer anticipation. 'Delighted to oblige.'

Fi turned and drifted away. 'Be quick,' she said. 'But not too quick.'

I smiled upon Silise and Brianne. It was low, to beat up people I'd already enthralled; they couldn't fight back, and there wasn't much honour in that.

Eh, fuck honour. These two pieces of shit hadn't a lick of it between them, and I didn't have the time.

By the time I'd finished relieving my feelings — er, securing our escape — Fi had found us the way out.

'They won't wake up for a while,' I cheerfully reported, catching up with her outside of Brianne's weird throne room.

'I trust they're still breathing,' said Fi.

'Confirmed.'

'For now,' said Phélan.

Fionn favoured him with a dark look.

He returned this without a blink, and without backing down.

'He's got a point,' I said. 'You *sure* you don't want to round off the week with a little murder, Fi?'

'Yes.'

'They *did* do unspeakable things.'

'Yes, and so have we, in our time.'

'Bollocks. None of us ever did anything *that* messed up.'

'Debatable.'

Phélan was shaking his head. 'And if you're finished *debating*, I'd like to get back to my life.'

'Sorry,' I said guiltily. I hadn't meant to drag Phélan down here, but that counted for little. 'You've been back in my life for five minutes and already I've embroiled you in high drama.'

'Par for the course.'

'Hey, at least you made new friends,' I tried. 'New, dead friends.' The spectre who'd taken a shine to him was nowhere in evidence, but I hadn't really the eyes to follow such things. Maybe he or she and Phélan were inseparable now. Cute.

Phélan looked at me like I was nuts, which felt all kinds of familiar. I smiled.

Brianne's palace didn't get noticeably less ornate outside of her inner sanctum, or whatever the hell it was supposed to be. I drifted after Fi as she conducted a search, her selkie-senses presumably engaged for odd patches of water.

Wasn't too long before she found one.

'Quick,' she said tersely, her hair and gown streaming in a spiralling flow of blue water. 'I'm not sure how long this thing will function.'

I hurried to catch up with her, and took firm hold of her arm. Phélan took the other. 'Oh,' I said, as the currents swirled up to claim us and the world began to fall away. 'Just before I rendered Brianne a senseless heap, I got intel. Mea and co were sent back to—'

The auction hall, I'd been going to say, but a roar of water drowned the rest of my sentence and we were swept away.

We emerged back where we'd started. The old car factory, front and centre, the same decayed, echoing hall we'd stepped into half a lifetime ago. Back when Mea was unaccounted for, Brianne remained a mystery, and Silise was still dead.

'You didn't truly want to kill her, did you?' Fionn said softly as I released her arm.

'Obviously, I did,' I said, but it wasn't the truth and we both knew it. Silise was our best friend, once, and whatever kind of a hell-bitch she's turned into now, you just don't run around eviscerating your buddies. I'd like to think even Daix would draw a line somewhere in there.

Maybe.

'Show's over,' said Phélan, and struck up a ghostly light.

The hall was empty, or, nearly so. Almost all of the auction attendees had gone; had left, presumably, once the bidding was over. Most of the witch-lights had gone out, casting the crumbling space into shadows only partly alleviated by Phélan's light.

Only a small gaggle of people remained. One leant against the far wall of the room; another slumped in a chair at one of the abandoned tables; and a third advanced upon the bedraggled, sodden group of Fionn, Phélan and me, grinning all over her petite little face.

'*Finally*,' she said, and to my immense surprise, tackled me in a ferocious hug.

'Daix?' I said dumbly. 'What the fuck.' Affection? From *Daix*?

She shrugged, and moved on to hug the stuffing out of Fionn. 'I don't know. You took an *age*, and once your room-mate and all the rest of them showed up and told me just what was going on down there—'

'Mea's here?' I scanned the faces of the few people remaining, or tried to. The shadows were deep, but I was pretty sure neither of them were Mea.

'Not now. She went home, and *yes*, I made sure she had suitable escort. She's safe. They all are.'

'How did you — what did you do, murder all their buyers?' I'd expected to have another battle on our hands; Brianne had whisked away our selkie friends before we'd managed to free them, and delivered them straight into the hands of those she'd sold them to.

'Don't be an idiot,' said Daix darkly.

'So I'm an idiot. Explain it to me.'

'We *are* their buyers.'

'We who?'

Daix gave a piercing whistle, and beckoned. The two mysterious figures separated themselves from the shadows at the back of the hall, and came forward.

I recognised one of them: the naga. She'd out-bid a few people for possession of at least two selkies.

The other was tall and cloaked. Conceivably the same tall, cloaked figure who'd won the bidding for a few more.

'Who the hell?' I said. Not my most intelligent utterance, but I was soaking wet, shivering violently with cold, and beginning to be aware of a vast and unconquerable exhaustion.

'May I introduce Ghian,' said Daix, tucking her arm through the cloaked person's. 'My husband.'

Ghian pushed back the hood of his cloak, and gave us a shy smile. He was a true ancient, I judged, though not because of any outward sign. He had the eternal youth of most of the fae, with light brown skin, a shock of silvery hair, emerald eyes that crinkled with mirth at the corners, and a tiny pair of curled horns. A faun.

I blinked.

'And Anat,' she said, repeating this gesture with the naga. 'My wife.'

Anat inclined her head, a faint smile turning up her red lips. Golden-skinned, dark-haired and glamorous, she had an effortless poise about her; she was probably no youngling, either.

'...Did I know you were married?' I said to Daix. 'Twice?'

'Probably not.'

'Wait. Did I know you had that kind of *money*?'

'Probably not.'

I felt a gentle touch on my shoulder, and I ceased to be wring-ing-wet. Fi. 'It's a pleasure to meet you,' said she.

'Er,' I said, still shivering. 'Right. Yes. It is! A pleasure.'

Phélan said nothing. He was hanging back, melding with the shadows behind me. When I turned, he met my gaze in silence.

'You can go right ahead with being not-here, if you want,' I said, drifting back to join him. 'We seem to be done.'

'Neat ploy there,' he observed, nodding at Daix and her en-tourage. 'It's what I would have done.'

'Didn't occur to me,' I admitted. 'Then again, I'm not filthy rich.' The fact that someone — presumably Brianne — had got away with that much money didn't sit easily with me, but we'd got the ladies back. That was the part that mattered.

Phélan nodded. And lingered.

'Is there something?' I asked after a while. 'I thought you were in a hurry to get back to your life.'

'Right,' said Phélan, after an instant's hesitation. 'Yes. See you around, Tai.' He nodded at me, and faded out. Where he'd been standing, nothing remained but shadow.

'Wait,' I said, cursing. I'd almost forgotten that trick of his. 'Thank you? For your help?'

No reply came. I had no idea if he'd heard me.

I suppressed a sigh, feeling oddly deflated. Weren't we the conquering heroes? We'd recovered the missing selkies, pun-ished the perpetrators (sort of), and made it home before dawn — *and* with all our eyes and limbs intact. Mea waited for me at home, already reunited with Coronis. Daix was happily married to two people at once, and Fionn was — sane, more or less, in spite of the events of the night. So what was my problem?

Fi, ever sensitive to atmosphere, was looking steadily at me.

I plastered a smile onto my face, and joined her. 'Thanks for the, er.' I twirled a finger in the air, indicating my now-dry self.

She just nodded. She had a drawn, too-pale look about her, and her eyes, far too huge in her face, held a haunted expression. I slightly revised my optimistic ideas about her sanity.

'You're tired,' I said immediately. 'I'm tired, too. Why don't we call it a night?'

She looked around, a faint frown creasing her brow. 'Can we? Are we — finished?'

'We'll probably have to do *something* about Brianne and Silise, but not right away.'

'I don't... know where to go.'

Meaning, she didn't want to go back to her flat yet, where she would be alone. 'Happily,' I said. 'I know the perfect place.'

A LITTLE LATER, MY cellar hideaway was full of people, and cosier than I'd ever seen it.

Part of that was due to the quantity of, well, fire.

Daix had started by kindling a fire in the hearth, which I appreciated. But the cellar was still perishingly cold, and Fionn couldn't stop shivering. So, Daix had set fire to one of my lampshades as well.

'*Hey,*' I objected, rushing to put it out.

'Oh, *please,*' said Daix, rolling her eyes. 'These are *my* fires, okay? Your lamp will be fine.'

Once I paused long enough to really look at it, I saw she was right. It was cheery, controlled blaze, even if it *did* flicker in weird shades of green, and my charming Art Deco lampshade appeared intact.

So I objected less when she lit up the other lampshade, too, and the only unoccupied chair.

By the time she was finished, I'd come right around. The cellar was rapidly warming up, all its dank darkness dispelled by green-and-golden light, and everybody appeared cheered.

'Fine, tipping my hat to the demon in the room,' I said, miming the gesture in Daix's direction.

'Hey,' she scowled. 'I identify as fae.'

'Oh, you do.'

'Keeps the smell of brimstone out of my hair.'

She'd commandeered the sofa, along with her two spouses. Ghian confirmed my initial impression of him, and maintained a shy silence. Anat, though, was voluble enough. Tucked up in my favourite armchair with three cups of hot chocolate all my own, I spent a half-hour or so catching her up on the entire adventure, prompted by regular questions.

Fi said even less than Ghian. Personally, I thought her tremors had little to do with her body temperature; Fi's a water-creature, a mere dunking in the ocean doesn't touch her. She sat in rigid silence with two sealskins wrapped over her shoulders — her own, and Narasel's — and grimly gripping the mug I'd given her without seeming to understand what to do with it.

I watched her, but I left her alone. She didn't need to be clucked over, or hassled with questions. Silise had thrown her into a state of minor trauma. It would take her some time to come out of it.

I *hoped* it was minor. The lost look in her eyes didn't encourage me. Wherever she was in her head... she was far, far away from my comfy cellar, and from me.

I wasn't surprised when, after an hour or so, she rose, and excused herself with a polite nod to Daix's guests. She gave me a hug on her way past — an actual *hug*, or, well, half a one. A brief pressure around my shoulders, her head tilted towards mine.

Then she was ghosting away up the stairs.

'Wait,' I said, hastily handing off the fresh mug of tea I'd been ferrying to Anat. 'Uh. Fi?'

She didn't seem to hear me.

I ran after her, caught up with her at the top of the stairs. 'Fi. Where you going? Home?'

She nodded. 'I'm... tired. I need to sleep.'

I wanted to go home, too. I wanted to see Mea with my own eyes, talk to her. Make sure she was all right. But she was with Coronis; she didn't need me, and I'd be a third wheel.

The cellar was almost as good as home, at least when it had Daix and Ghian and Anat in it. I wanted Fi to stay, too, but I couldn't oppose her desire to go.

'I know you'll hate my casting aspersions on your ability to cope,' I said. 'But. Are you going to be okay?'

'Fine.' She said it firmly, calmly.

'I'll be here if you need me.'

Fionn only nodded, not really looking at me. Not really listening.

So I grabbed her shoulders and shook her. Only a little bit; just enough to get her attention. 'Fi. Hear this. You've been alone for eighty years but that's *over*. Don't withdraw into silence. You don't have to deal with this by yourself anymore.'

It was too dark to be certain, but I thought I saw a sheen flicker over her eyes. Saltwater. Might be tears... might be some weird selkie thing I still didn't understand.

Fi would prefer explanation B, so let's say it's that one.

'I'll be okay,' she said, and since she met my eyes that time I more or less even believed her.

'Call me soon.'

She smiled, faintly. 'Don't you have a show to do?'

'So what? I'll always have time for you.'

Fionn's smile grew slightly bigger. Slightly.

'Call me, or I'll be showing up at your door,' I warned her. 'Frowning. Fiercely.'

'All right, all right.'

'Actually, I think I'll do that anyway. Maybe without the frown. Definitely with cake.'

'And Daix?'

'I don't know, do you feel lucky? Your flat may not survive.'

At last: a glimmer of a real smile, even a little laugh. And when I pulled her into a hug, she returned it.

'I don't like where my head went, tonight,' she admitted, pulling away from me. 'It'll take me a while to bring it back.'

'I understand.'

She turned, and opened the door leading back to the street.

'Fi?' I called after her.

'Mm?'

'I love you. So does Daix, even if she can only show it by stalking.'

'Love you, too,' answered Fionn. 'Both of you.'

And she was gone. I resisted a temptation to pull a Daix myself, and follow her home — just to make sure she got there all right. She wouldn't thank me.

I went back down the stairs smiling, following the sounds of Daix's laughter. It had been a hard week, but I liked the outcome. Fi and Daix and I, friends again. Working together, laughing together. Punching people in the face together.

It wasn't enough to erase eighty years of silence; nothing could ever do that.

But it was a start.

21

— · —

FIONN

I WASN'T ALTOGETHER SURPRISED, when I reached my flat, to find it somewhat less empty than expected.

As I let myself in at the front door, I became aware at once of a faint glow of light somewhere within. Someone sat in an armchair by the window, nearly in darkness, save for the small table-lamp she'd switched on.

Silise.

She watched me in silence as I carefully laid my precious sealskin over the back of my sofa.

'I can't believe you didn't change your damned hiding-place,' she said after a while. 'Really, how easy could you make it?'

'Clearly, I should have,' I agreed, keeping my eyes on her. 'Somehow I didn't expect that my erstwhile best friend might still be alive, and planning to enslave me with it.'

'That wasn't the *plan*,' she countered, sounding annoyed that I could even suspect her of it. 'Look, nobody wanted to do that to you. All right? Not even me.'

I remembered Brianne's words as she'd taken up my sealskin, and the flash of real regret in her eyes. Might be some truth there. 'Then why did you take it?'

She shrugged. 'Insurance. You always used to be stubborn as a mule. Nothing's changed there.'

'Sil.' By now it seemed apparent she wasn't planning to attack me; cautiously, I took a seat. 'If you'd needed the kind of help I could provide, you could have just *asked*.'

She looked long at me. 'I could have,' she agreed.

I waited, but Silise did not seem disposed to elaborate.

'What's it been for, Sil?' I said quietly. 'What were you trying to *do*?'

She shrugged again, avoiding my eye. 'A... game. At first. I was fucking angry, all right? They say everything gets better with time, but this *didn't*, and I...' She paused, and the anger in her faded. A kind of desolation replaced it. 'I wanted to hurt you. All of you. As much as you hurt me.'

'You enslaved half a dozen people. Sold them like cattle.'

'Please. They were in no real danger. I knew the *fatales* would save the day.' Her voice was acid.

'So they were what, a red flag? Some kind of twisted pantomime to get our *attention*?'

She actually had the effrontery to grin. 'You have to admit, it was a good game. We got you at every turn. Daix and her *intel*! So predictable.'

'Your *game* got a selkie killed.'

'That wasn't supposed to happen either.'

'But it did. If you couldn't call off your games *before* someone died, *that* was the point where it should've been over.'

Silise waved this off with an impatient gesture. 'Spare me your damned sanctimony, please? I *know*. But we'd gone too far to turn back.'

I just watched her for a time, trying to read the once-familiar contours of her face. Anger she had aplenty, and... something else. I didn't think it was regret, or, not much. 'You've had a small taste of what it's like to be someone's puppet,' I said at length. 'Courtesy of Tai. And while siren-thrall doesn't even touch the deep *wrongness* of a stolen sealskin, maybe you've a glimmer of an idea of what you did to me. To Mea, and Narasel, and Melly.'

'The thing is,' said Silise, rising from her chair. 'I'd do it again. All of it. Just for the sight of you bound and helpless at my feet.'

'What did we do that was so terrible?' I whispered, appalled by the burning resentment of her tone. 'We tried, Sil. We *tried*.'

'It wasn't enough.' She walked to the door; I didn't try to stop her. 'You abandoned me, Fionn. Left me for dead, walked away. Forgot me. And I won't let it go.'

No sense reasoning with her; she couldn't hear me. 'Watch your back, Sil,' I said quietly. 'We know you're out there, now.'

'Right,' she said. 'Why stab me in the back once, if you can do it over and over again?'

The door closed behind her, leaving me alone in the near-dark.

I bore the profound silence for all of five minutes before I took out my phone.

Tai answered so fast, she must have been watching for a call. 'Fi. You okay?'

'Not... not really, no. Are you still at the cellar?'

'All of us.'

I took a shaky breath, and let it out. 'Put the kettle on, will you? I'm coming back.'

ALSO BY CHARLOTTE E. ENGLISH

MODERN MAGICK:

The Road to Farringale
Toil and Trouble
The Striding Spire
The Fifth Britain
Royalty and Ruin
Music and Misadventure
The Wonders of Vale
The Heart of Hyndorin
Alchemy and Argent
The Magick of Merlin
Dancing and Disaster

HOUSE OF WERTH:

Wyrde and Wayward
Wyrde and Wicked
Wyrde and Wild
Wyrde and Wondrous

THE MALYKANT MYSTERIES:

Death's Detective
Death's Avenger
Death's Executioner

THE DRAYKON SERIES:

Draykon
Lokant
Orlind
Llandry
Evastany
Seven Dreams

WONDER TALES:

Faerie Fruit
Gloaming
Sands and Starlight
Summertide

TALES OF AYLFENHAME:

Miss Landon and Aubranael
Miss Ellerby and the Ferryman
Bessie Bell and the Goblin King
Mr Drake and My Lady Silver

CASTLE CHANSANY:

Dragonskin
The Best of All Chairs

The Far Below
The Queen's Philtre
Knight Errantry

www.charlotteenglish.com

About Author

English both by name and nationality, Charlotte hasn't permitted emigration to the Netherlands to change her essential Britishness (much). She writes (mostly) feelgood fantasy over copious quantities of tea, and rarely misses an opportunity to apologise for something. Ace and HSP, history buff and gamer, baker and voracious reader, she loves few things so much as peace and quiet, long walks, and really good cake. Her whimsical works include the House of Werth series, the Wonder Tales and Modern Magick.